PERISH BY
PEDICURE

A Bad Hair Day Mystery

PERISH BY PEDICURE

Nancy J. Cohen

KENSINGTON BOOKS
KENSINGTON PUBLISHING CORP.
http://www.kensingtonbooks.com

KENSINGTON BOOKS are published by

Kensington Publishing Corp.
850 Third Avenue
New York, NY 10022

All Kensington titles, imprints and distributed lines are available at special quantity discounts for bulk purchases for sales promotion, premiums, fund-raising, educational or institutional use.

Special book excerpts or customized printings can also be created to fit specific needs. For details, write or phone the office of the Kensington Special Sales Manager: Kensington Publishing Corp., 850 Third Avenue, New York, NY 10022. Attn. Special Sales Department. Phone: 1-800-221-2647.

ISBN-13: 978-0-7582-1226-9
ISBN-10: 0-7582-1226-7

First Hardcover Printing: December 2006
First Mass Market Paperback Printing: November 2007
10 9 8 7 6 5 4 3 2 1

Printed in the United States of America

ACKNOWLEDGMENTS

Dr. Richard S. Greene, Skin and Cancer Associates Dermatology Center, Plantation, FL, Diplomate, American Board of Dermatology:

Thank you for providing information on moles and the warning signs of skin cancer. Melanoma is a concern to all Floridians, who need to be vigilant about this disease. While education is the key to prevention, your expertise helps to save lives.

Nina Hallick, salon director, The Elite Group, Fort Lauderdale, FL:

With many thanks for sharing your experiences from beauty-trade shows, without which I wouldn't have been able to write this book. I appreciate the information you generously shared. As an active salon owner and stylist, you could serve as a role model for Marla.

Joanne Sinchuk, Murder on the Beach, Mystery Bookstore, Delray Beach, FL:

I'm glad we shared exhibit space at the hair show that inspired this story. We had a blast, and I probably wouldn't have gone without your participation. Let's plan on doing it again.

With special thanks to my agent, Evan Marshall, and to my editor, Karen Thomas:

I am grateful for your continued support and encouragement that allow me to continue Marla's adventures. Your suggestions always make the book stronger, and it's a pleasure working with you.

Chapter One

"I've probably made the biggest mistake in my life," hairstylist Marla Shore confided to her friend and colleague, Georgia Rogers. Driving onto the I-595 ramp exiting from the Fort Lauderdale Airport, she was headed east. "I mean, how stupid am I, to agree to let Dalton's former in-laws stay with me? It'll be a zoo at my house."

Georgia's sparkling dark eyes regarded her with amusement. "Don't worry about me getting in the way as another houseguest, hon. I'm, like, totally cool with the idea. You can't blame your fiancé for the foul-up, either. Weren't Pam's parents originally supposed to come for Christmas? It's not Dalton's fault that they changed their plans at the last minute and decided to pop in on you in January instead."

Keeping her eyes on the road, Marla plowed a hand through her chestnut hair. "If I had realized they'd be coming the same weekend as the hair show, I would've told Dalton to put them up at his house. He and Brianna are packing away Pam's things before we move into our new place, and he didn't want Pam's parents to see the boxes."

"That's more his problem than yours, hon."

Marla heard the rebuke in her friend's tone and inwardly agreed. But it wasn't as though her fiancé, Detective Dalton Vail, had given her much choice. His distress at the idea of his in-laws seeing Pam's prized possessions packed away had forced Marla's hand, and she'd reluctantly acquiesced to his request to house them.

After returning from her family reunion in November, she'd insisted they look at housing developments before setting a wedding date. Although she was quite willing to move from her town house, she refused to live in the same home where Vail had resided with his late wife, Pam. Too many memories haunted the place. Detective Vail had finally acknowledged it was time to move on.

She'd liked the models right away in the Royal Oaks community, located in southwest Palm Haven. Leaving nothing to chance, they had plunked down a deposit on a four-bedroom home with a two-car garage, formal dining room, living room with a vaulted ceiling, and a separate family room. One of the decisive factors had been the bright, airy kitchen that faced a screened pool in the back. Another had been the citrus trees in the yard. Vail missed the orange trees he'd lost to the citrus canker eradication program, and this area hadn't been affected by the disease. It would be a joint investment. She'd inherited enough money from Aunt Polly to pay back a loan she owed and to contribute to the new home. Renting out her town house would help with the payments.

"Are you sure you don't want to stop by my place first to leave your luggage?" she asked Georgia, who'd sagged in her seat. "You look tired. I'd think you would want to freshen up after a five-hour flight."

"That's okay, I can rest later. I'd rather go to the convention hotel and check in with the boss. Christine should have our schedule ready for the next few days."

Marla's passenger flashed her a quick smile, her face showing few wrinkles from the interceding years since they'd been college roommates. Hints of silver showed in her black curly hair, giving Marla a twinge of anxiety. At thirty-five, she was only a couple of months younger. Should she be worried about gray at her roots?

"Tell me what to expect," Marla said, heading north along Federal Highway. This wasn't the best part of town to show her guest. Rundown shop fronts bordered the road with nary a palm tree in sight. A truck zoomed past, spewing diesel fumes, while Marla got stuck behind a slow driver. Forced to slam on the brakes, she muttered a curse. Even for a Friday, traffic was heavy, thanks to the thousands of snowbirds who descended on Florida during the winter. Merchants loved the seasonal residents, while the natives barely tolerated them.

Georgia straightened her rose-colored cashmere sweater, careful not to snag the fabric on her chunky bracelet. She wore dangling earrings with rose quartz stones, a funky necklace, and carried a pink Coach purse. "I'm so excited," she said, glancing at Marla. "This is the first time Supreme Shows has come to Fort Lauderdale. Did you go to the one in Vegas last year? Luxor Products did a really good volume in sales at that show."

"The last one I went to was in Orlando. That always gets a good crowd," Marla said. "I attended most of the seminars on business management."

"Oh yeah? Our focus is on hair care and styling. Luxor will be introducing our new sunscreen products during the demos. You'll have to learn about them, so you can answer customer questions."

As sales rep for Luxor Products, Georgia had recommended Marla for a fill-in position as assistant hairdresser for this exhibition. It would be her first such experience and possibly the start of many more if she had a good time.

"When can we get inside to set up the exhibit?" Spotting the 17th Street causeway up ahead, Marla put on her right turn signal.

"Tomorrow morning, unless they plan to bring in the heavy equipment tonight. Christine Parks will tell us. She's the company director who's in charge of the whole shebang."

As Marla pulled into the parking lot by the convention center hotel, she wondered if she should reserve a room for herself. Once Vail picked up his former in-laws at the airport that evening, things could get hectic. It really annoyed her how he'd been more concerned about Justine and Larry's feelings than hers. But she was madder at herself for falling for his excuse, that the faster he packed, the faster they could move into the new place. She had her own packing to do, and now, with a house full of guests, she'd get nothing done.

"Don't be nervous," Georgia said, misinterpreting her friend's scrunching eyes as a sign of anxiety instead of anger. "I'll introduce you to everyone, and you'll find out when they're coming to do the photo shoot at your salon. I can't wait to see the Cut 'N Dye."

Thinking about the fact that each day away from her salon kept her from tending to clients, Marla frowned as she shut off the ignition, threw her car keys in her purse, and emerged into the chilly winter air. Not wishing to be burdened with a jacket, she'd dressed in a skirt-and-sweater set. Today was informal, but Sunday, when the trade show started, business attire would be *de rigueur*.

Fresh sea air blew off the harbor from Port Everglades, adjacent to the convention center. The wind whipped her skirt about her knees and tossed grit into her eyes. Blinking, she hurried across the asphalt toward the grand entrance. An interior concourse connected the hotel to the exhibit halls. It was a shorter walk, not to mention less costly, than the convention parking offered next door for a ten-dollar fee.

Inside the lobby Marla paused to survey the reception desk on the left, a bank of elevators, and a lounge situated just past a corridor on the right. Men in suits chatted at a nearby seating arrangement while a waiter pushed a catering cart full of rattling trays toward a wing that must have held the ballrooms.

"Where do we go?" Marla asked, watching a smartly dressed couple emerge from the elevator and stride purposefully down the hallway.

Georgia walked with a swinging gait, punching her arms in and out as though she carried weights. "I'll call Chris to see where she wants to meet us. Everyone may not have arrived yet." She pulled a cell phone from her bag and jabbed in a code. "Chris? It's Georgia. I'm here in the hotel lobby along with Marla. Okay. You got it." Clicking off, she stuffed the phone back inside her purse.

"So what's the score?" Marla asked, eager to meet everyone. She wasn't sure what an assistant hairdresser did at a show. She would need to learn her job here as well as the product line.

"She said they'll come downstairs. We should put some tables together at the café for about ten people." Grinning, Georgia grabbed her stomach. "I'm starving. Can I get you anything?"

"Just a cup of coffee, thanks." They approached the deli, where sandwiches and fresh salads were made to order. Self-service items were available down aisles and in refrigerated cases along the walls. While Georgia went to the counter, Marla explored a few paces down the corridor. Next to the café was a large, airy restaurant serving daily buffets, and beyond was an elegant, reservations-only dining room. The hallway stretched into the far distance, where Marla surmised it connected to the concourse leading to the convention center.

By the time Georgia returned with a take-out Caesar salad and apple juice for herself, and a Styrofoam cup of coffee for Marla, Marla had pulled two tables together and scattered several chairs around to accommodate later arrivals.

She had just burnt her tongue on her first sip of coffee when a woman with a confident smile and a cute turned-up pixie haircut reached them. Her hair was a color that matched her medium brown eyes, with gold highlights that gave a hint of contrast. "Hey, Georgia," she said in a sexy contralto voice.

"Christine Parks, this is Marla Shore," Georgia replied, standing to introduce them.

Marla rose, considering it proper to do so, and extended her hand. Christine gave a firm handshake. Her eyes, almond-shaped, were enhanced with mascara and a touch of peach eye shadow. With her high-cheekbone structure, she'd make a good model, Marla thought, admiring the other woman's haircut again and wishing she could wear her own hair short like that. On her, the style would lie flat because her hair was too straight.

"I'm so pleased to be part of your team," she said.

"We're glad to have you, Marla. Please call me Chris. We don't stand on formality." The other woman pursed her glossed lips. "Here comes Tyler. He's our area supervisor."

The man's mouth stretched in a wide grin as he sauntered closer. Deep creases on his face showed that he smiled often. Marla liked his outfit, a checkered camel vest over a white shirt, tan trousers, and a Union blue jacket with suede trim. It gave him a rakish look, especially with his caramel-colored hair tumbling across his forehead.

"Hey, Georgia, good to see you again," he said, giving the sales rep a two-fingered salute.

"Tyler Edgewater, this is Marla Shore, one of our assistant stylists," Chris told him. "Marla has been kind enough to offer her salon for our photo shoot next week."

"Awesome." His acorn brown eyes regarded her with interest. "I guess that means you live here?" he said, extending his hand. He squeezed hers a moment more than propriety dictated. "Maybe you can show us some sites in our off time. Like, we could use a local guide, especially to point out the hot spots."

"Sure, you can come along with Georgia and me. I'll ask my fiancé to accompany us, too," Marla replied in a smooth tone, folding her hands in such a way that he couldn't help but notice her diamond engagement ring.

"I doubt we'll have much free time," Chris said with a hint of disapproval. "Our schedule is pretty full."

"You're the bomb, boss." Tyler turned to Georgia. "Let's hope we rack in the orders like we did in Birmingham."

Georgia beamed at him. "Yeah, that was cool. Who else is here that I might know?"

"The usual gang. Here comes Jan." He turned toward Marla to add, "She's our regional manager."

Janice Davidson had chili red hair in a smart angled cut that dipped in at chin level and keen hazel eyes. She wore a New York look—black scoop-neck sweater and slacks, diamonds glittering in her ears.

"Welcome to the team," she told Marla in a pleasant voice. "I'm so thirsty. Did anyone notice if they sell carrot juice in the café?"

"Yuck." Tyler grimaced. "How can you drink that stuff?"

"You should try it sometime. Then you wouldn't be adding to your beer belly each time I see you." Smirking, Jan strode toward the counter to peruse the menu.

At least Jan's interplay with Tyler had seemed affectionate, Marla thought, unlike Chris's attitude toward him. The managing director's svelte looks had an icy edge—not in her clothing, a boldly colored patchwork jacket over an amethyst pant set, but in her facial expression. Chris narrowed her eyes whenever she glanced at Tyler, indicating that undercurrents rippled their relationship.

An African-American woman arrived, chewing gum as she greeted everyone with a welcoming wave. The gesture brought attention to her blue-painted fingernails with angel appliqués.

"Amy Jeanne Wiggs is our salon coordinator," Chris said to Marla, introducing them.

"I'd shake your hand, but I've just touched up my nails," Amy Jeanne said, blowing on her thumb for emphasis.

"That's okay. I love your hair," Marla responded, admiring Amy's glossy black ringlets.

"Marla, over here." Chris drew her away before

she could blink. "This is Ron Cassidy, our master stylist, and Liesl Wurner, our other assistant hairdresser."

The pair strolled arm-in-arm into the café, the woman a sultry blonde wearing a pout on her pink lips, and the guy sporting a cocky grin. His light, frosted hair stuck up in a short, spiky style like a rooster's comb.

Marla had just said her hellos to the trendy couple when a bald guy rushed up, spewing Spanish phrases. "Sorry I'm late," he finished in English. A gold hoop glittered in his left ear. "Hi, I'm Miguel Santiago," he addressed Marla after greeting the others. "And you are?"

"Marla Shore, assistant stylist."

"I'm one of the sales reps. Glad to have you join the gang." He pulled out a headset from his pocket and began twiddling with his iPod.

As the tenth person stormed onto the scene, Marla hoped no one would quiz her on their names. She felt dazed by meeting so many people at once. How would she ever fit in? They all knew each other from past shows.

The last man wore a navy turtleneck sweater and gray cargo pants. His ash-colored hair was swept back in a bold style that suited his serious demeanor and piercing dark eyes.

"Why did you call me down here?" he spat at Chris. "I don't have to attend your administrative meetings."

Chris arched an eyebrow. "You may be our artistic director, but you're part of the team, like everyone else. Need I remind you of your obligations?" Her sharp glare tamed his temper. He stepped back, clamping his lips shut. "Sampson York, this is Marla Shore. We'll be doing our photo shoot at her salon next week."

The master trainer pumped Marla's hand. "We have to prep our models for the stage demos," he told her in a lofty tone. "I was hoping we might use the facilities at your place."

"Huh?" Marla had no idea what he meant.

He scraped an empty chair closer and took a backwards seat on it, while Marla regained the place next to her friend. "One of your jobs is to get the models ready before the show," Sampson instructed, enunciating each word as though talking to a child. "We won't have much space in the exhibit hall. If we could do the coloring tomorrow at your salon, that would be *stupendous.*"

Marla stiffened, thinking of the Saturday clients she'd had to postpone and the busy scheduling for the rest of her staff. "I guess we could use my chair, and there's always the shampoo sinks. Sure, no problem. Then you could see the layout for the photo shoot ahead of time. Which day is that, by the way?"

Chris withdrew a sheaf of papers from a briefcase. "Here's a schedule for each one of you. Most of you know your jobs already. Amy Jeanne," she said to the nutmeg-skinned woman, "you're in charge of our local store managers. They're coming in tomorrow, and you can show them what to do. Georgia and Miguel will manage the cash registers. The rest of us will take turns manning the sales counters."

Sampson puffed out his chest. "I am removed from such common activities. It's *my* show that will bring in new customers. They are coming to observe my techniques."

The younger artist, Ron Cassidy, scowled at him. "How come my only demo is on Monday morning? I thought I was onstage twice. This schedule sucks."

"You're merely a master stylist," Sampson sniffed, "whereas I am reviewed in the trade magazines as a top educator. It is *my* vision that we bring to the show, my creation. You'll do what I've assigned you." He turned to the sullen blonde at Ron's side. "Liesl, you can instruct our replacement regarding her duties. Note that my demonstrations are at two o'clock each afternoon. I don't want any screwups, understand?"

Listen, pal, if you want to use my salon, take a lesson in courtesy. I don't like being called a replacement.

He must have noticed Marla's disquiet, because his intense gaze fixed on her. "I don't mean to be curt, but a lot is at stake here: my reputation, as well as the success of our new product line. People respect an artist's endorsement."

"I'm a quick learner," she said in a reassuring tone, "and I also hope to study your techniques and improve my skills under your tutelage."

As usual with big egos, flattery worked. He granted her a small smile. "Then I'll look forward to working with you."

"Our boys will move in the heavy equipment tonight," Chris announced. "We have all day tomorrow to set up the exhibit, starting at nine o'clock. You can pick up your exhibitor badges at the registration desk in the morning. Marla, I hope you'll come to our kickoff cocktail party tonight. It gives us the chance to get into the team spirit."

"Thanks, I'd love to come."

"Can we go to your salon Saturday afternoon to work with our models?"

"Sure. Do you want me here in the morning, or should I meet you at the salon later?" Either way, she'd have to pick up her badge and drop off Georgia.

"You're on our payroll now, dear. I expect you to be here with everyone else."

"Hey, the schedule says we don't do the photo

shoot until Wednesday," Ron griped. "What are we supposed to do after the show ends?" Grabbing a spoon from the table, he twirled it around and around before using it to check his reflection.

"Tuesday is for tear-down, whatever we don't get done by Monday night," Chris answered. "And if we finish early, we'll have some time off to relax before the photo shoot on Wednesday."

Marla pointed to the sheet of paper. "What's that item scheduled for next weekend?"

"We're doing another shoot in the Keys. Our publicist figured we should get some beach scenes for our new advertising campaign. Where better to showcase the product's sunscreen properties than in Florida? I hope you can come."

Oh joy, won't my clients be happy when I rearrange their appointments again? Maybe she could get out of it later, if Chris felt they had enough help without her. She didn't want to jeopardize her chance to work with Luxor in the future by backing out herself.

"What will I have to do?" she asked Liesl, who had sidled her chair closer to Tyler when Ron Cassidy ignored her. Tyler, making eyes at Georgia, didn't spare Liesl or Marla a glance.

Liesl replied with an insouciant shrug. "It's not so hard, luv. You'll help get the models prepped, and then you'll assist our artists at the show."

"I love your accent. Where are you from?" Marla remembered a character named Liesl in *The Sound Of Music.*

"I grew up in England. Anyway, when Sampson and Ron are onstage, we stand by with their combs, shears, and sprays. You can learn a lot if you watch them."

"It sounds exciting."

Her enthusiasm brought a reluctant smile to

Liesl's lips. "Bang on, luv. I get a real kick from doing the shows."

"You should watch me," Ron told Marla. "Someday people will call me The Great Rinaldo. That's the name I plan to use when I get famous."

"Excuse me?" Sampson sneered from across the table. "Rinaldo sounds like a magician's name, but, then, you'll need magic if you hope to replace me." Addressing the women, Sampson said, "Ronan is his real name. It means *little seal*. I guess his Irish mama thought it was cute for her eighth child."

"Shut up," Ron growled, and Marla saw the flash of hurt in his eyes.

"Hey, cut the crap, dudes," said Tyler. "We're supposed to be having fun. Listen to this joke I heard." Sipping from a Coke can, he told a story that made them laugh, followed by another and another.

This is just how I want to spend my week—getting caught up in company rivalries, Marla thought, shifting her feet to ease the tension in her back. Her colleagues would have to put aside their petty jealousies to function as a team, although she suspected that when crunch time came, they worked like a smoothly oiled machine. Otherwise, Chris wouldn't have brought these same people together again.

Personality differences aside, she couldn't wait to learn what the master stylists could teach her. She didn't know which excited her more: learning new techniques or benefiting from the publicity to her salon that association with Luxor would bring. It sure beat the unwanted publicity she had received from solving murders.

Chapter Two

"Can we stop by your salon on the way home?" Georgia asked, glancing at Marla rather than out the car window where traffic crawled west on I-595. Rush hour on Friday was not the best time to be on the highway. At least the sky was still light, since the sun didn't set until after six in January.

Marla tightened her grip on the wheel. "I'd love to show you the Cut 'N Dye, but my staff will be finishing up their last clients now. Besides, I might get stuck there if we stop off. If you don't mind waiting, we'll be there tomorrow. I would like to stop off at the police station, though, to make sure Dalton is ready to pick up Pam's parents tonight. I'd planned to go with him, but the cocktail party gives me the perfect excuse."

Georgia wriggled in her seat. "Way cool—I'm gonna meet your cop. Is he a real hunk?"

"You bet. Are you on the lookout, or do you have someone?" She hadn't exchanged much personal news with Georgia when her former roommate called. They'd both dropped out of college after two years to become hairdressers, and their relationship had lapsed until they met again at a hair show. They'd kept up a desultory correspondence since then.

"Oh, I'm on the prowl, hon." Georgia gave her a wicked grin. "Maybe your boyfriend has some single friends."

Veering into the right lane toward the exit, Marla spared her a quick glance. "What about the guys from Luxor? Tyler's cute, and Ron isn't any slouch, either. Miguel might look better if he grew his hair in. He looks like a pirate with that gold earring and bald head."

"Miguel is a teddy bear when you get to know him, but good luck detaching him from his iPod. Ron is too self-absorbed, and Tyler, well, he'll flirt with anyone in a skirt."

Marla didn't even mention Sampson York. The artistic director was out of their league, and her immediate impression hadn't been favorable. No doubt she could learn a lot from him, but his ego matched his height.

Focusing her attention forward, she drove off the exit ramp and turned north. "This is Palm Haven," she said when they entered her city limits. Stately royal palms lined the road leading toward the town center. A suburb of Fort Lauderdale, the city consisted mostly of tree-shaded lanes and brick public buildings sandwiched between the metropolis to the east and the Everglades to the west. Affluent residential communities fed the shopping malls, private schools, and parks.

The police station was located in an older part of town, where branches from overhanging ficus trees stretched across the road like the crossed swords of a military honor guard. Marla pulled into a parking space for visitors and grabbed her purse after shutting off the ignition. She touched up her lip gloss before emerging from her white Camry, signaling Georgia to follow her toward the entrance of the police station.

"Marla Shore and Georgia Rogers to see Detective Dalton Vail," she told the receptionist, who sat in a separate room behind a thick glass window. After presenting identification, they received visitor badges and were buzzed in. "This way," she told her friend, gesturing. They had to go upstairs, and she decided to take the elevator. A couple of uniformed officers passed by while they stood waiting for the lift to arrive.

Georgia giggled. "Would you believe I've never been inside a police station before? It kinda makes me nervous."

Marla's gaze traced the firm butts of the receding policemen and the equipment dangling from their utility belts. "I had that reaction my first few times, too, but now I'm used to it. Hiya, Ralph," she called to another guy down the hall.

"I suppose it helps if you know the people," Georgia replied, fluffing her raven locks. "How do I look?"

"You're gorgeous. Did I tell you I love your hair? Half my clients would kill to get those curls."

"Omigosh, when I was younger, all I wanted to do was straighten it, and they didn't have the processes like they do now. Luxor has a really good relaxer on the market. I'm hoping we can entice you to set up a display in your salon."

Georgia paused while they entered the elevator, and Marla pushed the button for the second floor. "As I'd mentioned when I called you about the job opening," she continued, "you can earn reward points for selling our products."

Marla adjusted her handbag strap. "And that gets me what?"

"Vacations, additional products, opportunities for more photo shoots. It's a great way to get free publicity."

"I know, and I can't wait. I've been wanting to expand—" She cut off her explanation when the elevator door opened. "I'll tell you about my plans later. There's the homicide division," she said, pointing. Threading her way through a cubicle warren, she led them toward a private office in the rear.

Lieutenant Vail spied them through the glass wall and rose from his desk chair. A few steps later, and Marla lifted on her tiptoes to kiss him on the lips. Wolf whistles played in the background as she turned to introduce Georgia to her fiancé.

His smoky gray eyes twinkled. "A pleasure, ma'am. Any friend of Marla's is a friend of mine." He inclined his peppery head in her direction. "This show has made her hyper for weeks. I hope she gets some benefit from it."

"It'll be a great learning experience," Georgia replied, her dark eyes wide with awe as she noticed the poster that read NAIL 'EM WITH GOOD FORENSICS.

Vail closed the door behind them as they entered his office. Although he wasn't in uniform, he wore his gold badge on his belt and a name tag over the breast pocket of his sky blue shirt. His navy sport coat lay draped over the desk chair. Papers littered the desktop and overflowed from a plastic garbage can. An empty coffee cup shared space with a sickly looking plant on the top of a metal file cabinet.

"How come you don't wear a uniform?" Georgia squeaked.

Marla smiled inwardly. Her friend was obviously

intimidated. Running a finger along the shelf, she winced at the layer of dust that came off.

"It's optional for detectives," Vail said, shooting Marla a look that melted her bones. With so many guests, they wouldn't be able to get together, in the intimate sense, for at least a week. "So, Marla, what's up? Did you have a reason for stopping by, or did you just want me to meet your friend?" Perching on the corner of his desk, he appeared to have all the time in the world for her whims.

She shuffled her feet. "I was, uh, wondering if everything is okay regarding your, uh, in-laws. Former in-laws. You know what I mean." Her anxious gaze lifted to his face. Even sitting, he stretched taller than her five feet six inches. "You'll call the airport to make sure their flight's on time, right? I have towels set out in their bedroom. Georgia is using the sleep sofa in the study, so Justine and Larry will have the guest room. I've stocked the refrigerator, too, since I won't have time to cook while the show runs."

"Aren't you going to the airport with me?"

"Sorry, but I've been invited to a cocktail party with the group from Luxor, and I got the impression it's more like a royal command, where people are expected to attend. Besides, this will present a good opportunity for me to get better acquainted with everyone. They're using my salon tomorrow to prep the models."

"Oh. And that's a good thing?" He looked doubtful.

She thought of all the shuffling she'd have to do with her staff and customers. "Yes, because then they'll see the layout before our photo shoot on Wednesday. This is a great opportunity, Dalton." She let enthusiasm invade her tone. "The publicity will be very useful, especially after we move to bigger quarters."

"How will the publicity help when you move into your new house?" Georgia interrupted. She'd been staring with fascination at a plaster mold of a footprint.

"I'm not talking about us," Marla explained. "This is what I started to tell you earlier. I'm moving the salon. But let's not keep Dalton from his work. I just wanted to let you know that I might be getting back late tonight," she told him. "Are you sure you can handle Justine and Larry on your own?"

His frown indicated his displeasure. "No problem."

Feeling awash in guilt, she reacted defensively. "Look, you could have had them stay at your place. So what if they saw your boxes? They know we're moving in together."

He slid to his feet. "It would hurt them to see Pam's dishes packed away, and her angel figurines missing from their cabinet, not to mention the furniture that's already gone to the auction house."

Marla suppressed a shudder. His home already looked brighter without those heavy wooden pieces. "Well, they'll have to get used to the idea. Brianna has kept the things that mean the most to her. You might offer Pam's folks some of the items neither of you want."

"I'll think about it," he said, crossing his arms over his chest.

Sure you will. "I won't have time to chauffeur them around. Why don't they rent a car for the week? Then you won't have to worry about picking them up, either."

"It's the least I can do."

She walked up to him and stroked his jaw. "I know this visit will be difficult for you. I said I'd be willing to help, but I'd like to see them acknowledge where you're coming from, too. You don't need to revisit your pain."

"They tried to get custody of Brianna after Pam died," he reminded her. "I don't want any roadblocks while they're here."

They stared at each other, each locked into a personal view of the situation.

Georgia cleared her throat. "Marla, I hate to interrupt, but it's getting late, and I need to shower before we dress for the cocktail party."

"Of course. See you later, Dalton. Don't forget my house key when you go to the airport. And watch out for Spooks when you bring their luggage in. I don't want him running loose outside."

"I forgot you have a dog," Georgia said on their way out.

"A poodle," Marla specified. "Dalton suggested I bring Spooks to his house, but he's already got Lucky, a golden retriever. They get along fine, but I'd rather keep Spooks with me."

As soon as they got home, Marla let her cream-colored pet into the fenced backyard. Georgia headed to the refrigerator to assuage her seemingly endless hunger pangs, while Marla retrieved phone messages, sorted through mail, and grabbed a drink of water.

"I love your house," Georgia gushed after Marla gave her a tour. "The rooms are so huge. I don't see how you can give it up unless you're moving into a larger place."

"I'm not selling; I've already got a renter lined up." She gestured to her living room. "The new house will be more modern, with high ceilings and the latest appliances. I'm really excited, although I don't know how I can handle two moves at the same time. Come on, I'll show you where to put your things."

She led her friend into the study, now converted into a spare room. Lemon scent lingered from her earlier cleaning.

Georgia slung her suitcase on the sleep sofa. "Did you already find a location to move your salon? What's the advantage?"

"I've been wanting to initiate day spa services for quite some time," Marla answered. "Many of my clients would like more choices than just a lip wax or facial, so we need to expand our service menu. Going more upscale means we'll be able to raise our profit margin as well. Working with your company will give us added exposure, and I can bring the new techniques that I learn at the shows to my staff."

"So you'll be getting married, moving into a new house, and expanding your salon, all at once? That's a heavy load, hon."

Marla grinned. "I get more accomplished by multitasking. Besides, the psychic I consulted in Cassadaga said change was very positive for me right now, and it involved a career aspect."

Georgia gave her a skeptical glance. "You don't believe in that stuff, do you?"

"Reverend Hazel Sherman was right about a number of things. She said I'd have a change of residence, and that's coming to pass. Then she predicted a family member would die on an upcoming trip, and I told you about Aunt Polly. But let's not dwell on the past. What are you wearing to the cocktail party?"

Before they left for the evening, Marla made sure everything was in readiness for her later houseguests. She left them a note apologizing for her absence, saying she'd see them in the morning if not that night. To make them feel welcome, she'd stopped off and bought a box of Godiva chocolates that she placed on the kitchen counter with her note. If she could just survive this weekend, she'd focus on the people who mattered in her life.

"Too bad your fiancé has to go to the airport tonight, or he could have joined us. I think Chris wouldn't have minded if you'd brought him," Georgia told her in the car on their way back to the hotel. She looked smart in a simple black dress and Swarovski jewelry. "In fact, Chris probably would be happier if you had an escort other than me."

"Why is that?" Marla hoped her Tahari suit would be proper. She'd bought it at an outlet mall, and it had still cost over one hundred dollars. The platinum-colored material had a satiny look and went well with the white gold necklace she'd inherited from Aunt Polly. She'd bought herself a pair of sparkly earrings to match.

Georgia grimaced. "Chris is in charge because she likes to control people. Try not to be too noticeable. She'll resent it if you get too much attention from the guys."

"But I'm engaged, so no one will hit on me."

"You'd be surprised."

Marla *was* surprised when Tyler offered to get her a drink at the company party. Elegantly dressed people milled about the hotel conference room reserved for their function. Other industry professionals had been invited, and leg room was getting tight by the time she and Georgia had entered. Georgia had just wandered off to greet someone when Tyler approached.

"Thank you," she told the area supervisor when

he returned with her glass of chardonnay. He'd gotten himself a beer, which went along with his football-hero looks. His broad shoulders, square jaw, and ruffled hairstyle were enhanced by two dimples. He had a killer smile, and he used it to his advantage. At the moment, he'd turned it on her.

"Yo, Marla, so where's your boyfriend? He's taking a risk letting you roam loose."

Marla couldn't tell if his leering grin was meant to entice her or was simply the result of too many pre-cocktail hour glasses of brew. "He had to go to the airport to pick up some other houseguests of mine. I feel bad about not going with him, but I felt that Chris would want me to be here."

"You got that right."

"Where do you live? Have you been to Fort Lauderdale before?"

"I'm from Atlanta. You wouldn't want to show us out-of-towners a good time while we're here, would you? I'm looking for, like, a personal tour guide."

Marla laughed. "You've already tried that line. Sorry, but my fiancé's former in-laws are visiting, and he expects me to help entertain them. Between coming to the show, working in my salon, and housing all these guests, I'll be lucky if I have space to breathe."

"Well, that sucks."

Marla noticed his glance toward the regional manager. "What about Jan? You could always go sight-seeing with her, or someone else from Luxor. Ask Georgia. She's looking to have some fun while she's here."

"Georgia is a blast, so maybe I'll do that. As for Jan, she wouldn't go out with me." Tyler's tone had turned sullen. "Our regional manager is too high-and-mighty after her promotion."

"Oh?"

"I qualified for her position, and I should have gotten it, but Chris passed me over. Watch out for that one. If you cross her path, she'll make you pay."

"Who do you mean? Christine or Janice?"

"Chris." Tyler frowned before leaning forward and lowering his voice. "I won't give her what she wants, no matter how hard she tries to crush me. And sooner or later the tables will get turned, and she'll be sorry."

With those words hanging in the air, he stalked off, leaving Marla alone. She stared after him for a few minutes, then decided to query Jan about what he'd said. The redhead had just broken off from a cluster of people and was heading toward the hors d'oeuvres table. Grabbing a plate, Marla slid next to her.

"I love your hair color," she said, eyeing the vibrant hue. "It goes so well with your eyes."

"Thanks. I like your mahogany, too. It suits your olive complexion."

"I may grow my hair longer. I'm tired of this length." Marla helped herself to some stuffed mushrooms, spring rolls, spinach wraps, and carrot sticks. "I'm hoping to learn more about Luxor's color products when we prep the models. What's really hot this season?" She figured that Jan would be willing to talk about the company, and then Marla could ease her into discussing the personalities involved.

Jan raised an arched eyebrow. "We've got a great look for a brunette who comes into your salon as a natural level five. You can take her to a rich red-mahogany. Or we have a technique called 'diffuse highlights' for someone who is more conservative.

You apply three different colors of the same tonal family. This leaves some depth at the scalp, meaning there isn't any grow-out factor. The ends are lighter, so it will look as though the sun colored the hair. If you have a medium blonde, we have a warm gold, a cognac blonde, or a vintage amber for variety. My favorites are the coppery reds."

Marla gestured to a couple of free seats at a small round table. She had trouble juggling her wineglass and plate until they were able to sit. "Is the UV protection in the coloring agents or the reconstructive treatments?" Laying a napkin on her lap, she popped a stuffed mushroom into her mouth.

"Both, but of course we're going to recommend our color-protection system. That's where you can bring up the point-of-sale. Dryness is another concern for people who get a lot of sun exposure."

"Maybe I should take home one of the catalogs so I can study the different products. I'd like to try some of them in my salon. I'm excited about learning new cutting techniques, too."

Jan snorted. "You'll learn plenty from Sampson. He likes showing off his skill."

"What about Ron? He didn't seem too happy that Sampson had assigned him only one stage show." Marla noticed that Jan only picked at her food, mostly raw vegetables.

"He's in too much of a hurry. If he's patient, he can benefit from his association with Sampson, who really is a brilliant artist. Sampson can be very demanding, but you put up with it. He knows his stuff."

"Chris must be used to dealing with his ego," Marla said, watching the director flit from person to person, acting as hostess. Her laughter trickled across the room.

"I don't know—she seems to be the one person

who doesn't bow down to him. Not that Chris bows down to anyone," Jan added bitterly.

"I understand she recently gave you a promotion."

Jan sniffed, her nose in the air. "As if."

"Pardon me?"

"As if that would make me happy." The redhead narrowed her eyes. "You're not one of us, so I can tell you things. Listen up, Marla. Don't try to get close to Chris or you'll get fried."

"Is that what happened to you?"

Jan's gaze shot loaded darts in Chris's direction. "You might say that. I know very well why Chris offered me this position. She thought it would make up for what she did to me, but she's wrong. The only way I'd feel better would be to get her job. I'd consider that to be the perfect revenge."

Chapter Three

After Jan's comments, Marla figured she'd better get on Chris's good side if she wanted to continue her association with Luxor Products. Finished with her appetizer, she mumbled an excuse to leave the table as Jan became engaged in conversation with another occupant. Pushing to her feet, she scanned the room and focused on the director.

Chris was hard to miss in her jewel-colored ensemble, surrounded by a bevy of male admirers. She had one arm draped around the neck of a red-faced fellow and her knee wedged against another guy's tailored suit. As she spoke, she moved her entire body in accompanying cues. The group seemed to be listening in rapt attention, or maybe they just hoped to get a piece of the action.

When Marla's glance caught hers, Chris beckoned. The crowd parted like the Red Sea, allowing Marla through to their hostess. Chris kissed one guy fully on the lips, blinked her mascaraed eyes at him, then stepped away. She grasped Marla's elbow and steered her clear.

"Are you having a good time, dear? I'm glad you were able to join us."

"Thanks. I was happy to be invited." Marla thrust aside a stray strand of hair.

"I saw you talking to Tyler." A hint of accusation colored the director's tone.

"He was asking me about sights in the area. I'd offer to show people around, but I'll be really busy between the exhibit and work at my salon. Plus I have other houseguests besides Georgia. My fiancé's ex in-laws are staying with me. You can imagine how comfortable I am with that idea."

Her attempt at levity failed to lighten the conversation. Chris simply said, "You should have brought your fiancé here tonight."

"He had to work. He's a police detective," Marla added, waiting for the widening eyes that usually resulted.

Chris merely smirked. A waiter approached, bearing a tray with a couple of red wineglasses, aged-cheese wedges, and salami slices on crackers. "The bartender told me to deliver this to you, ma'am," he said, handing Chris a glass.

"Oh, who's it from?" she demanded, glancing at the cash bar.

"Sorry, you'll have to ask the bartender. It's pretty crowded over there." He offered the other glass to Marla.

"Never mind. It could have been anyone," Chris said airily, as though accustomed to receiving gifts. Snatching a napkin, she selected a few appetizers. While she tasted one of the canapés, Marla thanked the waiter and accepted the other filled goblet. Her gaze swept the room, but no one seemed to be paying them undue attention. Had someone bought drinks for both of them, or mainly for Chris? The person responsible wouldn't reap many points by withholding his identity.

"So tell me about your salon, Marla, and what you hope to gain from this weekend."

Responding to the genuine interest in Chris's eyes, Marla expounded on her plans to grow her business operations. "I'm hoping the photo shoot will be successful enough that you'll want to come back," she concluded. "It seems like a great way to get publicity for the salon."

"Carrying our products will benefit you in that regard. Florida has the perfect climate to advertise our new line. You should encourage customers to continue their treatments at home. This will move more bottles off the shelves. We have a full line of shampoos, conditioners, sprays, and such. All contain aloe moisturizers and UV protection."

"Sounds exciting. I can't wait to try them myself. I assume we'll get to use these products when we prep the models?"

"You got it. A percentage from our sales gets donated to the American Melanoma Society. That's the angle we're promoting to the press."

"It's a good cause. I'm really happy to be involved."

Chris sipped at her wine, regarding Marla over the rim of her glass. "You'll do fine, just as long as you don't get in anyone's way." Giving a nod, the director spun on her heel and marched off just as Ron approached.

"Hi, Marla. How's it going?" said the light-haired stylist with a spark in his gray eyes. He wore a standard sport coat over an open collar shirt, a gold chain around his neck.

"I'm not really sure. It's hard to gauge how to act with some of the people here." She nodded at Chris's retreating back.

"The best tactic, if you take my advice, is to keep your ears open and your mouth shut." Ron leaned forward. "I hear you're looking to learn some new styling techniques. I can do wonders with my curling iron. Come to my room and I'll show you."

"No thanks." Marla chuckled. "That's an interesting variation on an old theme."

"Hey, I'm serious. I really like to teach people." He cracked his knuckles, holding his arms out like a wrestler before a match. "I have more patience than Sampson. He hogs the stage at these events, but his focus is showmanship rather than true education. He can be short-tempered when things don't go his way."

Marla glanced at Ron's earnest young face. "I imagine it's tough to work in someone's shadow when you have the skill to shine by yourself. Have you thought about jumping ship? I bet another company would be eager to nurture your talent."

He frowned. "I like working with the Luxor product line. Plus, Sampson's reign won't last forever. You can learn a lot from him, but you have to slough it off if he barks at you. Come to me if you have any questions."

"Thanks, I appreciate that."

She felt like a novice among this crowd, as though her background and experience didn't count. Tomorrow, would her nervousness show when she acted as assistant stylist? It was a new role for her, but it should be a piece of cake compared to some of the other things she'd done. *Don't worry, you'll manage,* she told herself. Besides, the work-related tasks would take her mind off the strangers sleeping in her guest room at home. Just thinking about Pam's parents made her stomach churn.

She circulated toward Amy Jeanne Wiggs, the salon coordinator, who was talking to Miguel Santiago. They halted their dialogue and gave her a friendly smile when she approached.

"Marla, we were just talking about your salon," Amy Jeanne said, her jaw moving up and down as she chewed a wad of gum. "It's so great that you're getting involved with the company."

"I hope I live up to everyone's expectations."

"Oh, you'll do fine. Then you can think about joining us at other exhibits." Amy Jeanne wore a royal blue shift dress, the pearls around her neck contrasting with the warm brown of her skin. As she spoke, she examined a fingertip as though searching for nicks in her nail polish. Miguel pulled out his iPod and busied himself with the controls.

"Do most of the same people show up at each event?" Marla asked.

"Depends on location and time of year." Amy Jeanne spit her gum into a cocktail napkin and rolled it into a ball. "A show's success depends upon the stage artists. Your role is crucial to their performance."

"So who's really in charge, Sampson or Chris?"

Miguel, who'd been swaying his hips to music no one else could hear, gave a snort. "Both of them, from their viewpoints." He'd dressed casually in a navy Cubavera shirt with white pants.

"A word of caution, girlfriend." Amy Jeanne twiddled the silver angel pendant she wore. "Steer clear from getting involved in anyone's personal problems. If Chris comes across as cruel in her remarks, let it go. You don't want to mess with her. Keep in mind that the company's reputation rests on Sampson's shoulders."

"So, for suck-up value, he's the one I need to address?"

Miguel stroked his bald head. "Flattery will get

you everywhere with Sampson, *querida*. Chris is the one who won't bend in a stiff wind. Ask her for a favor, and she'll stab you in the back. Isn't that right, Amy Jeanne?"

The girl's eyes flashed. "You got it, bro."

They wandered off, and Marla sought her friend for solace. She supposed any company had their conflicts, and she really didn't want to get involved in personnel strife. If she could just do a good job to benefit her salon, that was all that mattered. Political jostling held no interest for her.

"Hi, Georgia, are you getting tired yet? You've had a long day," Marla said, considerate of her friend's needs.

Georgia lifted a penciled brow. "I'm fine. How about you?"

"I've met a lot of interesting people." Marla wasn't shy about introducing herself to strangers, especially people who were exchanging industry news and gossip about who was doing what in her own field. Everyone seemed charged about the show and was eager to talk. Always the promoter, Marla had brought a supply of business cards and already had collected new ones to add to her files. She was thinking she should have brought a larger purse, because her small evening bag bulged ominously.

Glancing at her watch, she noted it was nearly ten o'clock. If they stayed later, maybe Pam's parents would be sleeping by the time they got home. She'd be putting off the inevitable, but she could face them with more fortitude in the morning.

"Ron hit on me, asking me to come upstairs and check out his curling iron," she added.

"It won't be the first time." Georgia chuckled. "You'll get used to these guys. Overall, I think they're a good bunch."

"Amy Jeanne and Miguel are pretty much sticking together. Are they an item?"

Georgia's glance spot-checked the room. "No way. Amy's kinda quiet, and I think she likes hanging with Miguel because he's so attached to his earphones. He has some beef against Chris that has to do with his brother."

Chris sauntered over as though she'd heard her name mentioned. Along the way, she linked arms with Tyler and dragged him close. A momentary frown crossed his face, but then he smiled blandly. Chris held another glass of red wine. Someone was keeping her well supplied tonight, Marla thought. The director's steps seemed a bit wobbly. Perhaps that was why she clung so tightly to Tyler.

"The party's breaking up," Chris said after a desultory conversation. "Let's go into the lounge. My head is starting to pound. I've got to sit down."

"Maybe you should go to your room," Tyler suggested in a flat tone.

Chris batted her eyelashes at him. "Will you come with me?"

He stiffened. "You can make it on your own."

"Nah, we'll go schmooze for a while longer. Into the lounge, people."

Marla found a seat between Janice and Liesl, whose wistful blue eyes focused on Tyler. The sultry blond stylist had chatted up a storm at the cocktail party. Marla had seen her with half a dozen men, at the very least. Each time, Chris had inserted herself into the circle and driven the conversation in another direction. Liesl had shrugged and moved on, making Marla wonder if the girl had already set her cap for someone else. She only hoped it wasn't Tyler, because Chris aimed to snag him, judging from the way she hung on his arm. Or maybe she'd just had too many glasses of wine. Refusing to be corralled, Tyler handed her off to an armchair before claiming a place beside Georgia on a cushioned loveseat. The rest of the crew had retired for the night.

Leaning back in her padded chair, Marla felt fatigue overwhelm her. She really ought to let the effects of her drinks wear off before she drove home, anyway, she thought, and ordered a cup of coffee, intending to sober up. Her mind blurred while Georgia's voice rang out with all the news she'd reaped.

Glancing at her watch, Marla couldn't believe how much time had passed. If she didn't get up soon, she'd end up sleeping in the hotel lobby. Her limbs wouldn't obey her mental commands, however. Her chair was just too plush, and the instrumental music playing in the background had lulled her into a state of tranquility. Dim lighting and tea lights on the round tables contributed to the soothing atmosphere. It wasn't until raised voices pierced the air that her mind snapped to attention.

"Tyler, don't you think you should ease up on the booze?" Chris's sharp tone lashed out.

The broad-shouldered male had sagged back on the couch, his arm draped around Georgia. Locks of caramel hair cascaded over his forehead, giving him a rakish look. He'd been stroking Georgia's shoulder when the director admonished him. Glancing up, he met her gaze with a dangerous gleam in his eyes.

"I'll have a good time if I want to," he told her. "You're not responsible for my personal behavior."

"No?" Chris's gaze narrowed. "Your decisions have gotten you into trouble in the past."

"I don't see a job description that says you're my keeper."

"If you make a fool of yourself, it'll reflect on the company. Making sure you behave *is* part of my job."

"What am I doing that offends you? Putting the move on Georgia? I've told you before that I won't play your game, so kindly retract your claws. What I do on my own time is my business."

Chris pressed her hand against her forehead. "Damn headache. I can't think straight."

"Then maybe you should retire," Georgia suggested, edging away from Tyler.

"Good idea," Jan answered instead, rubbing a hand wearily across her face. "I have to get up early to do my workout. Did you see the fitness center? I bet it'll be crowded in the morning." Pushing herself upright, she stood and stretched. "See ya later, guys."

An awkward silence descended after Jan left. Marla tried to catch her friend's eye to signal that they should leave, but Georgia was staring morosely into her beer glass.

"Really, I don't feel all that well. Tyler, walk me to my room," Chris demanded from her armchair.

He shook his head. "You can't manipulate me that way. I know what you're trying to do, and I'm sick of your attempts to pull my strings."

Marla winced. Is this what alcohol did to these people? If they fell apart during social hour, how would they pull it together for the show?

Chris's lips pursed as though she were in pain. "You'd better watch your tongue, or you'll be sorry," she told Tyler. "I can do a hell of a lot more to hurt you than just blocking your next promotion." Staggering to her feet, she wavered briefly before heading toward the elevators.

"Man, I shouldn't have shot off my mouth like

that," Tyler groaned after his boss left. He covered his face with his hands.

Georgia patted his knee. "She'll forget about it by tomorrow."

You hope, Marla thought. *After warning me to let Chris be the center of attention, you go and snuggle close to Tyler. Big mistake, when Chris obviously has her sights set on him.*

"We should go." Rising, Marla stretched her arms.

"Chris may fire me," Tyler said, lifting his head. "Or else she'll tell people things. I can't let her talk about me."

"You're too important to the team," Georgia replied. Her tone oozed sympathy, but Marla couldn't tell if she genuinely cared about Tyler, or if she felt obligated to reassure him. "She reminds me of a client who tells me how to use the curling iron every week at her appointment. It's annoying, but I realize she just naturally orders people around. I nod my head and go about my business. That's what you have to do with Chris. Act agreeable and then follow your own counsel."

"I don't agree." Marla sank back into her seat as an aching heaviness invaded her limbs. She needed to get home and go to sleep, but the thought of greeting her houseguests immobilized her. "One of my former customers, Bertha Kravitz, used to order me around, but I had to do what she said. She knew something about me that could have damaged my reputation."

Tyler's startled glance told her he understood, maybe even shared the same problem. "So how did you handle her?" he asked.

Her mouth twisted wryly. "I didn't charge for her hair appointments, and she came weekly. This went on for eight years, until she was murdered."

"No shit." Tyler's eyebrows soared. "Tell me about it."

"Yeah, Marla, you never mentioned this before," Georgia charged. She remained next to Tyler but kept a little distance from him.

"You don't want to hear the whole *megillah*. It's a long story," Marla said, her voice showing the strain of fatigue.

"Sure we do," her friend prompted.

"All right. Bertha died while she sat in my shampoo chair. I was giving her a perm, and we were alone in the salon. The cops suspected me."

"Omigosh, hon, is that how you met Detective Vail?"

"You got it." She related the rest of her sordid past, leaving out some of the details. "So it ended well, for me at least."

Georgia shrugged. "I can think of a few people who I wouldn't mind removing from my customer list, although not in that manner."

"Couldn't we all," Tyler put in. "I'm not a stylist, so I don't do hair, but some of the salon owners that I deal with don't know shit about the business." Marla noticed how his vocabulary had deteriorated with the passing hours. "There's one—"

"Wait, I gotta tell you about the flight attendant who wears her hair like airplane wings," Georgia cut in, renewed energy in her tone. Clearly, she enjoyed shop talk.

They traded stories into the night, until Marla's head drooped and she jerked herself awake. Rousing herself with effort, she grasped her purse and pushed up from her chair.

"Sorry to cut this short, but it's late. Georgia, let's go while I can still drive."

"Hey," Tyler said, plowing a hand through his

tousled hair. With his bristly jaw and bleary eyes, he appeared much less debonair than earlier that evening. "Maybe I should go apologize to Chris. She's gonna hate me for what I said."

"Don't worry about it," Georgia told him, yet she hovered as though concerned for him.

"She might say things that could cause trouble."

Marla sympathized with his concern, but it was late. "Why don't you catch her in the morning? You'll both feel better when you're refreshed."

"I won't be able to sleep."

"You're such a baby." Georgia rolled her eyes. "Marla, I should go with him. If he talks to Chris tonight, then we'll all get a good rest. Liesl has two beds in her room. She offered one to me if I wanted to stay at the hotel. Why don't I ring her and see if the offer still stands? It'll just be for the one night," she said in an apologetic tone.

"Okay." Marla would be just as glad to have one less guest. After Georgia instructed her on what to bring from her suitcase the next day, she left.

Inside her car, she turned the air-conditioning knob to its coldest temperature and put on the radio so she'd stay awake for the drive west. Her mind numb, she craved the comfort of home and prayed Pam's parents would be asleep.

Twenty minutes later, she saw that her prayers were answered when she entered her kitchen. Someone had left the light on, but only Spooks ran to greet her. Putting her purse on the counter, she stooped to pet him. His tongue darted out to lick her fingers. She could always count on his affection, she thought with a fond tug at his fur. When she straightened, the poodle trotted off to sniff at a pile of flight bags dumped on the floor. Holding her breath, Marla tuned her ears to the sounds in the house. Only the tick of the wall clock and the drone of the cooling unit filled the silence. Good, she hadn't disturbed her visitors.

Moving quietly, she slipped past the closed door of the guest room on her way to the master suite.

Her shoulders relaxed. Drained of energy, she prepared for bed in record time, and fell asleep soon after her head hit the pillow.

Dreams engulfed her: Bertha Kravitz's grinning face one minute and then the old lady's sightless stare the next. She saw again the wide-set eyes, pupils dilated, gazing blankly at the ceiling. Bertha's bagged head, immersed in perm solution, lolled back against the sink. Her face was distorted by an ugly grimace. Marla touched her hand, feeling for a pulse, the flesh feeling like a cold, dead fish. Images swirled and collided, mingling past and present.

She screamed, jerking upright, covered in sweat. The screams continued, but they didn't come from her mouth.

Her mind reoriented, and she focused on her bedroom where sunlight streamed through the cracks in the drapes.

Someone shrieked again, and she leapt out of bed.

Chapter
Four

Thrusting sleep-tossed hair behind her ears, Marla dashed into the kitchen from where the shrieks emanated. An older woman with brassy blond hair clutched her nose in front of the sliding glass doors that led outside. Beside her stood a tall, lean fellow wearing a collared shirt with a cardigan and looking very much like Mr. Rogers of television fame. Marla's poodle danced about their ankles, nudging for attention.

"What's wrong?" Marla said, foregoing introductions to Pam's parents.

"This glass door, that's what's wrong," Justine Keller retorted. "I walked right into it. My nose, did I break it?" she asked her husband.

"No, darling, I think you'll just end up with a bruise." He had a pleasant, smiling mouth and graying temples that contrasted with his dark hair.

"You must be Marla." Justine's scornful gaze raked Marla's rumpled nightshirt. "Don't you think you should put a big sign on this door, so people can see it's there?"

She swallowed, feeling like a schoolgirl. "You're

right, I'll have to add decals for visitors. Floridians are used to sliding glass doors."

"You don't say." Justine's hand dropped from her face. "I suppose I'll live."

"Here, let me show you how to unlock the door. Spooks needs to go out, anyway."

The cream-coated dog barked in response. Unlatching the lock, she slid it open and let him out to do his business.

"If you're okay, I'd like to get dressed," she said, feeling embarrassed by her lack of proper attire now that the crisis had dissolved. Her bare feet chilled on the cool tile floor. "Please help yourself to whatever you like in the kitchen."

"Tell me, my dear, how do you make coffee?" Lifting her chin, Justine sniffled. "I'm not familiar with this apparatus."

Who talks like that? "You don't know how to use an automatic coffeemaker?"

Justine gave her a haughty glare. "We use a French press at home, *and* we grind our own beans."

I see you dress for your meals, too. It was only eight o'clock, and Justine wore a white silk blouse tucked into a canary yellow skirt, white hose with matching heels, and gold button earrings with a matching choker at her neck.

Marla blinked. "You'll find a package of ground coffee in the fridge and filters in the pantry. When I come back, I'll make it for you if you haven't figured it out by then." Turning on her heel, she strode from the room.

Lord save me. If I survive this, Dalton owes me. Imagining how she'd exact restitution, she showered, blew out her hair, did her makeup, then pulled on a pair of black slacks and a ruby knit top. Not knowing what to expect at the convention center,

she snatched a black Ann Taylor jacket from its
hanger in case she would need it later. *One more
thing.* Picking up the telephone receiver, she dialed
her salon and left a message that she'd be there
that afternoon with the Luxor crew. Thank goodness Georgia had stayed overnight at the hotel, she
thought, finishing with a spritz of perfume. Dealing with two houseguests already had her frazzled.

"It's nice of you to accommodate us," Larry
Keller told her after she'd returned to the kitchen
and let Spooks inside. He'd spread the Saturday
issue of the *Sun-Sentinel* on the table, which someone had set with three plates and utensils. While
Larry read the news, his wife poured orange juice
into glasses.

The strong aroma of brewed coffee filled the
room. Actually, it smelled more like *burnt* coffee.
Sniffing, Marla sped to the counter, where liquid
spilled from the coffeemaker. Suppressing an ex-
clamation, she grabbed a sponge to mop up the
overflow. Obviously Justine didn't know how to
measure water.

Marla glanced at the woman. Justine had tied an
apron around her waist, making her look even
more like a housewife from the fifties. Who else
wore heels to breakfast—on vacation, yet?

"I'm sorry that I don't have more time to spend
with you this morning," Marla said. "Can I do anything for you before I leave?"

"No thanks, we'll be fine." Justine paused. "Dalton told us you have a friend staying here. Is she
still asleep? I imagine she must be tired when you
stayed out so late last night." Her light brown eyes
narrowed with disapproval.

Late for you, maybe. I don't have a curfew. "Georgia
decided to stay at the hotel for the evening. Luxor

Products sponsored a cocktail party last night. We were expected to attend."

"Yes, I got your note. I guess work keeps you pretty busy. It's going to be tough juggling two full-time careers once you're Brianna's stepmother."

Justine's voice broke on that last word, and she turned to stare out the window over the sink. A surge of sympathy engulfed Marla. This couldn't be easy on Pam's parents.

It's not easy for me, either, a selfish voice claimed inside her head. *Dalton should have made room for them at his house.*

"Where do you keep your eggs?" Larry said suddenly. Marla noticed how he didn't usually comment when his wife was speaking.

"Oh, sorry, I didn't put them in the egg bin because it needs to be washed out. They're still in the box in the back of the refrigerator."

"I like mine scrambled," he told her, returning his attention to the newspaper.

Clucking her tongue, Justine wheeled around, her gaze traveling over the kitchen. "It's so helpful when you have a woman coming in to clean every week, especially when you have a job outside the home."

Marla gritted her teeth. "I have a maid who comes twice a month for the heavy-duty work. I do the rest myself."

"You don't say. Well, if you talk to Dalton about it, I'm sure he'd be amenable to increasing her hours. With your combined incomes, that should-n't be a problem."

"We'll see. Did you want toast with your eggs?" she asked Larry, desperate to change the subject. Normally she would have eaten a breakfast bar on her way out the door, but she didn't want to hear

Justine's snide remarks about her dietary habits. Without further comment, she tossed together a cooked breakfast and choked down her portion. She couldn't wait to leave.

Pam's mother was insufferable, she thought during the drive to the hotel. Instead of being grateful for her hospitality, Justine had the chutzpah to criticize her housekeeping. At least Georgia would act as a buffer later on.

Arriving in the hotel lobby, she hadn't gone two feet toward the concourse to the convention center when Georgia rushed over to her.

"Omigod, Marla, omigod. You won't believe what's happened."

Tear marks stained her friend's cheeks, and her normally bouncy hair hung in limp waves about her shoulders.

"What's going on?" Marla asked with concern.

"It's Christine. She's dead, and I may have been the last person to see her alive."

Marla's jaw dropped in shock. "How can that be? She seemed fine last night, other than a headache. Not surprising, considering how much she drank."

Georgia drew her toward a quiet corner. "A room-service waiter found her this morning, collapsed on her bathroom floor. The police have been questioning everyone from Luxor, especially those of us in the lounge with her last night. Oh, God, what am I gonna do?" She covered her face with her hands.

"Whoa, slow down and start at the beginning. You said the room-service waiter found Chris?"

Georgia nodded. "Apparently she'd ordered breakfast the night before. When the steward came to deliver her tray, no one answered his knock. The door was ajar, so he entered and discovered Chris dead on the bathroom floor."

Marla motioned toward a couple of armchairs. "Go on," she told her friend, folding her hands in her lap. Georgia looked awful. And of course she hadn't put on any makeup, since Marla had brought her cosmetic bag from her suitcase only this morning, along with a change of clothes as requested.

"Christine had been soaking her feet in one of those portable foot baths. The cop said she might have had a seizure and toppled over. I guess that's their theory because she'd bitten her tongue. She ended up facedown in the water."

Marla pictured Chris with her head in the murky foot-spa water. "How horrible," she said, grimacing. "Was there enough water in there for her to drown?"

"They won't know the exact cause of death until the medical examiner does an autopsy." Georgia drew in a shaky breath. "They asked me if I knew anything about her medical history. Chris didn't confide in me. I wouldn't know if she was taking pills or had any problems."

"Maybe she had epilepsy or some disease no one knew about. In that case, I don't understand why you're so worried."

Georgia gave her a bleary-eyed look. "After you went home last night, Tyler headed upstairs to apologize to Christine. I came along to give him moral support, but the boss lady was in a bad mood and kicked us out. I stayed to argue with her, which was like trying to budge a tree trunk. I gave up, figuring we'd have a better chance to talk after a good night's rest."

"Can Liesl verify what time you entered her room?"

"She was sleeping. I'd gotten the key from the

front desk. I fell onto the other bed and slept until the police banged on our door."

Tapping her chin, Marla frowned. "How did they know to question you?"

"Tyler must have told them. But he was there, too. Chris was just as mad at him."

She crossed one leg over the other. Something didn't add up in this equation. "But he's the one who started it all. Chris got angry at Tyler's remark in the bar, and she left in a huff. I was witness to that much. You didn't do anything."

"Yes, I did." Georgia sniffed, wiping a tear from her cheek. "I let him sit next to me. That was enough to put me in Christine's black book. Listen, Marla," she began, but just then Sampson swooped down on them.

"There you are," the artistic director said, waving his arms. "What is going to happen to us? I am ruined, ruined!"

Marla shot to her feet. "Calm down. Tell me, who's in charge of the group now?"

"Jan would be the logical person to take over." He shook his head, as though to dismiss administrative duties as beneath his talent. "We'll have to cancel. What a disaster! Good God, the scandal will destroy me." His face was chalky white.

"That's not true," Marla said in a soothing tone, while Georgia rose slowly with a dazed look on her face. "I don't see any reason why the show can't go on. As long as the sales reps and salon owners manage the counters, you and Ron can proceed with your stage demos. How much stuff got unloaded last night?"

"All of the heavy equipment." Sampson had regained his composure and was now glowering at her. "But we'll be delayed in putting the exhibit together, and we still have to prep the models who are coming by this afternoon."

"No problem. Did you pick up your exhibitor badge?"

"I've got mine," he said, tapping his pocket.

"Georgia? Do you have yours?"

Georgia glanced at Marla as though she were from another planet. "Huh?"

"Come with me." Grasping Georgia's elbow, Marla marched her toward the registration desk and pushed her into the line for exhibitors. "Here's the stuff you told me to bring," she said, handing over the sack she'd brought from home.

"Thanks. I'll wash up in the restroom after we get our badges. I must look like a wreck."

Marla turned her attention to the registration clerk when their turn came and gave their names. Then she waited outside the ladies' room for Georgia to refresh herself.

Sampson trailed after her, pinning his badge onto his blue cotton dress shirt. He chatted up a storm as though needing to distract himself, asking Marla about her salon and offering advice until Georgia emerged. "Let's go," he said, loping toward the exhibition concourse.

The cavernous hall showed none of the finishing touches that would come tomorrow with the opening ceremony. Carpeting had not yet been rolled down the aisles, and wires trailed everywhere on the concrete floor. Sounds of hammering and the whine of electric drills resounded throughout. Searching for their booth number, Marla picked her way down rows strewn with half-emptied boxes, banners waiting to be hung, and large advertising posters.

"Clear the decks," yelled a voice from behind, accompanied by a beeping noise.

Marla stood aside while a forklift lumbered past, carrying shipping crates on its outstretched arms. *This counts as hazardous duty,* she thought, bumping into an exhibit table for a hairbrush display. Rubbing her hip, she was glad to spot Amy Jeanne Wiggs unpacking cartons at a large block of counters up ahead. A makeshift stage had been constructed beside the sales area, where folding chairs were stacked ready for placement. They had a good position, right at the intersection of two important junctions.

"Thank the Lord," Sampson cried, raising his arms as he rushed ahead. But then he stopped short, surveying the mess that needed organizing. "Incredible. How will we ever put this together in time?"

"Hi, guys." Amy Jeanne regarded them with sorrowful brown eyes. "I guess you heard about Christine."

"Yeah," Georgia answered, and the women hugged each other. "I can't believe she won't be here today."

"I've been trying to unpack stuff, but my heart isn't in it. Chris usually tells us where to put things." Amy cracked her gum, her mouth constantly in motion.

"How's the space behind the stage?" Sampson asked, standing tall. "Will we have room to put a chair there?"

"Go look for yourself," Ron snapped, emerging from behind the draped backdrop. "Has anyone seen my extra blow-dryer? I thought I'd put it in with the styling implements."

"Someone needs to get the posters up," Amy Jeanne said. "Where's the rest of the gang, bro?"

"I'm right here, *querida,*" Miguel hailed them as he danced a few salsa steps in their direction. The sales rep wore an embroidered Guayabera shirt and khaki shorts, in addition to a set of earbuds wired to his pocket-sized music device.

"Now what?" Georgia asked, spreading her arms. "We can unpack these boxes, but where do we put the stuff? Jan should be here to direct us."

"She's doing her workout routine," Ron remarked, yanking a hand mirror from a carton and holding it up while he ruffled his hair. "Speaking to the cops upset her, so she wanted to work off her energy. If she works off any more, she'll disappear."

"That woman eats rabbit food," Amy Jeanne agreed. "I can't get her to scarf down a decent meal. She's way too thin."

"Never mind that," Ron said. "If she's to take charge, she'll have to learn how to cope with last-minute setbacks. She should have been the first one here this morning."

"Oh, like you're so perfect?" Sampson sneered, peeking out from behind the curtain. "We're all out of whack because of Chris's death. Who wouldn't be? Hey, where's Tyler? Is Pretty Boy still getting his beauty sleep?"

"He hasn't come down yet," Georgia offered in a meek tone.

Marla realized the others were just going to mope around unless someone took command. "Amy Jeanne, why don't you and the sales reps unpack the products and arrange them on the counters? Set out the cash registers, the order forms, and whatever else you need to get started with sales. Meanwhile, I'll help Sampson and Ron with the stage work. Has anyone seen Liesl?"

Georgia raised her hand. "She went back to sleep after the police woke us."

"We'll get started without her. Let's go to work,

folks. If you put your best effort into this show, it'll be the most rewarding tribute you could give Chris. You know it's what she would want for the company."

Dispersing to their different duties, they left Marla to trail after the master stylists. Sampson seemed obsessed with the stage, gazing with dismay at the array of cartons.

"This will never do," he said, waving his hand imperiously. "Has anyone unpacked the lighting? I need my model's chair set over here under the spotlight. Will we have enough electrical outlets? Technician!" he hollered.

Stepping around the curtain, Marla offered to help Ron find the styling accoutrements. "Did you bring the products you're intending to use on the models? I could organize them into one container."

"Everything should be labeled," he said wearily. He kicked at a carton. "I still can't get it through my head that Chris is gone."

"I know." Needing to keep busy, Marla ripped open one of the boxes. A sharp cutter would be handy, she thought after chipping her nail polish. "What's this?" She pointed to an assortment of business cards, promotional pamphlets, a calculator, scissors, duct tape, a folded easel, and a glass fish bowl packed in foam inserts.

"That's Chris's stuff. She runs a contest to give away samples. People put their business cards in the bowl, and she draws half a dozen at the end of each day. Amy Jeanne adds the names to the company's mailing list. That's how we gain customers. We always notify people about new product releases."

"Clever idea. We can probably use the scissors and tape to put up our signs." She paused, curious about his personal background and why he'd chosen to work for Luxor. "How long have you been doing these shows?"

Stooping to tear open a carton, he spared her a glance. "Six years. I'm from L.A. Maybe you've heard of my salon—Ron's Hair Emporium?"

Marla grinned. "Not really, but I don't keep up with other parts of the country. So you have your own place, huh?"

"We specialize in hair design, not your weekly wash-and-blow. My average tab runs about four hundred dollars."

Marla gaped. "You must be well-known on the West Coast. What do you gain from being in the shows?"

His eyes sparked, making Marla surmise that his enthusiasm helped draw patrons to his chair. "As I told you before, I like to teach," he said simply. "Being in front of people lets me share my vision. When I create a style, it's the perfect complement to a certain facial structure and personality. You have to consider what's inside the person that wants to come out. It's more than just a look—it's a form of self-expression."

"I see." She could tell Ron genuinely wanted to mentor others and felt herself warm toward him. "I can't wait to observe what you do with the models."

"You'll be blown away," Ron said, grinning. "But taking center stage is nothing compared to my big plan. Someday I'll have celebrities seeking me out. That's when I'll take my stage name, Rinaldo."

"As a platform artist?"

"Hell, no. As owner of Rinaldo's Hair Emporium of Beverly Hills. The time isn't ripe just yet, but you'll see. One day I'll be famous for my artistic creations."

Just don't let your ego get too inflated, pal. The aroma of warm baked cinnamon rolls drifted into her nostrils. "The food court must have opened. I'm hungry." As her stomach rumbled in confirmation, she reached for a piece of paper wedged inside the glass fish bowl. Unfolding what appeared to be a bank check, she deciphered the handwriting. The draft was made out to Christine Parks and signed by Sampson York.

Clanging noises sounded from around the corner. Still holding the check, Marla straightened and rounded the stage. She saw a guy setting up lighting tracks while Sampson yelled orders to another man hanging publicity shots of models against the black backdrop.

"I found something of yours," she said, approaching the artistic director.

He glanced at her. "My chair?"

"No, not that." She could understand his obsession, since the chair would be the focal point for his stage action. "I imagine it's packed with the bigger equipment. All of the crates haven't been opened yet. Anyway, that isn't what I'm talking about. This check belongs to you," she said, handing it over.

Viewing the handwriting, he paled. "Where did you get this?"

"I found it among Chris's things and figured you'd want it returned. Five thousand dollars is a lot of money."

He looked as though he'd choke on his tongue. "Thanks," he muttered, crushing the paper into his pants pocket. "Where the hell is Liesl? She should be here by now. Chris would never let her sleep so late. Why don't you go and kick her out of bed? Oh, and Marla," Sampson added, just as she shifted her foot to turn away, "I know you'll be a sport and won't mention this check to anybody." He patted his trousers, giving her a distinct glare. "We wouldn't want your first experience with Luxor to be your last. Understand?"

Chapter
Five

Marla spotted the blond stylist in line at the food court. Waving, she hastened over. "Liesl, I've been looking for you. We're getting set up for the show."

"Hiya, luv. I ran into Janice outside. She said the cops wanted to ask me some more questions. Do you know how early that detective chap woke us?" She yawned for emphasis.

The aroma of brewed coffee made Marla eager to get in line, but first she had a question for the other stylist. "Do you remember what time Georgia came in last night?"

Liesl shrugged. "I'd called the front desk so she could get her own key. I must have been conked out because I wasn't aware of anything until the police rapped on our door. Why do you ask?"

"Tyler went up to Chris's room last night to apologize for something he'd said earlier in the lounge. Georgia accompanied him for moral support."

"So?" Liesl moved up her place in line, while

Marla glanced at the fruit cups and yogurt on display.

"I'm trying to get a sense of the timing. Georgia indicated that Tyler had left Chris's room first, while she lingered behind."

"Did I hear my name?" Tyler drawled, tapping Marla on the shoulder.

She spun to face him. "Where have you been? We need help at the booth."

"No sweat, sweetheart. I'm on my way." He didn't look too energetic, with dark circles under his eyes and an unshaven jaw.

"Tyler, can I get you a Danish?" Liesl said in a suggestive tone, her pout indicating she'd rather offer something more personal. Dressed in a tight-fitting amethyst sweater and jeans, she was attracting envious glances from other females.

Hello, did I suddenly turn invisible? Marla thought. *You could include me in your breakfast offer. I'd like a bagel.*

"No thanks," Tyler replied, "I lost my appetite, after what happened to Chris and all."

"What did happen last night?" Marla asked, her hunger fleeing. "Georgia said you both went up to Chris's room. Chris threw you out, but Georgia stayed to argue your case."

Tugging her elbow, Tyler drew her aside. "Chris accused us of having an affair behind her back. It made her furious to see us together, and she hadn't been feeling well to begin with."

"How so?"

"Remember in the lounge, she'd complained of a headache? She looked really bad when she opened her door. Very pale, her eyes kinda glazed. I thought she'd drunk too much."

"Did you know of any medical problems she might have had?"

"Are you kidding? I tried to steer clear of any personal business between us. Not that she didn't keep trying," he added bitterly.

"Okay, so she wasn't receptive to your apology last night. What did Georgia say in your defense?" Marla asked.

"She tried to reason with Chris, but the more she said, the angrier Chris got. They ended up shouting at each other."

"That couldn't have helped Chris's headache." Perhaps the guests in the neighboring room had heard their raised voices and reported the incident to the police. "Did you tell the cops about your disagreement? They knocked on Liesl's door to question Georgia this morning."

He shifted his feet. "Hey, they questioned all of us, ya know?" Gesturing at Liesl, who'd emerged from the line holding a croissant in one hand and a coffee cup in the other, he said, "You heading over to the booth? I'll go with you. Man, this is going to be a crappy day."

Realizing she still lacked a clear sequence of events, Marla decided to report to Jan. The regional manager might need help making arrangements for Chris's body after it was released. Pulling her cell phone from her purse, she exited the exhibit hall and dialed her salon. It would be easier to hear out in the main lobby, away from the construction noise.

"Luis," she told her receptionist when he answered, "please tell Nicole that there's been a setback. I'm not sure we'll make it into the salon today. The company director died in the night under strange circumstances."

"Ayie, that's horrible."

"They're going to continue with the show, but I don't know if anyone will be able to focus on the models. We'll have to get them done somehow, I suppose. Anyway, I may not get there until much later, if at all. Were there any calls for me that I have to return?"

After receiving her messages, she hung up and punched in the code for Palm Haven's police station. "Lieutenant Dalton Vail in Homicide," she told the operator. Then, "Dalton? Sorry to bother you at work. Just wanted to touch bases and let you know what's going on. I met Justine and Larry this morning. I hope they can entertain themselves until you pick them up later, when Brianna comes home from school. I'm stuck at the convention center all day and don't know if we'll get to my salon to do the models' hair. The company director was found dead this morning."

"You're kidding, right?"

"Actually, I'm not. The cops think she may have had a seizure. Do you think you can find out anything from your buddies in Fort Lauderdale?"

After a pause to digest the news, he said, "I'll give them a call. Give me the victim's name."

"Christine Parks. Uh-oh, I've got to go. Here comes the regional manager, and I need to talk to her. I'll get back to you later. Love you." Stuffing her cell phone back into her purse, she hustled toward Jan.

"Morning, Marla," Jan said, looking svelte in a black turtleneck sweater and a leather miniskirt. Her hazel eyes shone with clarity of purpose, while her hips swung with confidence. She looked the consummate professional, ready to take charge.

"Is that your breakfast?" Marla asked, pointing to the bottle of yogurt fruit shake in Jan's hand.

"Yep. You should try one of these drinks. They're rich in nutrients."

"That's okay. I need solid food for energy in the morning."

"Exercising helps, too. I get sluggish if I don't do my morning routine. Where's the rest of the crew?"

"Everyone is inside setting up the booth," Marla told her. "I'm so sorry about Chris. This must be very difficult for you."

Jan tossed her sleek red head. "I'm not surprised that Chris worked herself into a frenzy. She micromanaged everyone's job. I won't be like that if I get her position."

"I see," Marla said, taken aback by Jan's callous attitude. Taking advantage of the opportunity presented, she threw out a probe. "Were you surprised when she promoted you to regional manager? I understand Tyler would have liked the job."

"He was really in line for it. Tyler wouldn't give her what she wanted, though, so she passed him over. You learned quickly not to cross the boss lady, but trust was another issue. I came by that lesson the hard way."

"How so?"

"Come on, let's go inside." Jan headed for the exhibit hall. "I believed her about something and got totally messed as a result. It taught me to verify whatever she said."

"It sounds like she had a way of offending people."

Jan gave her a sly glance. "If you keep your nose down, you can get ahead at Luxor. There's plenty of opportunity for people who put the team ahead of their personal ambitions."

Like you? Give me a break. "Thanks for the advice," she murmured.

Jan halted at the main concourse inside the exhibit hall. "Have any of the models arrived yet?" she asked, peering around at the bustling scene. "Sampson told me what time they were supposed to arrive, but I forgot. How much did you get done at the booth?"

"Quite a lot, but everyone is upset by Chris's death. They need your calming influence. What did you tell the police?" Marla added in an idle tone, hoping to catch Jan off guard.

"They needed a list of company employees working on the show plus a rundown of anyone who'd spoken to Chris yesterday. That was tough, because she'd greeted a lot of folks at the cocktail party. I mean, why did they ask so many questions when she obviously had some medical problem no one recognized?"

Marla wondered if Jan had heard of the discourse between Chris and Tyler later that night, and of Chris's subsequent accusation. "It's just routine in cases with an unaccompanied death," she replied.

Veering left, Jan proceeded to their exhibit space. "I mean, who knew Chris was taking antidepressants? Someone on the hotel staff found out and told me. She had a prescription bottle in her bathroom."

"Oh, yeah? Was it something she took regularly? I wonder if seizures might be an adverse side effect."

"I'm not a pharmacist—how should I know?" Jan shrugged. "I gather people don't usually pop those pills like tranquilizers. It's likely Chris had some sort of disorder."

"Was she close enough to anyone on the Luxor team to have shared confidences?" Marla asked.

"Not in the way you mean, darling. No one knew her secrets, not even the guys she bedded. With her, it was more a control thing, you know?"

They arrived at the booth, and Marla abandoned further speculation for the moment. Jan assessed their progress and smoothly got the operation underway. By noon they'd set the stage and laid out all the products on the sales counters.

"Let's grab lunch," Jan told the assembled crew, "and then we'll head over to Marla's salon. The models are supposed to arrive by one o'clock. Amy Jeanne, you'll stay here to orient the store managers when they come in."

Miguel, bobbing his head to music from his iPod, raised his hand. "I don't have to go, do I? If I stay here, I can pass out flyers to the other exhibitors."

"Good point. Tyler, why don't you guard the booth and talk up our products to anyone who walks by? And you'll have to dispose of those empty cartons. There's not supposed to be any visible trash."

Listening to her made Marla weary. For an energy boost, she bought a mandarin orange chicken salad in a takeout container at the food court. Wandering into the convention center lobby, she elected to eat at one of the tables set up by a coffee bar, away from the loud din of drills and hammers. Georgia, who'd trailed after her, slumped into the opposite seat.

"I'm glad a few people are staying behind," Marla confessed. "That will make for less confusion at the salon. You and Jan from the sales team, Liesl and myself to assist Sampson and Ron. How many models will there be?"

Georgia scrunched her eyes. "Six for the cut-

and-style demos. Sampson wants them to display our spring palette. We need to work on their coloring today, although some are scheduled for perms or other processing first."

Bless my bones, how are they going to crowd so many people into the salon? "Just how do you expect us to get all these models done? I hadn't planned to keep my place open late."

"Don't worry, Amy got their costume measurements already, and we still have tomorrow morning for prep work. Ron said we could use his hotel room if we need extra space."

By one-thirty only five girls had checked in, and Ron was missing. Standing by the curb outside, Jan hailed a couple of taxis. "I'll go over to your salon with Sampson and this bunch. Liesl, you're with me since you have to assist our artistic director. Find Ron," she ordered Marla and her friend, "then meet us there. I have a hunch you might find him in his room. He may have already started prepping one of the models."

"I'll go look," Marla told Georgia, whose haggard expression concerned her. Back inside the hotel lobby, she pointed to a comfy seating arrangement. "Wait for me there. If you need a brief snooze, go ahead."

Anxious to proceed to her salon to head off whatever disasters might occur, she hustled to the elevators. Ron's room was on the tenth floor. Once inside the lift, she sagged against a wall. This day kept getting longer, and if every show was so exhausting, she'd rethink her decision to participate next time. But it could just be that Chris's death had put a pall over their energy. Sighing, she added another cup of coffee to her mental priority list.

"I'll be right there," Ron's voice shouted in response to her knocking on his door. A moment later, he swung the door wide while she blinked at him. He wore a white towel tucked around his waist and nothing else. Behind him, she heard a feminine giggle and saw a streaking figure clutching a sheet around itself.

"Marla, what do you want?" Ron said, raising an eyebrow.

Caught you in the act, hot shot. "You're supposed to be downstairs. We're going to my salon to do the models, remember? Jan has already left with Sampson and Liesl. She has five of the girls with her. Am I to assume that your visitor is the sixth?"

Ron had the grace to blush. "Er, I was only getting started. My sink works just as well as the ones in your shop."

"Really? Does that mean you won't be joining us?" She peered around him, but the girl had vanished into the bathroom.

"We'll come over in a while. Heather's highlights will take more time."

"Oh, yeah, I see how she'll take up your time, all right."

Ron's lip curled in a snarl. "Hey, no offense, but I do things my way. We'll show up at your salon, even if we're late. Sampson can't possibly get everyone done by himself. Tell Jan to chill in the meantime."

After handing Ron one of her business cards, Marla strode down the corridor toward the bank of elevators. If this was how he conducted business, he wouldn't be hobnobbing with Hollywood celebrities anytime soon. It could also be the reason why Ron remained in Sampson's shadow. Being a womanizer on his own time was one thing, but Chris wouldn't have permitted any male to upstage her. In her book, she stayed on top. Of course, now that she was gone, all bets were off. Did Ron hope to gain from her death? If so, Sampson remained his main obstacle at Luxor.

She remembered the check Sampson had written to Chris. What was that all about? Had he owed her money? Certainly, he hadn't been happy when Marla presented the uncashed check back to him. You'd think he would have been glad to have his debt cancelled, especially if Chris used it as a means to control him.

And these were just the stylists, she thought as she arrived at the ground floor, retrieved Georgia, and headed for the parking lot. Now that Chris's seat was open, Jan had a chance for promotion. That meant Tyler could move up to regional manager, the position that Chris had denied him.

Why am I even bothering to think this way? Force of habit, that's why. Vail's influence already had her contemplating suspects. Chris's unattended death raised some questions, including what had really happened last night between Georgia, Tyler, and the company director. Likely, the interpersonal dynamics were similar to what went on in most other firms, but then, no one ended up dead with their face in a foot bath at other firms.

It's not your concern, she told herself, withdrawing her car keys from her purse. Georgia remained silent, so Marla spent the drive trying to rally her friend's spirits.

She did a good job, because by the time they arrived at the shopping center housing the Cut 'N Dye, Georgia was chatting happily about the restaurants in San Francisco, where she lived. Her appetite had returned with gusto, necessitating a stop at Burger King on the way west. Fortunately, the afternoon air had warmed to a balmy seventy degrees with a light sea breeze.

"This is why I love living in Florida," Marla said, sipping a Diet Coke in the parking lot of her shopping strip. "It's worth the risk of hurricanes. Besides, most of the tempests I've confronted have been caused by people."

But she felt as though a whirlwind hit as soon as they walked through the door at her salon. Nicole had a panicked look on her face. "Marla, thank God," the cinnamon-skinned stylist called out from her station. "I didn't know where to put everyone."

The seats up front were filled with regular customers and a couple of the models. Glancing toward the rear, Marla noticed Sampson using her chair for a coloring job, while another model sat at an empty manicure console with foils in her hair. The fifth girl occupied a seat by the shampoo sinks. Liesl stood by Sampson's side, looking bored.

What am I supposed to do when Ron gets here, hand him his styling combs? Marla wondered. *Is that all my role requires?*

"How's it going, guys?" She waved to her staff members. Other than Nicole, whom she'd left in charge, the rest of her crew seemed oblivious to the commotion. Not surprising, considering some of the other interruptions they'd experienced in the past, thanks to Marla's sleuthing.

Jan intercepted her. "Did you find Ron? We're on a time schedule, you know." The redhead tapped her watch.

"He wanted to start the other model in his room. He'll be along shortly."

Jan must have heard something in her voice, because she snorted. "Don't count on it."

"I can do one of the girls in the meantime," Marla offered.

"Not yet. Let's review the setup for our photo shoot." She signaled for Marla to follow her to the reception area.

As Marla passed the front desk, Luis grinned. She imagined the handsome Hispanic enjoyed having the models close by. One of them had evidently gotten tired of sitting around. The tall raven-haired beauty flipped through a magazine on his counter, sneaking glances at his dark eyes and trim beard. *Wait until Ron arrives, pal. You'll have competition.*

Her attention turned to Georgia, who'd removed an entire display case worth of goods. The sales rep had placed Luxor products on the shelves instead and was now occupied in arranging them in a certain order.

"Can I help you with those?" Marla asked, scurrying over.

She didn't want to incur the disfavor of her other accounts.

"Listen, hon, you're representing Luxor now. We have to show off our merchandise to its best advantage." Georgia had tied a bandanna around her head to keep her curly black hair off her face. Her eyes sparkled as she put a sign in front of a promotional videotape for sale. "We have a unique straightening process that Sampson will be applying next if you want to watch. He's certified to perform thermal hair reconditioning. Customers can buy this video if they want to see how it works."

"Wonderful, but perhaps we should replace this stock—"

"Marla, let's not quibble over minor stuff. Georgia is one of our top sales reps," Jan chided. "Look, this is a good spot for the photographer. He can place the backdrop screen over there, and the lights will go in these two spots. Do you have any potted plants to soften the scene?"

"Sure," Marla mumbled, feeling as though a steamroller had overtaken her salon. Better to go with the flow, and fix things later.

She didn't realize how much time passed while shuffling around following Jan's orders, assisting Ron, who sauntered in the door two hours late, and fitting in one of her own clients with a rush job. Jan was haranguing everyone to finish and get back to the hotel when Detective Dalton Vail strode through the door with his daughter and her grand-parents in tow.

"Marla," he cried, his craggy face breaking into a smile, "I just stopped by to show Justine and Larry your place, but I didn't expect to see you here. How about joining us for dinner?"

Marla glanced at a wall clock. It was past five already? "I'm afraid not. The show opens tomorrow morning at nine. We need to make sure the ex-hibit is ready as well as the models." She swept her hand to indicate the preening girls, adjusting their costumes in front of the mirror.

Justine's eyes widened as she took in Ron's out-fit, a khaki shirt open to the waist and hip-hugging leather pants. But that was nothing compared to the shimmering sequined tops and miniskirts on the models.

"Dear heavens, Marla, is this the norm for your clients?" the older woman exclaimed, staring at the rainbow of hair colors the models displayed. One girl sported shades of red alternating with plum. It made her nose ring stand out.

"Not really," Marla replied, her cheeks warming. "It's purely for razzle-dazzle at the show."

"Maybe if this were Las Vegas." Justine sniffed.

"You and Georgia can have the evening off," Jan told Marla with a knowing smile. "We'll be outta here soon, before your doors close at six. So run along, and have a good time."

Oh joy. Marla plastered a smile on her face as she turned to Vail. At least Georgia would be there to give her moral support. "If you don't mind having us tag along . . ."

"Don't be silly, sweetcakes," her fiancé said, beaming. "We're all one big happy family. Aren't we?" he asked his daughter.

"Sure," said the thirteen-year-old, swinging her ponytail. "We'd love for you to come. Right, Nana?"

Chapter
Six

Vail decided to take his former in-laws to Padrino's for dinner, because they'd never eaten Cuban food. Marla had her doubts that they'd like black beans and rice, but Georgia might find it fun. Personally, she liked the restaurant for its white-clothed tables, lively atmosphere, and tasty fare. Located in the Fountains Shopping Center, it held its place among the competition. She often went there for lunch, choosing the reasonably priced buffet.

"You certainly have your choice of malls nearby," Justine commented when their party met up with Marla and her friend at the entrance. Marla had driven separately, giving Vail time with his family. After a harassing day, she'd rather have gone home and changed first, but she was curious to know if Vail had learned anything about Christine's death from his cronies. Nor could she constantly avoid her guests. She'd accepted the responsibility, and it wasn't her policy to shirk her duties, however unpleasant.

"I looked for a space here when I considered

moving my salon," she confessed, ducking under Vail's outstretched arm while he held the restaurant door open. "But I prefer the idea of pedestrian traffic, and Palm Haven has a town square under construction. It's going to be really neat, with upscale boutiques, bistros, and a cutting-edge technology museum that'll draw young people to the area. The opportunity to get in at the ground level was too good to miss."

"That's awesome, Marla," Georgia gushed. "We'll have to drive over there so I can take a look. When will the place be ready?"

Marla stood aside while Vail gave his name to the hostess. "They say it'll take six more months, but you know how those things go. Meanwhile, I'm hoping to decide what sinks I want, the fixtures, and all the other stuff that goes into a salon."

"Won't you take anything from Cut 'N Dye?"

"No. I really want to start fresh. Probably I'll sell most of the old equipment. I'm hoping to look around at the show, see what's new."

"What did you gals accomplish today?" Vail asked, filing behind them into the dining room. Their round table seated six, and Marla found herself wedged between him and Georgia. His in-laws flanked Brianna, who grabbed for the sliced bread as soon as the waiter set a basket on the table.

Marla saved her answer until after their drinks arrived. She and Georgia shared a pitcher of sangria. Swallowing a gulp of the chilled fruity wine, she proceeded. "We set up the exhibit, got the stage ready for tomorrow's demos, and prepped the models in my salon. I'm amazed we got that much done, considering how the day started."

"Oh, yeah—about that call you wanted me to make," Vail began, twirling his water glass.

"Justine and Larry probably aren't interested in hearing about our jobs," Georgia interrupted, lifting her glass in a mock toast. "I'm so glad to finally meet you," she told them. "You and Brianna must have a lot of catching up to do."

Marla gave her a sly glance. Had she diverted the conversation on purpose? If so, for whose benefit?

"Brie is so grown up now." Larry puffed out his chest. "Did she tell you she got an A on her last English test? And she's trying out for soccer in the spring term? Way to go, pumpkin."

"Soccer?" Marla said. "You didn't tell me about that, sweetie," she added, turning to Brianna. "I think you'd be great at it, with your long legs." At thirteen, Brianna already showed promise of being tall. She'd started filling out, and height wasn't the only manifestation of her growth. Soccer would be really good to keep her in shape. But who would take her to the games if Vail had to work late?

"I don't know, Marla," Justine said, glaring at her over a slightly uptilted nose. "Raising a teenager is a big responsibility. Brie will need someone to drive her around, and that's only the beginning. These can be tumultuous years."

"I drove Brianna to ballet class for a while, so I know what to expect," she retorted, her muscles tensing. "And Brie already looks to me for guidance on grooming matters, right?" she asked the girl, who nodded. "We'll work things out."

Justine's lips tightened, making Marla wonder how Vail had described their arrangement. He'd promised she wouldn't get stuck with housekeeping duties or attending school functions unless it was her choice. Knowing how she felt about children, he understood the reason for making these promises, but Justine and Larry had no knowledge of the tragedy in her past or even about her previous marriage.

"I'll bet your daughter would be proud of the young lady Brie has turned into," Georgia said to Justine as she nudged Marla's knee under the table. What was she trying to do, forge a mutual admiration society? Pam's parents would never accept her as a substitute for Brianna's mother.

Justine's eyes misted. "You're right. Brianna has her same dark eyes, too. She'd only want what's best for you, dear," she told the girl.

"Mom would want Daddy to be happy, too." Fiddling with her fork, Brie spoke quietly. Marla's heart went out to her. Caught in the middle, she shouldn't be forced to choose sides.

"Your father needs a strong woman to support him. He works long hours in the police force, and some nights he doesn't come home at all. That's not the proper forum in which to raise children, unless he has a wife who cares more about her family than her job."

Marla half rose from her seat. "Excuse me? Today a lot of families have two-career households. I can provide the same level of care as a stay-at-home mom. In addition, I'll be a good role model for Brie."

"Marla is there for us when we need her," Vail added, his fierce scowl challenging his in-laws to defy him. "She may wear a lot of hats, but she puts her heart where it counts."

"No kidding," Georgia put in with a teasing grin. "It's true that if Marla says she'll do something, she'll follow through to the end—and that doesn't always work to her advantage. Like when we were college freshmen and she was put in charge of the light-bulb sale to raise money for our sorority. When the day came to distribute the bulbs, Marla noticed the supply fell short. She went around and unscrewed all the lights in the common rooms that weren't being used and gave them to people to sell. She'd planned to run to the hardware store later to buy more, but before she could replace the bulbs in the empty sockets, the dean dropped by for a surprise visit. Needless to say, she got in a heap of trouble."

Marla flushed in embarrassment while the others laughed, all except Justine, who didn't appear amused. Marla remembered how she'd tried to live up to her commitment and had fully intended to replace the missing bulbs before the day's end. That lesson taught her to expect the unexpected and to assess a situation before she got involved in it. Of course, sometimes she got sucked into things she'd rather avoid anyway, like this conversation.

"Let's talk about something else," she suggested, leaning back while the waitress delivered their meals.

"Yeah, Marla, let's talk about that woman who died this morning," Brianna said, making Marla nearly choke on the forkful of pan-fried tilapia in her mouth. "We often discuss cases over dinner," the girl told her shocked grandparents.

"Well, I never," Justine remarked, giving Marla a scathing glance.

"It helps to talk things out," Marla said. "Brianna is pretty smart, and sometimes she comes up with a new angle. We consider it an intellectual exercise. Right, honey?"

Georgia cut in. "This may not be the best place to talk about Christine. I'd rather tell you about our new line of sunscreen products. We're totally going to *rule* at the show."

Sensing that Georgia was revving up for a sales pitch, Marla pressed forward. "Dalton, did you speak to your colleagues in the Fort Lauderdale precinct about their findings?"

Looking like a piece of meat being haggled over by a group of squawking vultures, Vail pounced on her opening. "Actually, I did. It doesn't appear as though the victim's death resulted from natural causes."

"That makes it a homicide case, right, Dad?" Brianna said proudly. "Like, don't keep us in the dark. What did you learn?"

He gave her an indulgent grin. "The deceased had a labeled prescription bottle in her bathroom. She took antidepressants, but the preliminary toxicology report showed a different type of medication in her system, something called a monoamine oxidase inhibitor."

"What's that?" Marla swallowed a bite of fried plantains.

"It's a drug that's dangerous when taken with certain foods. Together, they can produce a hypertensive crisis. But Chris's regular prescription was for a newer medicine that doesn't cause this adverse reaction."

"I don't understand. What foods do you mean?"

"Red wine and aged cheese, for example. She may have ingested these items at your cocktail party last evening."

"Are you saying someone may have slipped her a riskier drug, or that her prescription was wrong?"

He peered at her from beneath his thick eyebrows. "The pills in her bottle were analyzed. They matched the label."

"I don't get it." Marla tilted her head. "Somebody gave her a different antidepressant? Why? To produce a deadly interaction, and yet let it seem as though she had collapsed from a seizure?"

"But she did have a seizure," Georgia put in.

"That's one of the outcomes of a hypertensive crisis," Vail explained. "In this situation, not of natural causes."

"Chris drank wine last night," Marla added. "Her glass always seemed to be full. I saw her nibble on cheese and crackers, too. How can that be harmful?"

Vail pulled a sheaf of folded papers from his pocket. "The forensics guy faxed this over because I didn't understand the whole thing myself." He consulted his printout. "If you want to get technical, the first generation of drugs known as MAO inhibitors had a major side effect called the cheese reaction. There's a substance present in certain foods that has the ability to release noradrenaline. This substance is called tyramine."

"Really, Dalton, is this necessary?" Justine said with a sniff.

He spared her a glance. "Just let me finish. The MAO inhibitors prevent noradrenaline from metabolizing. That means when you combine those foods with this type of drug, you get an increase in sympathetic nervous activity."

"Huh?" Marla took a sip of sangria, hoping the red wine it contained wouldn't produce any adverse reactions.

Vail summarized from his notes. "MAO-A is the specific enzyme responsible for noradrenaline metabolism. After this was identified, the newer drugs were developed."

"Didn't you say Chris's medicine was not harmful?" Marla asked while another gulp of fruity wine slid down her throat.

"Correct. She was taking one of the safer reversible inhibitors. The classic antidepressants are rarely prescribed anymore, but they may still be used for depressed people who don't respond to other meds. In other words, you can still get hold of them."

"So if you're taking the classic drugs, you have to avoid red wine and cheese?"

"Any foods with tyramine, including aged cheeses, processed meats, wine, beer, yogurt, chocolate, and caffeine."

"All the good stuff," Marla muttered, thinking she'd almost prefer to risk illness than give up her morning coffee.

"What are the symptoms of a bad reaction?" Brianna inserted, buttering another piece of bread. Marla noticed she'd polished off half the loaf.

Vail shuffled through his pages until he found the response. "Headache, palpitations, nausea, chest pain, seizures, then circulatory collapse."

"Chris complained of a headache last night," Georgia said, twisting her napkin. "Oh gosh, I remember she ate some salami."

Justine gave them all chastising looks. "This is a horrible topic to discuss at the dinner table. I swear, Dalton, if Pam were alive, she'd have your hide for exposing the child to this sordid business."

"You're right," Marla said, agreeing for once. She glanced at Vail, who wore a sheepish expression while stuffing the papers back into his pocket. No time like the present for a change of subject. "Tell me, Justine, what did Pam like to do for fun? Dalton mentioned that she took walks in the park."

It wouldn't hurt for her to meet Pam's parents at the halfway mark. They meant to guard Brianna's future, so they'd probably scrutinize anyone Dalton chose for a second wife. She shouldn't regard their remarks as personal criticism. It was time to dismiss Pam as a rival for Dalton's affection and move on. He'd been willing to put his wife's ghost to rest; now it was her turn. Fixing an interested expression on her face, she leaned forward.

Justine's eyes lit up. "Pam was an old-fashioned girl at heart. She grew up with traditional values. Being a stay-at-home mom was important to her, but she also liked entertaining and getting involved in parent activities."

Marla half-listened while Justine droned on about Pam's sterling qualities. She had intended to pay attention, but Vail's drug explanations echoed in her mind, being of much more interest.

After they got home and her guests had retired to their rooms, Marla pushed aside her concerns and decided to get caught up on her phone calls. She spoke to her mother and brother, then phoned her best friend, Tally. Tally owned the Dress to Kill boutique where Marla bought a lot of her clothes.

"How's the hair show?" Tally asked. "Or would you rather tell me how you're getting along with your visitors?"

"You won't believe this, but the company director was found dead this morning. Someone may have slipped her a drug similar to pills she was taking but with deadlier side effects."

"No way. Marla, don't tell me you're involved in another murder investigation."

"Of course not." Marla filled her in on events so far. "Isn't it curious that Chris's demise happened under these circumstances? Think about it. A group of people get together only for these trade shows. Someone among them knows that Chris takes antidepressants. It's possible this person obtained the more dangerous drug and either substituted some tablets in Chris's container or slipped it to her through another means."

"Like in her drink at the cocktail party."

"Exactly. What does this add up to in your mind?"

"A premeditated crime," Tally said.

"I got the impression that a lot of folks didn't care for Chris. She rubbed people the wrong way. Tyler, our area supervisor, was pissed that she promoted Janice Davidson over him. Jan made a remark that the promotion wouldn't make up for what Chris did to her, and even Sampson got spooked when I tried to return a check he'd written to Chris."

"Sounds like you've already been snooping." Her friend's tone held amusement.

"I'm keeping my ears open, that's all." Marla lowered her voice. "I can't talk about it to Georgia. She keeps changing the subject. I'm wondering what really happened between her, Chris, and Tyler last night."

"It's been a long time since you've seen each other. I'd be careful what you say around her."

"Georgia can't be guilty. She wouldn't harm a soul. She certainly isn't capable of committing murder."

"No? Then perhaps you can find out what, if anything, she stands to gain from Chris's death."

"Who, me? I'm not getting involved. My job is to assist the master stylists at the show and host a photo shoot at my salon. That'll be enough to keep me busy."

Tally's low, throaty chuckle didn't come as a surprise. "Yeah, right. Since when has a hectic work schedule stopped you from sticking your nose where it doesn't belong?"

Sitting on her bed, Marla grinned. "You have a

point. I'm really trying to be good, though, with Pam's parents here. It isn't easy when they keep comparing me unfavorably to their daughter."

"You can't blame them. They must miss her terribly."

Marla traced the pattern on her bedspread. "I guess so." An uncomfortable lump rose in her throat. Justine and Larry brought home the fact that Pam had been a living and breathing individual, a loving mother to the family that Marla wanted to join, and a vibrant woman who had been taken from life too soon. Could it be that the pain of loss was reminding her once again of her own past mistakes and inadequacies?

"How is Ken? Any progress in that department?" she asked Tally to defer the conversation from herself. Her friend had been trying to get pregnant for months now. Since fertility tests had shown there wasn't any physical problem, that left stress as a possible culprit. Ken had urged her to hire a manager for her dress shop so she could take more time off. Tally had resented his implication of blame, and they'd embarked on rocky waters in their relationship.

"We're thinking about taking a cruise," Tally replied. "Ken won't admit that his job makes him tense, and we could both use the break. I don't know if I could stand being on a ship for an entire week, though."

"You know what they say—a relaxing cruise washes away your worries. I wouldn't mind trying one."

"What about those brochures in your purse? Doesn't look as if you'll get to Tahiti anytime soon."

"How about never? I can still dream, though. I'd be lucky to get as far as the Caribbean islands."

Even the Caribbean seemed a lifetime away when

Marla entered the trade-show exhibit hall early the next morning. Pounding music blared from loud-speakers as she strode past a flashing neon siren at the Code Blue display of wigs and accessories. Red carpeting had been laid down the aisles, and bright lights glared from tracks on the cavernous ceiling. Her pulse jumped as opening hour approached. Anticipation charged the air, and she had to force herself to stay on course to Luxor's booth instead of straying to browse the exhibits.

Marla spied Tyler examining some Lado styling tools and stopped to tap on his shoulder. Georgia had already gone ahead, disappearing around the corner occupied by tooth-whitening products. Wares beckoned from all directions, making her wish she was attending the show instead of working it. She'd really like to take some of the classes offered in the advertised seminars.

"Morning," she said to Tyler, who wore a suede jacket over a delft blue shirt. "It's easy to get distracted, isn't it?" She pointed across the way. "I need to check out those capes later. I'm going with a new color scheme when I move my salon."

Grinning, he fell into step beside her. "You'll have time during your lunch break to scout around."

"Are we sticking to Chris's schedule, or did Jan change things?"

His smile disappeared. "She's made some adjustments. The cops wanna talk to us again, so Jan set up interview times."

"That's a bummer," Marla said, using his type of language.

"Not so much for me as for your pal."

"What do you mean?"

Tyler stopped by a video displaying an application of permanent makeup. "Didn't Georgia tell you? When we spoke to Chris the night before last, she accused us of having an affair. Like, that's totally false. You were there in the lounge, and you heard our conversation. Chris was way out of line. Worse, she was even angrier at Georgia than at me. I felt bad because Georgia had tried to do me a favor by coming along, but Chris wouldn't listen to us." He paused. "She fired Georgia on the spot."

Chapter
Seven

Tyler's voice deepened. "No one else knows, except for us. But now that Chris is gone, Georgia can keep her job. Things worked out to her benefit."

Marla hadn't realized her jaw had dropped open, but now she snapped it shut. Why hadn't Georgia mentioned anything about this to her? She recalled how her friend kept avoiding the subject of Chris's death. What else did Georgia have to hide?

"And then?" she said. "Is that when you left?"

"I gave up, figuring Chris might be in a better mood in the morning. Like, I tried to tell Georgia, man, but she was too upset. I could hear them arguing as I walked down the hall."

"Did you notice the time?"

"It was, like, after one o'clock." He resumed his pace toward their exhibit.

Marla shifted her purse as she strode beside him down the aisle. "Were you aware that Chris took antidepressants?" Vail might have wanted her to withhold that information, but Jan knew about it already from the hotel staff.

Tyler gave her an oblique look. "Chris's personal life wasn't my concern."

Before she could question him further, they arrived at their booth. Jan, looking stunning in a black suit with gold trim, descended upon them, clipboard in hand. She meted out assignments without so much as a greeting.

"Tyler, allow me to introduce you to Lou and Nina. They're local store managers who will be helping Miguel and Georgia at the sales counter this morning. Amy Jeanne will oversee their operation, while you and I will follow up on our accounts."

Marla glanced at the stage, where Ron was setting up equipment. Liesl, who'd been helping him, bustled over.

"Hi, Tyler," the young stylist said, wiggling her body, dressed in a metallic grape-colored sheath.

"Hiya," Tyler said, barely sparing her a glance. But then he seemed to have second thoughts and winked at her. "Cute outfit, babe. Where's Sampson?"

"The maestro is still upstairs," Ron called out. He wore a flashy black jacket emblazoned with silver studs. "Hey, Marla, come over here. You're doing a demo this morning."

Startled, she gazed at him. "Huh? What demo?" She approached the stage, noting he'd laid out his cutting implements on a tray.

"We thought it would be instructional to correct your technique in a live performance. One of the models is coming in at ten. You'll do a cut-and-style, and I'll critique your work."

"Are you kidding? I'm not prepared for anything like that."

He tossed her a smock to wear over her suit. Earlier, she'd refused to wear a costume like a showgirl. "You'll do fine," he said with a reassuring grin. "Just be careful with my tools, okay?"

As the show got underway, she had to raise her voice to be heard. A cluster of bejeweled models swept past the aisle, their hips swaying to the music as though they were on a runway. They represented Farouk Systems, which apparently had a presentation coming up. She needed to see a program.

"Is there anything on extensions?" she asked Liesl during a momentary lull. "I see they're doing braiding over at Donado International." Not all the companies had big stage productions or their own theater like Paul Mitchell's artists. Many of the companies offered exhibit-hall education at their booths. Creative hair design interested her, because she was thinking she'd like to do more of that in her new salon location. The more elaborate jobs brought in bigger bucks, and she'd need added income to balance her expense sheet.

"You have several choices for extensions," the blonde said, consulting the schedule. "Torain is doing a class. He's well-known as an author, teacher, and cosmetology demonstrator. 'Torain introduced the contemporary adhesive hair-extension system called Fusion,'" Liesl read. "'Learn techniques that will allow you to perform one of today's highest-paying salon services.'"

"That sounds good," Marla replied. "Anything else?" She peered over Liesl's shoulder.

"Here's a demo that specializes in products for the Hispanic market. That could be useful for you in South Florida. Or else, Baha is presenting their Ultratress hair-extension technique. Get this, luv. You could win a free class valued at five hundred dollars if you attend."

"Nice, but I wouldn't have time to take advantage of it."

"How about this one? 'Increase your ticket price by learning about wigs, weaves, and extensions.'"

"Too complicated. I need to concentrate on one technique at a time. Actually, I'm hoping to learn the most from watching Ron and Sampson."

Liesl gave her a guarded smile, as though she wanted to be Marla's friend but couldn't quite loosen her reserve. "Sampson acts like a blooming prima donna, but he knows his stuff. He's a Platform Artist of the Year winner and was nominated for Top International Stylist. I plan to stick with the bloke."

"Did he enter any of the professional competitions at this show?" The first fifteen contestants in each hair competition received a free mannequin. That hardly made up for the hundred-dollar registration fee, in Marla's opinion. Then again, entering contests served as a means to garner recognition. It might be worthwhile to consider for the future, especially if winning could raise her profile with Luxor.

"Not that I'm aware of. Look, there goes Adam Phelan. He won the GQ Image of the Year and Next Generation Fellowship awards. I think he's doing a workshop on razor cutting."

"You seem to know a lot of these people." Marla was familiar only with the big names, but, then, she didn't attend as many shows as Luxor's team.

"It's part of the job."

"What do you get out of it, aside from having your travel expenses paid?"

Liesl's gaze slid to Tyler. "It helps me improve my skills, luv. I don't have any ambition to open my own place, but I aim to work in a high-class London salon one day. For now, I'm not tied down. Chris appreciated my ability to join the group at short notice. She wouldn't bring anyone in who was too rigid. I guess you're lucky there was a last-minute opening for another stylist."

"Thanks to Georgia. She's pretty much a free soul, isn't she?" Marla said with affection.

"Rubbish. Georgia is looking to get hitched." Liesl brushed a stray strand of hair behind her ear. "She almost got married at our last show in Vegas. I'm surprised she agreed to work with Chris again after what happened."

Ron signaled them with an annoyed frown on his face. Pushing aside her nervousness at her upcoming performance, Marla pressed Liesl for more information as they headed toward the master stylist. "And what was that?"

"Why, don't you know? That's when Georgia discovered Christine in bed with her fiancé."

"You're kidding, right?"

Liesl gave her a knowing glance. "I'm serious. Georgia and Nick were thinking about getting married in one of the wedding chapels. She broke off the engagement after catching him with Chris. Chris let on that he'd seduced her, but Georgia didn't believe it. She figured Chris had to assert control as a reminder that she was in charge. When you worked for Chris, it was her way or no way. Personal issues had no place on her ground, or she'd mow you down."

Turning away, Liesl left while Marla stared after her. *Why didn't Georgia tell me?* she thought, narrowing her eyes as she glanced at her friend, who worked the counter blithely as though nothing untoward had happened. Had Georgia used this show as a cover to get revenge? If so, why wait until now?

Maybe that hadn't been enough to motivate Georgia to murder her boss. Maybe getting fired had lit the fuse. But that didn't make sense, if Chris ingested the wrong drug in time for the cocktail party, or even at the event. Presumably it was the food she ate there that interacted adversely with the medication in her system. That meant someone had slipped it to her before she'd fired Georgia, right?

Chewing her bottom lip, Marla contemplated the possibility that she had housed a murderess under her roof this weekend. Even though it seemed illogical, she couldn't help adding Georgia to her list of suspects. What would Georgia do when the police got her alone for more intensive questioning?

I have to help her, Marla decided. Despite her suspicions, she didn't believe Georgia had done in their bossy director. No one had cared for Chris, and someone else was just as likely to have slipped her the dangerous drug. Marla could try to find out who would have the requisite medical knowledge as well as access to prescription medications, like the earlier class of antidepressant that wasn't much used today.

With her concentration elsewhere, Marla had trouble focusing on her stage demo. Ron shouted orders while she snipped and styled the model's hair. She fumbled the shears more than once, aware of the growing crowd, but all she could think of was Chris's absence.

Ron lifted her elbow. "Hold this section closer to the head and take smaller cuts," he said, speaking into his lapel microphone. "You want it to fall back in just this way." Grabbing a segment of hair, he showed her the proper technique. The silver studs on his jacket shimmered from the overhead lights. He drew aside with a flourish but not before she saw his glowing expression.

Of course. Sampson was the only one on the schedule today for giving a presentation at Luxor's exhibit, so Ron had arranged for this little lesson out of spite. It gave him a chance to showcase his talent under the guise of teaching Marla. How clever.

But how did Ron know that Sampson would be late? Probably the artistic director slept in at every show. Or he'd entered an early competition so he could strut his stuff twice in one day. Marla wouldn't put it past him.

Sampson strolled into view just as she prepared to take a break. She'd ended up acquitting herself rather well at the demo, pleased with how the model's hair turned out. From the rapt faces on the audience, it appeared people had enjoyed the display. Marla hadn't realized how much satisfaction could come from instructing others. This time she had been a student under Ron's tutelage. Maybe next time, she'd try the role as teacher.

"Want to walk around with me?" she asked Georgia. They had enough people to man the counters. Every hour, someone left to speak to the police investigator. Marla's turn came after lunch, which wouldn't be beneficial to her digestive system. Better grab a snack now so she'd have her wits about her later.

"Sure, hon." Georgia reached under the counter to snatch her purse. "You wanted to check out the salon furniture, didn't you? I think there's a whole section just before the nail polishes. And I'd like to get into the Ace discount store if we have time. The line was too long when I went by there earlier."

"I'm glad to see you're in a better mood. Shopping always gives me a lift, too." With a grin, Marla started down the aisle. She and Georgia both wore their smocks with the company logo.

Farther along, she gaped at a group of male dancers gyrating on a stage to a pounding beat of loud rock music. They wore tight black pants and body-hugging shirts, except for a pumpkin-haired guy in a kilt. Waving his arms over his head, he rotated his hips in an erotic motion that brought cat-calls from the female audience. Another troupe of dancers trounced around on stage, women wearing tube tops adorned with blinking lights, their spiked hair in sunburst colors.

She didn't realize she'd stopped until Georgia yanked her onward. "You wanna ogle guys? Check out the Menswork performance later. They're showing their punk collection in rock-and-roll hair."

"That's okay. Now here's something I need." She pointed to another exhibit. "Bridal services. New graduates don't realize all the things you can do with wedding parties."

"Come on over, ladies." The educator, a svelte brunette, signaled to them. "We're demonstrating spectacular hair for your spring and summer brides. Create an unforgettable look that your customers will remember for a lifetime. Spend a few minutes with us and you'll see how to accessorize with veils and jewelry. Learn folding, knotting, lacing, and banding techniques. Wait, don't leave. Take one of our promotional packets."

The salesgirl handed Marla a stuffed bag full of sample products and literature. *I should have brought a shopping cart for all the freebies,* Marla reflected. The bridal market was another area in which she could expand, with pre-wedding consultations as well as onsite service packages. But that would have to wait until she moved into her new salon.

"I always feel overwhelmed at these shows," she admitted to Georgia, turning down a row where brooms for sweeping hair were on sale along with tattoo jewelry, hair clips, styling books, and ceramic straightening irons. Smells of garlic and onions reached her nostrils as they arrived at the far end near the food court, where they got in line at Starbucks.

Georgia shifted from one foot to the other. "I love having the opportunity to travel and learn new techniques. I wouldn't be able to go to so many places just on my salary."

"Do you rent your chair or work on commission?"

"I'm a renter, so I can reschedule my clients if a show comes up. I like being independent."

"I don't do chair rentals at my salon anymore. It gives me more control and makes for better team spirit when we split a commission. I think your owner can be more involved that way."

"You also have more responsibilities, like restocking shelves and continuing the education for your stylists," Georgia pointed out.

"That's why I go to classes, so I can bring home the things I learn." At the window, Marla ordered a tall black coffee and a piece of the low-fat cinnamon cake. Offering to treat her friend, she stood back while Georgia placed her order.

"I'd like to take you out to dinner," Georgia said. "It's the least I can do in return for your letting me stay at your place."

"Let's see what Dalton has planned with Larry and Justine." Balancing her hot coffee cup and plate, Marla advanced to the condiment station. "I guess you've never had to worry about in-laws, let alone a man's in-laws from his previous marriage."

She kept her tone idle, as though not expecting a reply. In truth, Marla hoped to prod Georgia into telling her about Las Vegas.

Finding a seat at an unoccupied table, Georgia claimed the spot, and Marla followed suit after adding cream and sugar to her coffee. "I almost had the chance for a family, but Chris ruined it for me," Georgia said, the corners of her mouth turned down.

Marla blew on the hot liquid in her cup. "How so?"

"I finally met a man I really dug. We were talking about getting married. He'd even gone so far as to buy me a ring." Georgia cast her eyes downward, twirling a plastic spoon in her cappuccino. "He came to the last show in Vegas with me. Nick attended the cocktail party and had a good time meeting everyone. But that was a mistake."

"Go on." Marla leaned forward so she could hear over the background chatter echoing in the huge hall. Dipping her tongue into her drink, she determined the coffee had cooled enough for her to sip.

"It was so awesome, us being there together, but I let it distract me," Georgia said. "Chris felt I wasn't up to par. Nick and I were thinking about hiring one of those wedding chapels, and we had arrangements to make. Chris got mad when I told her what we had in mind."

"What did she care what you did on your personal time? Besides, she should have been happy for you."

"Not when Luxor paid my way. Anyway, I went off with some of the girls to go shopping, but I felt guilty leaving Nick behind. So I returned early. Chris was in bed with him." Georgia lifted her face, her eyes filled with remembered pain.

"You must have been furious."

"Furious doesn't begin to describe how I felt. It was my room, so I kicked them out, and I threw Nick's suitcase in the hall after him. I never wanted to see him again."

"What about Chris? I'd blame her for seducing the guy. What a rotten thing to do behind your back."

"I hated her, but I understood her reasons. It was never about stealing Nick from me. Chris, ever the control freak, expected my full devotion, and our romance interfered. She probably figured we'd have a spat and make up later, but I couldn't forgive Nick for betraying me."

"So you just went back to work?"

"I told Chris I didn't have to like working for her, but I had an obligation to Luxor, and I wouldn't abandon the crew. I guess I was kinda hoping she wouldn't be around for the Beauty Classic trade show that I'd signed on for next."

"Why didn't you tell me about this before?"

Georgia shrugged. "It's history. What matters now is that I'm single and looking."

"It matters that Chris is dead and you have a possible motive, if her death proves to be a deliberate act."

"Excuse me? It's a far reach to believe I'd knock Chris off over something that happened months ago."

"Combined with the fact that she just fired you, I'd say you're a prime suspect." Marla forked a piece of cake into her mouth. The moist cinnamon flavor melted on her tongue.

"Who told you that?"

"Tyler remarked that you're lucky to still have a job. He said how convenient it was for you that Chris died, and no one is the wiser."

"He'd better keep his mouth shut. I hope he didn't rat on me to the detective. You're not gonna say anything, are you?"

"I've learned not to volunteer information." They fell silent, consuming their snacks. "Can I ask you something?" Marla said after swallowing her last bite. "Liesl answers my questions well enough, but she seems hard to get to know. I notice she acts more relaxed around you."

"Don't take it personally. She feels guilty about her family history. Once when she was tipsy, she told me about it. Liesl's grandfather served in the Gestapo. His wife fled to England with their children, one of whom married an American and moved to the United States. That was Liesl's mother."

"Why should she feel bad about what her grandfather did?"

"Collective guilt. I imagine she feels awkward around you."

"Tell me about it." Marla rolled her shoulders to shrug off worldly concerns. They had enough problems without worrying about buried hatreds and generational atonement.

She consulted her floor map for the booth with AB Salon Equipment. "Number thirty-four hundred is at the south end opposite the OPI exhibit. Let's move on."

Tossing her trash into a garbage can, she started down the nearest aisle. She couldn't decide what to look at first: gleaming shears at Ashai Scissors, titanium brushes at Interfashion USA, or Turbo Power hair dryers. Georgia lingered by a collection of shiny metal tweezers.

Some guy was arguing with a security guard at another hairbrush booth. "When I opened the package I'd bought, the brush wasn't the same model this fellow showed me. I want the one I paid for," he said in a loud voice.

Uh-oh. Marla hastened forward, dodging a surge of nail techs who stomped by discussing the latest China Glaze collection.

"Tell me again what happened last night," she said to Georgia, hoping to spot a discrepancy in Tyler's report.

"I'm getting sick of repeating myself." Glancing at her, Georgia sighed. "Sorry, I know you're trying to help. I went along to give Tyler moral support, and Chris accused us of having an affair. She thought I wanted revenge for what she did to me and Nick. I tried to convince her otherwise, but she wouldn't listen. She kept shouting at me, and her face was so red, I thought she'd burst a blood vessel."

"She complained of a headache earlier, remember? She might have been feeling ill by then."

"Oh, she was ill all right. That woman had mental problems."

Alarm shot up Marla's spine. Did Georgia know that Chris had a history of depression before they learned about the antidepressants? Jostled by the crowd, she consulted her map to get her bearings. They should make a right at the Creative Nail corner.

"You saw how Chris ordered you around," Georgia continued. "She didn't respect anyone, not even Sampson. He's our leading design artist, and yet she made him dance to her tune same as everyone else."

Marla recalled the check he'd written to Chris. "I wonder what hold she had on him."

"Good question."

"Let's keep our ears open. If you hear anything that might be important, let me know, okay?"

"I'm more likely to add to your problems. Gosh, hon, I've brought a load of trouble on you, haven't I?" Georgia patted Marla's shoulder.

Marla thought about Justine and Larry waiting back in her town house to offer more criticisms, Dalton's probable resentment that he was left to deal with them alone, and Brianna caught in the middle. Never mind that she found herself in the midst of another murder.

"Don't worry about it," she replied with a wry twist to her lips. "I manage to find enough trouble on my own."

Chapter
Eight

The homicide detective appropriated an un-used classroom on the second floor for his in-terviews. Marla wiped her sweaty palms on her smock as she approached the door and gave her name to a deputy standing guard. She should be used to this by now, but it wasn't Vail questioning her this time.

Sergeant Masterson had a craggy face like Columbo's and wore a rumpled blue shirt with a diagonally striped tie. He'd discarded his jacket, draping it over an empty chair. At his motion to enter, Marla strolled inside and sank into the seat he indicated. She hadn't passed anyone in the hallway, making her wonder whom he'd interviewed last. Steeling herself, she clutched her hands in her lap while primly crossing her ankles.

After she answered the standard opening ques-tions, he got down to business. His keen brown eyes narrowed as he fired the first salvo. "Tell me how you first met Christine Parks." She noticed that his shoulders hunched while he waited for her reply.

"My friend Georgia introduced me to her on Friday." She compressed her lips, having learned not to offer extra information. She waited to see where he would lead her.

"This was your first experience working with this group, correct?" he said, consulting his notes. He clicked on a ballpoint pen in his hand.

"Yes, that's right. Georgia told me there was an opening for an assistant stylist. I thought it would be a great opportunity to try something new."

"You've known Miss Rogers for how long?"

"We were college roommates. We both dropped out after our sophomore year to go to beauty school." Her gaze slid to the floor. That wasn't the only reason why she'd dropped out, but the tragedy that had set her on her current path had no relevance to this investigation. She lifted her glance, staring at him defiantly. "I lost contact with Georgia for a while, but then she found my e-mail address. We got back in touch and sent each other holiday cards."

The sergeant smirked, as though he knew all her secrets. "And then?"

"Then she called to tell me about the job opening. I offered to put her up at my house, so we could visit while she was here."

"So she arrived on . . . ?"

"Friday. I drove directly to the convention hotel so we could check in. That's when I met Christine Parks for the first time. She brought down the rest of the staff for a preliminary meeting so we could go over the schedule."

"How was her demeanor on this occasion?"

"Very much in charge." *Chris wore flashy clothes to attract attention*, Marla wanted to add, but she bit her lower lip instead.

"Did her behavior seem off-kilter in any manner?"

"Not really, and she appeared to be perfectly healthy," she said, anticipating his next question.

He gave her a sharp look. "Tell me about the others who were present."

Lighten up, pal. I'm on your side. In a concise manner, she rattled off her basic impressions of her colleagues.

"And how did your friend Georgia react toward Miss Parks?"

Marla shifted her position. "No problems there. Everyone knew Chris was the boss."

"Please answer my question."

"I said, there weren't any problems. Georgia acted respectfully toward the director. If anything, Sampson was the one who had a problem with Chris. He seemed to resent her for requiring him to attend what he deemed to be an administrative session. Chris put him in his place."

"What about Janice Davidson, who has assumed command now?"

"Jan wasn't particularly grateful for her promotion to regional manager. I don't think she was angling for Chris's position." Oh no? Hadn't Jan said something about the perfect revenge being her getting Chris's job? And what about Tyler, who felt he should have moved up the ladder? If Jan got the directorship, that left a vacancy for her position. Tyler could end up being promoted after all. Was it possible that political maneuvering was behind Chris's death? That seemed too obvious. On the other hand, Georgia could have a hidden agenda. Who had the best motive, if not a woman betrayed by her lover?

"Not everyone liked Chris," she blurted out. "At

the cocktail party, Tyler warned me about crossing her path. I heard the same thing from Jan and Amy."

"Did they say why they felt this way?"

"Not specifically, but I got the impression there were personal issues involved. I really don't know any of these people well enough for them to confide in me."

"Not even your friend, Miss Rogers?"

She squirmed. "What do you mean?"

"Didn't Miss Rogers have an altercation with the deceased later that evening?"

"Well, yes," she said, wondering who had ratted on them. "But it started with Tyler. We were sitting in the lounge after the cocktail party. Chris wasn't feeling well. She had a headache, and she asked Tyler to walk her to her room. He turned her down in a rather nasty manner."

"Wasn't your friend seated next to him?"

"What about it?"

"If she knew Chris had an interest in Tyler, she could have deliberately tried to provoke the victim."

"That's absurd. Tyler was the one making the move on Georgia. He'd put his arm around her."

"And how did she react?"

"She slid away from him."

"But not until she'd started an argument between Chris and Tyler."

"Their disagreement had nothing to do with Georgia."

"No? Didn't Christine Parks once come between Georgia Rogers and her fiancé? Couldn't Rogers, having detected the director's interest in Tyler, have deliberately interfered in their relationship?"

Marla's muscles tensed, and she gripped her hands together. "Tyler and Chris didn't have a relationship. He wasn't interested."

"Precisely."

"I tell you, that was not Georgia's doing."

"Rogers has been attending these shows for years. She's probably gotten to know people's habits. She could use that knowledge against them."

"I don't believe this. Georgia wouldn't harm anyone, certainly not for an incident that happened months ago."

"Someone wanted Chris dead." The detective watched her carefully, gauging her response.

"I know all about the switch in antidepressant drugs," she said, deciding to come clean. "My boyfriend is Detective Dalton Vail with the Palm Haven Police Force. He told me about the preliminary toxicology report."

"Ah." His neutral expression didn't give away his opinion of this revelation.

"When do you think someone slipped her this drug? Presumably, she had an adverse reaction by taking the more dangerous medicine with the wrong foods. Doesn't this imply the perpetrator had a degree of medical knowledge? Like, I didn't know that drinking red wine and eating cheese could cause problems with some medications."

"I'm considering the accessibility factor. Tell me, did Miss Parks obtain her own drinks from the bar?"

"Actually, at the cocktail party, a waiter came over and offered her a glass of wine. He said someone had paid the bartender. Did you talk to him?"

"I'll ask the questions here, Marla. I may call you by your first name?" Scratching his head, he peered at his notes. "Did you see Chris helping herself to the appetizers? Or did one of your friends deliver a plate of hors d'oeuvres?"

"We were jostled by so many people, I can't remember." She pictured the scene, but had no memory of Chris standing in line at the buffet table. "Could you tell how many hours the drug had been in her system at the time of death?"

"It had a short half-life, so it wouldn't have taken long to work its effects. I don't think it's anything Miss Parks took by mistake. I'm with you in that somebody gave it to her at the cocktail party."

Marla leaned forward. "I'd like to help, because I don't think Georgia would be capable. I've assisted Dalton with cases before with good results."

Masterson's face eased into a smile. "I'd be grateful for any tidbits of information you pass along, but I wouldn't discount your friend if I were you. Rogers didn't tell you about her engagement, did she?"

"Liesl told me, but Georgia was okay talking about it."

"Close friends confide in each other. Did she also tell you she'd been fired?"

Tyler must have opened his big mouth. She met the detective's hard gaze. "I learned that through the grapevine, too. Georgia didn't deny it when I mentioned it to her."

"Mr. Edgewater informed me about events that night," he said, confirming her notion. "Evidently, the victim accused him of having an affair with Rogers. Despite their protests, Miss Parks dismissed your friend. Rogers stayed behind to argue her case after Tyler left. He'd decided to explain in the morning, after Miss Parks had a good night's rest."

"That's because Chris looked ill. Don't you see?" She leaned forward. "The guilty party gave Chris the wrong drug *before* she fired Georgia."

"It doesn't prove anything. Rogers could still have held a grudge since the show in Las Vegas."

Marla's blood boiled at the officer's single-minded attitude. "Is there anything else you want to ask me? Because you seem to have decided who's to blame already. I don't agree, and I'll do everything in my power to uncover the person who really bumped off Chris."

Departing in a huff, Marla sought Georgia at their exhibit. As she approached, she noticed the dance troupe on stage, having already attracted a crowd with their wild gyrations. Sampson peeked out from behind the curtain and signaled to her. All the electronic cables from the sound system and lighting had been hooked into a laptop computer, where a guy in blue jeans sat monitoring the equipment. Marla's stomach clenched. It was almost time for their artist's presentation.

Liesl issued last-minute instructions to the two models who hovered together backstage, glittery makeup shimmering on their cheekbones. This particular workshop would demonstrate layering techniques and the use of finishing products. Marla's job was to joggle the spray bottles while Liesl managed Sampson's tools.

"Marla, where have you been?" Sampson shouted, pacing backstage. In contrast to the models' dazzling costumes, he wore all black. With his gray hair and piercing dark eyes, he looked like a maestro. Her heartbeat accelerated. This was her chance to observe an award-winning educator up close.

Grabbing the supplies she'd prepared earlier, she nodded to him. "I'm ready," she said, her voice squeaky. After her morning performance, she figured she should be less nervous, but being in the spotlight still left her breathless.

Concentrating on her tasks when their turn came, she was barely aware of the colored spotlights focused on the chair in the center of the stage, the pounding music blaring from the stereo speakers, or the upturned faces of the crowd. Sampson pranced around the first model, snipping and trimming while spewing instructions. He held his scissors and comb in one hand, while he lifted strands of hair with his other. He worked with quick, deft movements that Marla envied. His commentary included references to their new product line.

He waved at her, and she squirted water on the section of hair he'd just separated. Lifting the hank with his comb, he addressed the audience. "You'll want to preserve this brilliant red mahogany with our unique protection system. Our natural extracts extend the life of hair color with their essential sunscreen properties. Use of our four-part system protects the hair from damaging UVL effects, reducing fading and keeping hair healthy and conditioned."

Marla handed him the locking spray. "This contains silicon and panthenol that help to extend the life of your color," he added. "See this intensified shine? Beautiful, isn't it?" *Lift, comb out to ends, snip.* "Your clients will be energized by this remarkable treatment system."

By the time he went on to a second demo, the audience had grown. He took a brief intermission to get a drink of water while Marla swept the stage and the other stylist changed tools.

Returning onstage, he donned a cape embellished with flashing blue lights and a glove with shearlike claws on his right hand. This time, he enhanced his act with flourishes worthy of a magician. Drumbeats vibrated through Marla's bones, reverberating through her head.

Her reactions became automatic as she handed

over the products he'd preselected while Liesl dealt with his implements. Her mind reeling, Marla felt as though she were part of some tribal ritual, especially when he displayed the model like a sacrifice to thunderous applause at the end. Exhausted, she hung back while he took his bows.

Hairdressers bombarded them with questions afterward, and she was too busy describing their product line and referring customers to the sales force to consult with Georgia until later. It wasn't until they were on their way home that she finally had a chance to discuss the police interview.

"I'm so tired," she said, sinking against the car seat cushion during the drive west. She'd promised to pick up dinner to feed everyone. Dalton and Brianna were coming over, and just the thought of all that company made her bone-weary.

Georgia gave her a sympathetic glance. "You get used to it after you've done a few shows. I thought you did great."

"Thanks. I noticed that Ron disappeared during Sampson's demo. Doesn't he like to watch?"

"I think he had to go upstairs for an interview then. That police detective made me very uncomfortable. How did you feel?"

Marla gripped the wheel tighter. "He knew about Chris firing you. Tyler told him."

"Shoot. Now the sergeant will have even more against me. As for Tyler, I'm not surprised that he'd think about covering his own ass. He's the type who looks out for number one."

Oh yeah? Maybe you should do the same. First you forgive Chris for screwing your fiancé, then you go out on a limb for Tyler, who stabs you in the back. Are you really such a schmuck? It's time to stand up for yourself and focus on your goals.

"Masterson asked how I felt about Chris seducing my fiancé," Georgia said, filling the silence. "He didn't believe me when I said it didn't matter anymore. Really, hon, does he think I killed Chris because of what she did to me? If anyone, I should off Nick. He's the one who ruined my life. Besides, Chris annoyed plenty of other people."

"You got that right," Marla agreed.

"Speaking of Tyler, Chris knew something about him that he's hiding from the rest of us. I overheard them talking once. Chris threatened him, and it sounded pretty serious. Tyler warned her that if she came 'between them,' she'd be sorry."

"Between who?"

"I don't know." Georgia hesitated. "Maybe you can find out. Like, I'd be grateful if you diverted that detective's attention away from me."

"I'll do my best," Marla promised.

"Jan was talking about sending flowers to Chris's relatives. I think she has a sister."

"That would be a nice gesture." Marla's concern returned to more immediate matters. "What should we get for dinner?" Her tone lacked enthusiasm. Entertaining visitors seemed like a burden right now.

Brightening, Georgia pointed out the window. "How about Kentucky Fried Chicken? It's quick, and you won't have to prepare anything."

"Works for me." Disregarding the fact that this would prompt Justine to complain about her nutritionally deficient meals, she flicked on the turn signal. "Tell me, what do we have planned for Tuesday?"

"Nothing yet. We have a free day before the photo shoot at your salon."

"I'd like to go in to work that morning. I'll check

with Dalton before making plans for the rest of the day. Justine and Larry are here to see Brianna, and I don't want to interfere with his arrangements."

Brianna's grandparents had other ideas as they sat in her living room after dinner. True to form, Justine had made a snide remark about the fast food, but Marla had deftly switched the topic to the show's highlights. She gave the older couple a gift of skin-care products, which seemed to please them. Brianna's saucy eyes lit up when Marla presented her with a brightly colored nail polish collection, a package of nail-art tattoos, and a medley of lip glosses. For Vail, she'd bought shampoo and conditioner and an aftershave moisturizer.

"Thanks, Marla," he said with a delighted smile. "You didn't have to bring us anything."

"This is so cool," Brianna exclaimed as she sifted through her booty. "I love this glitter topcoat."

"Thank you, dear," Justine said, lifting her nose. "It was thoughtful of you to think of us, but isn't Brianna too young to fuss with her appearance? Teenagers have enough problems today, without worrying excessively over how they look. It leads them to eating disorders, coloring their hair with toxic dyes, and ruining their complexions. She'll have plenty of time to resort to artifice to cover up her age lines."

"Come on, Nana, all my friends wear makeup and nail polish. This isn't the Dark Ages."

"Girls nowadays grow up quicker than we did," Marla said a bit cautiously, exchanging glances with the child. She didn't want to start an argument between Brie and her grandparents.

"That doesn't mean you have to hurry them along the road to maturity," Justine said. "As Brianna's stepmother, you'll be responsible for establishing standards. If you're too lenient, a moral wasteland lies ahead."

"Thank you for those words of wisdom." Marla shot a glance at Vail. He was perched on the edge of his armchair, his attention fixated on a photograph peeking out from Justine's handbag. Viewing it from an angle, she identified the handsome couple, arms entwined, against a background of leafy branches in a park. Dalton Vail and his wife, Pam.

Marla gritted her teeth, swinging her gaze to the elder woman smiling benignly from the camel sofa. It took all her willpower not to comment, but she held her tongue, forcing herself to breathe evenly until her nerves calmed.

Tension hung in the air as thick as a slab of meat. Grateful when Georgia's prattle disrupted the ensuing silence, Marla surveyed her treasured possessions. She'd miss her living-room arrangement when she moved; it would remain behind for the renters. That had been part of her deal with Vail, in exchange for him selling the heavy antiques Pam had favored. They'd both start fresh, a new chapter in their lives. With all that she had on her plate, Marla couldn't even begin to think of home decorating, but she was sure about one thing. She didn't want any photos of Vail and Pam staring her in the face.

"I'll have some free time on Tuesday," she said to Vail, acting her role as gracious hostess. "Did you have plans for Justine and Larry?"

He regarded her with a hopeful expression. "I've got some work at the office. Justine said she'd like to check out the Festival Flea Market while she's here."

"Or we could visit the Swap Shop in Sunrise. It's

closer, if you don't want to drive to Pompano," Georgia suggested.

"Outlet shopping at Sawgrass Mills is another possibility," Marla told them. "It doesn't matter to me. I have a few clients to do early in the morning, but I'm hoping to be done by eleven at the latest."

"Couldn't you take the entire day off?" Justine asked, smoothing the folds on her pleated skirt. She sat properly, her heels crossed at the ankles. Marla noticed with irritation that not a single hair on Justine's brassy head was out of place. What did she use for holding spray, paint lacquer? And her bouffant hairdo had gone out of style years ago. Talk about preservation. Justine could pass as a monument to the fifties.

"I've had to reschedule my clients already this week," Marla explained, "and Luxor Products still has a couple of photo shoots coming up. I can't spare so much time away from the salon." An idea popped into her head. "We're going to the Keys on Friday with the Luxor team. Maybe you'd like to come along?" She grinned at her houseguests, aware that her bared teeth might look more like a snarl.

Larry scratched his chin, marred with gray stubble. "Can we swim with the dolphins at that marine park in Islamorada?"

"I'd better find out for sure where we're going first. We may not have enough time for a detour, now that I think about it, because I have to take Georgia to the Fort Lauderdale airport that night. What time does your flight leave?" she asked her friend.

"Nine-thirty."

"I'll need to drop you at the terminal before eight. Will it bother you if I don't park and go inside?"

"Not at all." Georgia pointed to Spooks, who had emerged from his nap in the study. The dog rolled his head against the couch. "Look who's decided to join us."

Justine glanced beyond the poodle and gasped. "Oh dear, I think your pet did something bad."

Chapter Nine

"Spooks, what did you do?" Marla said, jumping from her seat. Rounding the couch, she dropped her jaw when she regarded the suspicious mound on the carpet and its soft, lumpy consistency. *Oh, yuck. That looks like dog poop, although it usually isn't light tan in color.* And Spooks never had accidents indoors unless he was sick.

The poodle stretched out at Vail's feet, resting his head on his front paws and gazing at her with baleful eyes.

"Did you throw up?" she asked him, but instead of barking a reply, he rubbed his head against the floor. "He must have eaten something that didn't agree with him," she said, eyeing her houseguests. "Did anyone give him human food?"

Larry waved a hand. "He gobbled up my leftovers from the China Bowl. I thought he'd enjoy getting a treat." His gravelly voice indicated an absence of malice, merely puzzlement.

"No wonder. Regular food doesn't agree with him. Please don't give him any meal extras in the future."

She cleaned up the mess with paper towels, then sprayed the stain with a foaming cleanser. Scrubbing the spot with a damp rag, she was pleased to see no residual effects.

Washing her hands in the kitchen, she glanced over her shoulder when Vail entered. Reaching from behind, he encircled her waist with his arms and planted a kiss on her neck. "You're a saint to put up with them," he growled in her ear.

"I'm Jewish. We don't have saints." Snatching a dish towel, she dried her hands before turning into his embrace. Her lips met his, and she savored his passion before pushing him away. "Look, something is still wrong with the dog." Spooks, who had followed her into the kitchen, ran along the baseboard rubbing his head against the wall. "Maybe he has an ear infection." Concerned, she watched her poodle dash into the family room and repeat the bizarre behavior.

"Tomorrow is Monday. You could take him to the vet in the morning." Standing at her side, Vail stroked her back with a swirling motion that made her wish she had time to indulge in sensual pleasures.

"Great, just what I need on top of everything else is for Spooks to get sick."

Early the next morning, she dropped him off at the animal hospital with instructions for the doctor to do a thorough exam. He'd thrown up once more and still exhibited strange behavior, running from one room to the next, breathing fast, and scraping his head against the furniture. Marla felt guilty leaving him, but she and Georgia had to get to the convention center.

"Don't worry, they'll take good care of him,"

Georgia said reassuringly when they were back on the road.

Feeling groggily in need of a second cup of coffee, Marla pressed the accelerator. Traffic was a lot heavier than on the previous day, but that was to be expected during rush hour heading east on I-595. Thank goodness this was the last day she'd have to commute. She had the feeling that when the show ended, however, her responsibilities would continue.

Ron Cassidy waited for her at their exhibit booth. "Where have you been?" the master stylist said, shoving stiff fingers through his frosted blond hair. Marla noticed most of the others were present, except for Sampson, who must still be asleep. Detective Masterson roamed around backstage, poking at their equipment.

"It's nine o'clock," she replied. "We're right on time." She watched Georgia slide into place behind the product displays. "What do you want me to do?" With an hour left before Ron's scheduled presentation, she was supposed to log in the models and assist with costuming and makeup.

The stylist jerked his thumb. "Get rid of him," he urged, meaning the police officer. "He'll upset the girls when they arrive."

"Maybe he wants to talk to them."

"Why would he do that? They don't know anything."

"Chris might have spoken to the models on the phone. I imagine he has to interview anyone who had contact with her."

"Oh yeah?" Ron moistened his lips. "I need the models to focus. Take them back to the prep area until it's show time."

Marla had hoped to question the subjects herself, but there was too much commotion in the curtained-off zone at the far end of the convention center. Sounds of splashing water, whirring blow dryers, and people chattering made private conversation impossible. Ron had commandeered three models, one of them the leggy gal Marla had spied in his hotel room. Heather showed up with a wide-eyed glow that suggested this might be her first job. The skinny blonde who accompanied her wore a bored expression, while the flaming redhead bounced from foot to foot in a manner that displayed her assets and drew admiring glances from some of the male hairdressers.

After putting the finishing touches on the models' makeup, Marla rattled off last-minute instructions. Following a musical prelude, she would march the girls onstage and seat the first model in the chair. While the others flanked them, she'd assist Ron as he proceeded with his popular hair-design workshop. Marla looked forward to observing his texturing methods and precision-cutting techniques.

"Look who's in the audience," Heather cried as they paraded down the aisle and came within sight of Luxor's booth. Marla's heart sank as she spied Masterson in a front-row seat. He looked out of place in his business suit among the casually dressed stylists beside him.

"Never mind," Marla said in a sharp tone. "Just listen for your cue." A drumroll preceded their appearance onstage.

"But I should talk to him. There's something I noticed that could be important. When I—"

Marla never heard the rest of Heather's sentence, because the tempo changed, drowning out the girl's words. And then she forgot all about Heather's statement as she tried to keep up with Ron's movements and get an education at the same time. He spoke rapidly as he worked, maintaining a continuous commentary while he cut and shaped and texturized. His energy drew more people, whom he soon had enthralled. He even cracked jokes, unlike Sampson, who played the serious diva. Marla liked his style immensely and wished he would offer day-long seminars. No wonder he yearned to be hairdresser to the stars. He deserved the recognition, which he wouldn't achieve in Sampson's shadow.

"You did great," she told him later, after the crowd had dissipated. Sweat beaded his brow from the hot spotlights.

"Thanks," he said, grinning as he packed away his gear. "So did you. I hope you stay on the team."

"We'll see if the new director invites me." She paused. "Have you any idea if Jan will get the position permanently?"

"Ask her yourself. She's right behind you. Hey, boss lady, Marla wants to come to our next big show."

"Don't call me that," Jan said, her tone cool. She held a clipboard and pen, looking sleekly business-like in a moss green suit that enhanced her flaming red hair.

"No offense, but you're in charge now," Marla said, not wanting to get Ron in trouble. "How long will it last?"

"Until the board meets, and I have no idea what they'll decide. Ron, I've fit you in at three-thirty with Yolanda to demonstrate our straightening system. Will that work for you?"

"Super. You know how I've been wanting to share

my technique. It's light-years ahead of any other process. Here's what I'll need . . ."

Closing her ears to the rest of Ron's request, Marla searched the throng for Heather's coppery head, but the models had zipped out as soon as their stint was completed. No matter, they'd show up again at her salon for the photo shoot on Wednesday. Then she could ask Heather what she'd been about to say before they went onstage. It might be important, but right now, she wanted to follow up on what Georgia had mentioned about Tyler. Her friend had hinted that the area supervisor might be hiding something from the rest of them. Was that why Tyler had told the homicide investigator that Chris had fired Georgia, to throw suspicion on her? Because he couldn't risk the heat falling on himself?

Her gaze halted on Amy Jeanne, who stood behind the counter obsessively rearranging shampoo bottles into perfect rows. Her cascade of black ringlets functioned as a showpiece for their shine products, while her nail art could have won contests. Momentarily at a loss for a task to perform, Marla approached the counter.

"Can I help you with anything?" she offered the salon coordinator. "I've got a break until Sampson comes down."

Amy Jeanne grinned widely enough to give Marla a glimpse of her gums. "That means you can take a long lunch. The maestro makes his grand entrance just in time for his demo."

"Really? You don't want me to take a shift at sales?"

"We have more than enough help. You're lucky. If Chris were still around, she'd find something for you to do. She couldn't stand it if anyone was idle."

The salon coordinator fingered her pearl necklace. The beads contrasted with her warm mahogany skin and made her nut brown eyes appear to glisten. "Jan's management style is completely different. I sure hope she gets to keep the job."

Marla raised her eyebrows. "This isn't how you'd want Chris to lose her position, though."

"I know. Sergeant Masterson suggested one of us may have given her a bad drug." Amy's face sobered. "I didn't know she took stuff for depression. She always seemed so on top of everything, and everyone."

Marla spied Tyler chatting with Miguel behind the display of holding sprays and anti-humectants. "I understand Tyler wasn't happy with her."

"They had a long-standing feud. She'd always had the hots for him, but he didn't reciprocate. Tyler may act like a flake, but he keeps to himself a lot of the time. You don't really know what's going on in his head. Chris couldn't get through to him, and that annoyed the hell out of her. She liked to pull the strings where people were concerned."

"Are you speaking from personal experience?" Marla said, noting Amy Jeanne's bitter tone.

"You could say that."

Hoping she'd elaborate, Marla reverted to the original topic when Amy remained silent. "Did Chris try to coerce Tyler?"

The other woman drew forward a pack of order forms, shuffling them like cards. "She claimed to know things about him that would chase women away. Tyler didn't care. He flung her off like water, until recently."

Marla leaned forward. "What do you mean?"

She didn't get the chance to find out, because a customer snagged Amy's attention, and it looked to be a long conversation. Gritting her teeth in frustration, Marla retrieved the program from her purse. Her fingers brushed her cell phone, and she decided to call the vet to see if they'd diagnosed Spooks. First, she had to leave the exhibit hall to get away from the noise.

"He's perfectly healthy," the doctor's assistant told Marla on the telephone. "We took his temperature, listened to his heart, and checked him over, and there's nothing wrong. He probably just ate something that didn't agree with him."

"Okay, thanks," she said with a sense of relief. "I'll pick him up later." She called her mother, then Vail, but he was out of the office.

Sauntering back inside the exhibit hall toward the food court, she spotted Sergeant Masterson stuffing down a burger at one of the crowded tables. After buying a chicken salad at the place with the shortest line, she claimed the seat beside him.

"Do you mind if I join you?"

His curious eyes regarded her. "Not at all," he said between bites. "How's it going? I thought you handled the presentation this morning pretty smoothly."

"Thanks. I was afraid I'd drop something, but once I got absorbed in Ron's act, I didn't think about anything else."

"The show must go on, even if one of your team is dead."

She resented his sardonic tone. "That doesn't mean no one cares. We've talked about sending flowers to Christine's family."

"I see. Does anyone talk about who might have killed her? Who was intimate enough with her to know she was depressed and taking medications? Who had the medical knowledge to switch drugs?

And who bought her drinks and fed her the wrong foods at the cocktail party?"

Marla nearly choked on a piece of chicken. "I'm working on it. How much do you know so far?"

"I'm running background checks on your teammates."

"Not me?"

"You wouldn't have known her long enough to bear a grudge. Besides, I had a nice chat with your boyfriend."

She could just imagine the earful Dalton had given him. "Will you keep me posted? I can be more useful if I'm clued in."

"As long as you don't play sleuth all by yourself. Detective Vail warned me that you can be impulsive."

"He did, did he?" She tapped her fingers on the table.

"I'm requesting that no one leave town until this case is solved. Will that be a problem? I know Miss Rogers is your houseguest. Liesl Wurner has an empty bed in her hotel room. Rogers could always move in with her if she overstays her welcome at your place."

"It's okay, Georgia and I have a lot of catching up to do." True, but she hadn't counted on Georgia being there past Friday. She'd been looking forward to having time alone with Vail, his daughter, and Brie's grandparents. Her heart sank at the thought of juggling them all for a few more days and the continued disruption to her work schedule.

The detective studied her reaction. "I'll be telling your crew soon. The bad guy won't be happy about remaining."

"No kidding. I'll do my best to assist you, Sergeant."

After lunch, she got too busy to pursue her queries. The afternoon passed quickly with Sampson's performance. He outdid himself with the show's creative design, including costumes, choreography, and music, receiving a standing ovation while a reporter snapped photographs.

Still hyper from the demo, Marla slipped out to attend a career-development seminar, a demo on extensions, and a class on updo styles from Nexxus. She felt like the odd person in the group, at loose ends when she wasn't assisting either Sampson or Ron. It would be good to have the day to herself tomorrow, except for her guests. If Masterson was smart, he'd look into her colleagues' activities during their spare time. Forced to remain in town, the killer would be trying to cover his tracks. He might leave clues for a sharp investigator.

Why did she assume the perpetrator was male? Marla contemplated the possibilities during the drive home, while Georgia sat silently in the passenger seat. It could just as well have been Janice, who wanted to move up the corporate ladder, or Liesl, who'd sent venomous glances toward Chris at the cocktail party. Don't discount Amy Jeanne, either. The salon coordinator appeared the quiet type who worked in the background, listening to everyone else, but even she'd had a reason to resent Chris.

Thank goodness I won't have to see these people again until Wednesday for the photo shoot at my salon. Vail would say it wasn't her battle, even though Chris's death happened on turf close to home. Her only reasons for getting involved were to clear Georgia of any blame, and to ensure her own continued employment by Luxor. She really liked working behind the scenes and could benefit from the travel opportunities. If she played her cards right, her attempts to remain in the company's graces wouldn't get derailed by the apparent homicide. She just had to keep her nose out of trouble.

Traffic slowed, and she cursed under her breath. She had to pick Spooks up at the vet before their office closed at seven. Nervous energy kept her fatigue at bay. She still had to plan dinner, yet she hadn't given the meal any thought.

Georgia waited in the car while she retrieved the poodle. It took more time than expected, because the veterinarian insisted on speaking to her in an examination room.

"Spooks seems perfectly healthy to me," the lady doctor said, giving Marla a kindly smile. "His blood work came out fine, and his heart is strong. It's likely he just experienced an upset stomach." She handed Marla a can of special dog food. "Give him a couple of tablespoons at a time to ease his digestion back to normal. If he keeps it down, you can go back to his regular Science Diet Canine Maintenance. Here are a few antinausea pills in case you need them."

Marla almost barfed herself when she got the bill. "One hundred ninety-five dollars? What for?"

The receptionist raised an eyebrow. "The diagnostic profile came to one hundred fifty; the exam was thirty-five, and these pills add another ten dollars."

"Oh. Well, I suppose it's good to get his blood count every so often." She stooped to scratch her pet's ears after an attendant brought him to the front station. Fumbling with his leash, she stepped out of the way of his prancing legs. He certainly acted healthy enough, she observed as he charged ahead to her car once outside.

"Hey, Spooks, how are you feeling?" Georgia said, a look of relief on her flushed face when she spied them. She raised her car window after Marla turned on the air-conditioning.

"He's okay, and I'm nearly two hundred dollars in the hole," Marla replied, backing her Camry from the parking space. "My own doctor doesn't even charge that much." Spooks barked, his voice sounding hoarse. She had hated leaving him at the vets. "Anyway, we have to think about food. There isn't enough chicken left over for all of us."

She didn't have to worry. A pizza box sat on her kitchen counter at home. Evidently Vail had taken Brianna's grandparents out for dinner. He'd ordered the pizza, knowing Marla wouldn't have had time to plan ahead. *What a wonderful guy*, she thought, reading the note he'd left. She missed him already.

"He's a lucky catch," Georgia told her when they were relaxing in Marla's family room. They'd finished their meal, put the leftovers away, and had settled in for a quiet night to watch a movie. "I can tell he's devoted to you."

"He needs me, and so does Brianna. They've been lonely since Pam died. And I didn't realize how much I wanted a family until I met him. Stan, my first husband, only thought about himself. Dalton is special, and so is Brie."

"Are you going to have more children?"

Marla rolled her eyes. "No way. It's enough to have one teenage girl around. But I'm finding it very gratifying in a way I'd never expected. I've really become very fond of Brianna." She chuckled. "Besides, I get to take her shopping and teach her how to use makeup. That's fun. In turn, Brie keeps me clued in to what young people like to do these days." Marla grabbed the remote, but her hand stilled when the phone rang. "Darn, not a moment's peace around here. Hold on."

"Hi, it's Heather Morrison," said a familiar voice at the other end of the line. "You know, I'm one of the models at the beauty show."

"Sure, Heather. What can I do for you?" Did the girl need directions to her salon on Wednesday? Marla couldn't conceive of any of other reason why she'd call.

"I have something important to tell you." Heather's voice hushed. "I can't talk now. He'll hear me. Meet me tomorrow morning at eleven o'clock inside the Turkish Bath down by Bal Harbour. We'll talk then. There are plenty of private nooks where no one can hear us." The girl rattled off an address while Marla scribbled on a scrap of paper.

"North Miami Beach?" Marla said. "Isn't there anywhere closer for us to meet?"

"Just be there, okay? I have to go. Be careful who you trust, Marla. I'll explain when I see you in person." *Click.*

Marla hung up, frustration seething inside her. What could this be about? Did it relate to Chris's death?

Her mind swept back to earlier in the day, when she'd trotted toward the exhibit booth with the crush of models, and Heather had spied the detective in the audience. The girl had begun to speak, but events interceded and she'd gotten cut off. Aware of Marla's connection to a cop, she might be hoping to use Marla as a conduit to relay information.

Or it could be a trap. The killer, threatened by Marla's inquiries, might be working in concert with Heather. That seemed a bit far-fetched, but she wouldn't toss out any possibilities. Nonetheless, it presented her with a dilemma for the next morning, not the least of which was the ten o'clock client she'd have to cancel.

"What did the model want?" Georgia demanded. She'd turned on the TV, putting it on mute while Marla carried on her conversation.

The truth trembled on her tongue until she recalled Heather's warning. Had the girl meant for Marla to beware of her houseguest as well as the others on Luxor's team? A needle of doubt pricked her mind.

"She wants to talk to me. I agreed to meet her tomorrow. Maybe we'll all go for a ride," she said, thinking about her plans for the day with Larry and Justine.

Georgia ignored her response. "Omigosh, Marla. Look at Spooks. He's acting weird again."

Chapter Ten

Spooks dashed from the family room, scraping his head along the wall in his mad rush down the hallway. Concerned, Marla stumbled after him. Was he still sick? She halted at the foyer when Justine and Larry burst in the front door, followed by Vail and Brianna. Hearing their laughter, Marla experienced a twinge of longing. She still felt like the outsider in their relationship.

Greeting the arrivals, she forced a friendly smile. "How was your dinner?" she asked her guests. Without waiting for their reply, she addressed her fiancé. "Thanks for the pizza, Dalton. It was thoughtful of you. Where did you go?"

"We ate at the Macaroni Grill. Brie has to do homework, so we're leaving." Stepping forward, he gave her a quick peck on the lips.

Her nose picked up his favorite spice scent, but she tamped down her reaction. Bad timing. She turned her attention to the teenager, who'd bent over to pet Spooks.

Brianna's ponytail swung as she tilted her head. "What's wrong with the dog? He's pulling away from me." She sifted her fingers through his crown. "Oh, yuck. Look here, Marla," she said, parting his hair. She held the squirming animal while Marla knelt beside her.

Spotting the black round blob attached to his scalp, Marla grimaced. "Ew, that looks like a tick. I can't believe the vet didn't find it."

"It must be hurting him," Brianna said in a sympathetic tone. "Think how it must feel to have an insect digging into your head and sucking your blood."

"No wonder he's been running around the house acting nuts." Her heart went out to the poor creature, who licked her hand, a forlorn expression on his doggy face.

"We have to go." Vail propped an arm on his daughter's shoulder. "Or do you want us to stay and help you?"

She felt his in-laws' eyes boring into her from behind. "Thanks, but I'll manage," she said, rising.

"Listen, I realize you have to go into work tomorrow morning, but can you phone me and let me know your plans?"

His gray eyes seared hers, and for an instant she felt as though she could peer into his soul. It couldn't be easy on him, having Pam's parents visit just when he'd prepared to move forward in life. Yet he'd put her in a tough position, and his attempts to mitigate the pressure weren't working. *Like, you should have thought of this before you invited them to stay at my place. It's disruptive to my routine, too.*

"I got a call from one of the models at the show," she said. "She has something important to tell me, so I'm meeting her tomorrow down on North Miami Beach. Maybe we'll all take a ride.

It's near Bal Harbour, if we want to go shopping afterward."

"Okay, but be careful. One person has already been killed."

His words echoing in her mind, she grinned at her guests, who stood staring at her after Vail and his daughter left. "All right, who knows how to remove a tick? Or should I wait until I can take Spooks to the vet in the morning?"

Georgia shook her head, waves of curly black hair fanning her face. "It'll just drink more of his blood and get bigger. That's so gross." Turning away, she scurried off.

Marla glanced at Justine, primly dressed in an ivory skirt, a white shell under a yellow jacket, matching white heels, and mother-of-pearl jewelry. Her ensemble clearly identified her as a tourist since the natives, many of whom were transplanted northerners, traditionally changed to autumn colors after Labor Day.

"Don't look at me, dear," the older lady said, raising her hands. "I wouldn't permit animals at my house. They shed all over and bring germs in from outside."

"I'm going to watch the game," Larry said, vanishing toward the family room along with his wife.

Gathering the poodle in her arms, Marla regarded the empty foyer. "Cowards. Would you believe I paid the veterinarian a couple of hundred dollars for a physical exam, and she found nothing? I told her Spooks had been rubbing his head," she shouted after them. "Don't you think the doctor should have looked him over more closely?"

Resolving to call the vet's office in the morning with the correct diagnosis, she pondered her next step. She had no idea how to remove a tick, but

Georgia was right. She didn't want the dog to suffer all evening.

"I think you light a match, then blow it out, and touch the end to the tick to free it," Georgia called from the hallway, "but I'm no expert."

"Gee, thanks." Her stomach clenched.

As a delaying tactic, she released the dog and went to her computer to search the Internet. She found an article that claimed the burned-match trick was a fallacy. "Disgusting," she said, pressing a hand to her mouth at the sight of the silhouette of an eight-legged insect in the article. She might have a reputation for facing down bad guys, but bugs rattled her every time.

Forcing her eyes back to the page, she read the instructions.

To remove a tick, gently (so it doesn't squish) grip its body with a tweezer. Loosen the head, then carefully pull back until the body is fully detached. Swab the area with antiseptic. Place the tick in a small jar in case the veterinarian wants to examine it.

"At least Spooks is up to date on his Lyme disease shots," Marla muttered to herself. "There's no way I can do this."

Fortunately, her neighbor Goat was home, and when she pleaded for his help, the rangy man who worked as a pet groomer appeared at her front door within minutes. His straw hair askew, he looked like a beach bum, with his scrawny beard, colorful Hawaiian shirt, shorts, and boat shoes. "Ugamaka, ugamaka, chugga, chugga, ush," he sang, dancing a jig to her relieved grin. "Your dog has cooties, but I've worn my booties. If you want my help, just give a yelp. We'll be snug as a bug in a rug."

Marla was used to his riddles. "The bug is at-

tached to Spooks's head, not a rug. I hope you
know what to do."

"Whoa, dude, who's that?" He did a double-take
when Georgia rounded the corner and stopped
abruptly. She'd changed from her work clothes
into a pair of capris and a turquoise tank top, making Marla marvel at how she didn't seem affected
by the cooler weather. The low-cut bodice offered
a nice view of her bosom.

Marla introduced them. An amused smile lifted
her lips when she saw Goat's face flush.

He cleared his throat. "Let's get the patient
ready," he said, taking the dog from her arms.

"Do you need a nurse?" Georgia said in a sim-
pering tone.

His face turned a deeper shade of red. "Sure,
whatever."

"You didn't offer to help me," Marla told her
friend.

"Goat knows what he's doing."

"Oh, and I don't?"

"Actually, no." Georgia trailed her neighbor
into the kitchen while he rattled off a list of supplies for Marla to obtain. Larry gave them an annoyed glance from the family room couch. Justine
didn't even look up from the book in her lap.

Goat performed the operation while Marla held
her squirming pet and Georgia handed him tools
like a trained assistant. The stylist prattled on about
the show, Chris's demise, and what a funk the investigation made for company employees. By the
time they finished the surgery, Marla's temples
pounded. If she didn't know her neighbor better,
she'd think he was working extra slow to extend
his visit.

"This Christine person," he said to her, "did she know anyone else in the neighborhood?"

Throwing out a used alcohol swab, Marla gave him a startled glance. "What do you mean?"

"Like, why does everybody think one of your friends killed her? Did she fly into town and go directly to the hotel for the show? Or did she have other, you know, people in Fort Lauderdale that she might have seen?"

"We've assumed the guilty person was at the cocktail party."

"Oh yeah? And could you identify everyone there as belonging to the hair show?"

Her gaze met Georgia's surprised brown eyes. "Well, no."

"Omigosh," Georgia said. "I kinda wondered if Chris had come in a couple of days early for a reason. I just figured she wanted to confirm our arrangements."

"Whoever she met could be important," Marla replied. "I'll ask Heather tomorrow. Chris might have contacted the models ahead of time. Heather has something to relate," she informed Goat, "and it may have to do with Chris. I can't wait to find out what she has to say."

Marla's anticipation swung into high gear on Tuesday morning as she searched the street numbers for the address Heather had given her. The bathhouse was located in the Sea Breeze Hotel, just up the road from a famed beach resort on Collins Avenue. Palms lined the roadway. Condominium buildings obstructed the ocean view toward the east.

"Why can't you just drop us off at the shops,

dear?" Justine asked, fingering her pearls in the rearview mirror. Larry was reading the newspaper beside her.

"I thought we'd get there in time for lunch. Besides, you might enjoy the spa." *Not to mention there's safety in numbers.* She didn't know what to expect from Heather, but her companions could cover her back while she scuttled into a corner with the young model. She hoped Georgia's presence wouldn't put a damper on their meeting, but she couldn't very well get rid of just Georgia. "If you want a mud facial, I'll treat you," she told Justine. If this was an upscale day spa, they'd offer a complete range of services. She wouldn't mind a soothing aromatherapy wrap herself.

They'd brought swimsuits, just to be prepared, and after Marla parked the car, they emerged carrying beach bags. The Sea Breeze Hotel promised to have a pool as well as a sandy shore. Its faded turquoise exterior needed a fresh coat of paint, Marla noted as they trudged from the parking lot. The midday heat warmed her skin; the temperature had risen into the mid-seventies. It was a relief to walk into the cool, filtered air of the hotel lobby.

Following directions from a clerk, they climbed down a spiral stairway to a set of double glass doors. And then they seemed to enter a time warp. A pair of hanging lamps cast a dim glow over an elaborately designed reception area, where a sign said, RUSSIAN AND TURKISH BATHS SINCE 1892, NEW YORK AND MIAMI. The lamps, with their bulbous shapes, studded with colored stones, would have been at home in ancient Morocco. In a corner stood a pedestal holding a vase with a bouquet of jade, carnelian, and quartz gemstone flowers. It made a colorful splash against the wall, constructed of

brown-flecked rocks. A collection of brass orna-
ments reminded Marla of Asian hookahs.

"You've got to be kidding," Georgia breathed,
her eyes wide with awe.

"Holy moley, I've always wanted to see a *shvitz*,"
Larry said in the most enthusiastic tone she'd ever
heard him muster.

"Well, I never," Justine huffed, regarding the
decor with a moue of distaste.

Marla wasn't certain where Heather expected to
meet her, so she approached the reception desk.
She had to veer around an icy white marble statue
of a goddess in the center of the floor, where it
stood under a crystal chandelier hanging from the
gold-painted ceiling. Its dim lighting was enhanced
by flickering wall sconces that added to the eerie
atmosphere. Benches placed around the lobby
were carved from dark wood, further weighting
the mood.

Glad she hadn't come alone, Marla spotted another sign: JACUZZI PIPES IN SALT WATER FROM THE
OCEAN. Under this was a list of admission prices and
special services offered. Besides a massage or a soap
wash, you could get a Dead Sea salt scrub or a black
mud treatment. *No thanks,* Marla thought. *I just
want to meet Heather and get out of here.*

"I'm supposed to meet a friend of mine," she
told the mustached man behind the counter. Giving Heather's name and description, she was grati-
fied by his nod of recognition.

"She came in not so long ago. How many?"

"Excuse me?"

"How many of you are going into the baths?"

"Oh." She glanced over her shoulder at the others and counted. "There's four of us." Realizing

she'd have to pay for her guests, she withdrew her wallet from her purse.

The swarthy-complexioned man waved his hand. "You pay when you leave." He laid on the counter a set of small metal rectangular boxes like the kind in a bank vault. "Put your valuables in here, please. Wallets, cell phones, jewelry. I give you each your own keys, see?"

He held up a wristband from which two keys dangled. "One key is for safety deposit box. When you check out, I give you back your valuables. Other key is for locker inside."

Oh joy. Justine and Larry are going to love this.

"Maybe we should wait outside, dear," Justine suggested, looking affronted when Marla said she had to empty her purse.

"Not me," Larry countered, for once going against his wife's wishes. "I could use the Jacuzzi. It'll help my arthritis."

"Jacuzzis breed germs. All that heat and moisture, and then you sit in the water with other people." Justine shuddered.

"Do what you want, but I'm going inside," Marla said, plunking her cell phone and other important items into the lockbox. In exchange, the man gave her a wristband.

"It sounds like fun to me," Georgia said, following suit. When Larry had cast his lot with them as well, Justine gave in.

"I'm not going to sit out here all by myself. Who knows what sort of undesirables frequent this place?" With a disapproving frown, she joined the gang.

Pushing through the inner door, Marla led the way into a curved corridor lined with oil paintings that depicted plump ladies in colorful scenes from days of old. Onion-shaped frames made of twisted rope reminded her of mosques in the Middle East. One picture showed a lady in a rose gown about to kiss a bearded man, a table laden with food behind them. Other tableaux showed elegantly dressed couples picnicking by a lake, a family at dinner, and a naked woman reclining on a couch. They all seemed to feature a more realistic view of women, one in which a rail-thin model like Heather wouldn't be worshiped as the feminine ideal. She wondered how the girl had come to find this place.

They split up at the locker rooms, Larry heading into the men's area and Marla with her companions into the women's. It was a small space, with a row of lockers, mirrored marble sinks, a single shower, and a toilet stall. A wave-shaped painted bench faced the lockers. On the counter stood another bouquet of coral, amber, and jade gemstone flowers. The tile floor had a drain in its center, and rivulets of water flowed into it. A set of double glass doors moist with condensation led to the Jacuzzi.

Marla found the number assigned her on the wooden locker door and opened it with her key. "I don't know where Heather's gone, but I suppose I'll have to hunt for her," she said, noting a sign saying HAVE A HAMAM WASH, TRADITIONAL TURKISH SOAP, TWENTY MINUTES FOR $35. After pulling a swimsuit from her bag, she stuffed her belongings into the locker.

"Where are we supposed to change?" Justine asked, wrinkling her nose.

Just then a brunette entered the room, opened her locker, and stripped right in front of them. Oblivious to their shocked stares, she donned a bikini and trotted out to the Jacuzzi, carrying the towel provided with their entry fee.

"That answers your question," Georgia said, giggling. Turning her back to them, she pulled off her shirt.

"You can wait for us if you want," Marla told the older woman, "but I don't know how long this will take. Heather has to be somewhere inside." She managed to don her two-piece swimsuit with a modicum of modesty. Dipping her fingers into a square red vat leaning against the wall, she withdrew a pair of plastic slippers for her feet. *All the comforts of home,* she thought, adjusting her wristband.

"I'm going ahead," Georgia said. "We don't have much time, and I want to make the best of it. See you inside." She pushed open one of the doors to the Jacuzzi, letting in a cloud of steam. "Whoa, Marla. Get a load of these hunks."

Marla peeked over her shoulder, her jaw dropping. She'd expected stooped old men to come to a place like this, not beefy young athletes. These guys weren't gay, either, judging from the fellow sitting under the waterfall and smooching the bikini-clad gal. They kissed in plain sight of three muscular guys in the tile-lined pool.

Justine had ducked into the toilet stall to change clothes. When she stepped inside the Jacuzzi room with Marla, she gasped.

"Good gracious, this place is a cesspool for hedonism."

"I wouldn't go that far," Marla said, remembering the Perfect Fit Sports Club where Jolene Myer's body had been discovered in the whirlpool. "It looks quite relaxing."

A large pipe shot heated seawater from a well seventy-five feet below the ground into the Jacuzzi, creating a pillar of steam and a steady roar. Marla padded carefully along, aware that it would be easy to slip on the wet ceramic tiles. The cavelike walls made her feel as though she were in a grotto, and the mist added to the effect. Blue tiles ringed the ceiling, but she focused on the man emerging with a towel around his waist from the men's locker room. Larry grasped the metal rail at the mouth of the pool and lowered himself into the frothing water.

"I'll just wait for you here," he said with a sigh of pleasure. He tossed his towel onto a ledge and submerged up to his neck, his folds of flesh disappearing beneath the surface.

"I thought you wanted to try the *shvitz*," Marla said, peering at the bubbles with apprehension. A weighted body could vanish in there and no one would notice.

"Later," he replied, closing his eyes.

They had to speak in loud voices to be heard over the rushing water. Justine and Georgia traipsed behind as Marla entered another section, calling Heather's name. She closed her mouth as soon as she realized the girl wasn't there. On her left was a waterfall cascading over a stone ledge where another couple sat entwined, their passion evident. Sulfur emanating from the minerals added to the mystical swirl of steam from an aromatherapy room, heat from a sauna, and vapors from the Jacuzzi. Dim overhead lighting reminded Marla of a subterranean setting: oblong bulbs protruding into cagelike fixtures.

In the corner rose a stone-rimmed pool of ice water with buckets stacked alongside. Patrons who got overheated were supposed to dump the frigid water over their heads. More closed doors faced off this little nook, which also held a stall shower and a rack for towels. Gargoyles decorated the far wall, while a marble sculpture of a winged creature dominated the center of the gray tile floor.

Marla couldn't understand where Heather would be hiding, or why she'd chosen this place to meet her. Did she come here regularly and feel that sticking to her routine would avert suspicions? If so, who had made her so afraid?

"I can't take the heat," Justine complained, wiping her flushed face with her towel.

"Sweating is good for you," Georgia stated in a bubbly tone. "It gets rid of your toxins. Look at this sign for the Finnish sauna. It says the dry heat stimulates blood circulation and induces perspiration, leading to a thorough cleansing of the skin and relaxing muscles and joints."

Marla could feel the heat radiating from the glass door. She peered inside the sauna, which was lined with cherrywood paneling. Brightly lit, it showed one long wood bench on the left side and a double decker on the right. There was nowhere for anyone to hide, and the room was empty. Disappointed, she turned to the aromatherapy room, where eucalyptus-scented steam billowed out when she opened the door.

"Ooh," Georgia yelped, "I bet that will open my sinuses. I'm going in there." The door slapped shut behind her.

"And I'm leaving," Justine said, turning on her heel. Her foot slipped, shooting out from under her. She flailed her arms, tumbling backward. Marla caught her, and they fell together. Marla's rump hit the tiles but at least she cushioned the blow for the older woman. Spray from the waterfall wet their bodies while Marla disentangled herself.

"Are you all right?" The young couple parted and sprang to their assistance.

Justine waved them off. "Well, I never. It's a good thing I'm not injured, or I'd have cause for a lawsuit." After adjusting the strap on her one-piece swimsuit with its matronly skirt, she regained her feet. "If this is how you spend your spare time, Marla, I can't say that it's the proper environment for my granddaughter. We'll discuss this later." Placing one foot carefully in front of the other, she departed.

Rubbing her lower back, Marla asked the young man and woman if they had seen Heather.

"I think she was heading for the Radiant Room," said the guy, a broad-shouldered fellow with slicked-back ebony hair. He could have passed for a college football star.

"What's that?"

"You know, the *shvitz*. If you want to get cooked, that's the place to go. It's got fifteen tons of rocks sitting on brick arches, and they're heated all night. You sit on a bench on a wood slat, and when you feel as though you're about to pass out, you dump cold water on yourself. There's an ice-water pool with buckets to fill in the anteroom. I recommend the *platza*."

At her confused look, he explained. "The *platza* specialist beats you with a broom made of fresh oak leaves, sopping with olive-oil soap. It opens your pores, removes toxins, along with layers of dead skin, and is incredibly relaxing."

"Sounds like something I'd send my enemies to do," Marla muttered. Aloud, she thanked them and passed through another door, feeling as though she were in a weird underground maze on a steamy planet. A dingy corridor stretched in front of her, heavy wooden doors leading to individual massage rooms. Crossing the intricately tiled floor, she noticed a massive door with a porthole at the far end. She figured that must be the famed Russian shvitz.

The anteroom, with its stone walls and single tiny window located high up, near the ceiling, appeared much like a dungeon. On one side, a raised stone pool held ice water that trickled from an overhead pipe. Was this medieval, or what?

No sign of Heather.

Moving forward, she yanked open the sauna door. A wave of heat hit her face, but not before she glimpsed two men lounging on a bench, pipes crisscrossing the ceiling, and a drain sucking water from the floor. Slamming the *shvitz* door shut, she retreated, perspiration drenching her body.

Sweat and moisture permeated the air in the anteroom along with something else. She could almost taste the metallic scent on her tongue.

Dread prickled the hairs on her nape. Recessed in the gloom, two Swedish shower stalls were barely visible on the right. Should she look in there?

She'd barely cracked the first frosted-glass door when a glance inside chilled her blood.

She screamed, shattering the silence.

Chapter
Eleven

Heather's body lay twisted in the shower stall, sightless eyes staring upward. Water dripped onto her skin and the knife that protruded from her midsection. She wore a bikini, and the hot pink fabric seemed to leach into a growing red tide on the floor. Even in the dim light, Marla could discern the stain.

She clapped a hand to her mouth. *Think rationally. What would Dalton do?*

See if the girl has a pulse.

Crouching, she gritted her teeth and forced herself to touch Heather's clammy wrist. No pulse. Not surprising.

Jerking backward, she inadvertently jostled Heather's hand, and a piece of paper slipped out. Not wanting this possible clue to get wet, Marla was in the process of gingerly lifting it when the door to the *shvitz* crashed open. Without thinking, she tucked the paper into her swimsuit. The two men from the Russian sauna rushed toward her. Clutching her stomach, she pointed to the stall.

"Are you okay?" one man asked while the other ran for help. Gripping her elbow, the fellow assisted her to her feet. "Come away from there. You can't do anything for the poor soul."

"I . . . I opened the shower stall, and . . ." Compelled to explain, she couldn't continue. Her voice choked, and a wave of light-headedness made her vision swim.

"Put your head down," the man's voice said from afar.

He pushed her to her knees and bent her neck forward. While she struggled to regain equilibrium, other bystanders arrived. Someone dumped a bucket of ice water on her head. The shock jolted her, but it cleared her mind. Shivering, she wrapped her arms around herself.

"I'm fine," she said, scooting onto the stone ledge that served as a bench.

"The cops are on their way," said a bare-chested young man with soft brown eyes. "They said for everybody to stay put." He studied her with alarm, as though afraid she'd be the next victim to need resuscitation.

No one would be able to revive Heather. Had one of the people in this room killed her?

Marla's gaze darted from face to face. Goosebumps covered her flesh. Most of them had left their belongings in a safety deposit box at the entrance. Their skimpy swimwear might not accommodate a weapon, but a rolled-up towel could.

She wasn't safe. *Better go get dressed.*

"I don't feel well," she mumbled. "I need to get cooled off. I'm getting changed, and then I'll be in the lobby."

Rising, she stumbled her way through the gathering throng. Where was Georgia? Scanning the people in the hallway, she didn't see her friend. Could Georgia be oblivious to what was going on?

Sure enough, Marla discovered her soaking in the fragrant steam of the aromatherapy room. She hadn't heard anything through its thick walls.

Sticking her head inside while vaporous clouds exuded into the anteroom, Marla called to her, "Come on, we have to leave." Immediately she felt her sinuses clear from the eucalyptus scent. Breathing in the mist, she filled her lungs, hoping to calm her nerves.

"What's wrong?" Georgia asked, wrapping a towel around her body as she emerged. Her hair hung in damp ringlets about her head. Moisture beaded the skin above her upper lip.

Marla had to raise her voice. The roar from the waterfall and bubbling Jacuzzi combined with the hiss of water hitting hot stones made hearing difficult. "Heather is dead. Someone stabbed her, and I suspect it happened not too long ago. She was in the shower, so she might have just come from the *shvitz.*"

Ushering Georgia into the women's dressing room, she surveyed the small space. Fortunately, they were alone, everyone else having gone to play witness.

"You mean the killer may still be here?" Georgia's eyes bulged.

"It's possible. I didn't recognize anyone, if that helps."

"What do you mean?"

Marla toweled herself dry. "Heather had something to tell me, and I presume it related to Chris's death. That means someone from Luxor might be involved . . . or not. Like the cops, I've been assuming it must be one of us, but maybe we're wrong. Goat suggested we trace Chris's movements since her arrival, in case somebody else in her life held a grudge."

Stripping naked without any show of modesty, Georgia nodded at her. "I agree Heather may have been killed because she knew something about Chris's murder. Omigosh, Marla. That makes you a target, too. And me, by association."

Quickly changing into her street clothes, Marla glanced at the scrap of paper she'd salvaged from the dead girl's hand. *Bell Farms*. Those two words scrawled in hasty handwriting meant nothing to Marla. She'd have to decipher them later.

"Since I'm the one who discovered Heather's body, I'll be under suspicion until the police examine the evidence," she said, folding the paper into her pants pocket. "I'm damned if I'll ask Dalton to intervene on my behalf again. If we're lucky, the detective in charge of this case will get answers faster than Sergeant Masterson."

Grabbing her belongings, she pulled on Georgia's elbow. "Justine and Larry must be having a fit," she said and then gasped. "Oh no, I forgot about Larry. Is he still in the Jacuzzi?" She hadn't even looked at the pool in her haste to depart.

Georgia's grin lifted her spirits. "Nah, he peeked his head inside the sauna earlier and told me he was calling it quits."

Exiting the locker room, they entered the corridor where uniformed police officers tramped past the walls lined with onion-shaped paintings. The well-endowed painted ladies seemed to stare at Marla, their eyes shifting to follow along.

"Go through that door," Marla told the cops, pointing to the men's locker room.

"Thanks, miss," one of them said, hesitating.

"I'll be outside if you need me," she replied, moving forward before his questions impeded her progress.

Relief settled over her when she and Georgia reached the lobby. Her shoulders sagged, and her knees wobbled. It took all her strength to remain upright and appear calm. Justine and Larry, seated on one of the carved wooden benches, rose to greet them. The older couple looked weary.

"Marla, what's going on? Why are the police here?" Justine demanded. Her concerned eyes belied her terse voice.

"I found a dead woman in the shower stall."

"Good gracious, how shocking."

"Yeah, well, those things kinda happen around me." Lacking the energy for a full explanation, she approached the front desk. A stout woman had taken over for the man with the mustache.

"Who's the police officer in charge?" Marla asked the lady, whose purple hair color could only have come from a home dye job. "I'd like to give my statement and leave."

The woman summoned the proper authority, who patiently questioned each one of them before getting their contact info for follow-up. After Marla paid their bill and retrieved their valuables, they left.

"Where to?" Marla said to her companions once they were on the road. Her watch indicated it was just past one o'clock.

"Can we still go to Bal Harbour?" Georgia asked in a meek voice from the passenger seat. "I know you're upset and shaky from what happened, but it would do you good to get your mind off it. There's nothing more you can do for Heather now, and you'll be able to think better after lunch."

Marla gave an inward sigh. The last thing she needed was food. She felt gritty, tired, and badly in need of a rest, but going home wouldn't be any fun for her visitors.

"Justine, what would you like to do?" Gazing into the rearview mirror, she gulped at Justine's sad expression, and a wave of guilt slammed her. Brianna's grandmother must be remembering her dead daughter. Instead of going out of her way to make the woman feel at home, Marla had dragged her along on a dangerous venture that merely reinforced the memory of a premature loss of life. She kept making things worse.

"I don't care, dear," Justine replied in a listless tone.

Marla put on her turn signal. "Shopping will lift our spirits," she said, although her last word conjured the image of Heather's body and made her want to gag. "Besides, I could use a strong cup of coffee right about now."

Stopping at a traffic signal, she waited until the light changed to steer into the shopping mall parking lot. The air outside had warmed considerably, and the bright sun cheered her. After locking her car, she guided her company to Carpaccio. They got a table outdoors in the pleasant tropical setting and ordered salads. Well, except for Larry, who tried the linguine with lobster in a spicy tomato sauce. To her surprise, he snatched the bill when they'd finished.

"It's our treat," he said, giving her a genuine smile. "You're being nice enough to house us for the week. I realize it's inconvenient when you have another guest. We didn't mean for it to work out that way."

Picking up her water glass, she plunked it back down. "I know you were originally supposed to come for Christmas but got delayed. You couldn't help it if Justine needed a root canal."

"Yeah, but we would have chosen a different week to stay at your place if we'd known about the hair show."

She gave him a startled glance. "I thought you were supposed to stay with Dalton, and he couldn't, er . . ."

"Couldn't handle it?" Justine pitched in with a smirk. "I suppose he told you that he didn't want to hurt our feelings by having us stay there while he's packing. We're aware you're moving in together. It's only logical that he'd put away Pam's things." Folding her hands, she cocked her head. "Brianna asked me if we wanted her mother's plate collection. She didn't think you'd want them around."

Marla's throat constricted. She glanced at her friend, but Georgia was studiously gazing at a lizard crawling up a nearby palm tree. "What are you saying?"

"We chose to stay with you, to get to know you better. You'll be responsible for our granddaughter when you marry her father. We meant to see what kind of person you are. I have my reservations, but I have to admit, I like your tenacity. You don't give up on things easily."

Marla swallowed. "No, I don't, if it's something worthwhile. I care about Brianna a great deal. I'm not claiming that I'll make a great mother, and I certainly never intend to take Pam's place, but I'll do my best." *So Dalton didn't push them on me. It was*

*their decision to stay at my house. Why did he lead me to
believe otherwise? Probably to avoid raising my stress
level, knowing Justine came to evaluate my mothering
abilities. As if my own doubts aren't enough to shake me.*

"I don't expect you to involve my granddaughter in solving murders," Justine said, lifting her nose. "She needs to concentrate on her schoolwork."

"Naturally," Marla murmured. *Here comes a lecture.* But Justine dropped the subject, leaving Marla to wonder when she'd address it again. In the meantime, their conversation turned superficial as they strolled past exclusive shops with overpriced wares. Georgia browsed inside the Escada boutique, while Marla merely window-shopped at Versace.

Justine halted in front of Tiffany & Co. "Oh, look," she commanded, peering at the display. "I'd like to get that for Brianna." Breezing inside, she let the door snap back in Marla's face.

Marla examined the items in the window. Surely Justine didn't mean that cross pendant in sterling silver on a sixteen-inch chain. Brianna had never favored religious jewelry, and Marla could think of other necklaces the teen would appreciate more, like that Loving Heart design. What did kids wear these days? None of the necklaces were cheap, and even the silver ones cost more than one hundred dollars.

"Are you coming in?" she asked Georgia, while Larry strolled ahead to look in the Brooks Brothers window. They entered the hallowed domain inside Tiffany's.

"Way cool," Georgia said, fixing her dark eyes on a round-link bracelet. "I wish I could afford this stuff. Or rather, find a boyfriend who could buy it for me."

Marla glanced at her friend's wrist, which already held a collection of bangles. "You don't have room for anything else."

"There's always room, hon. Besides, I need something to match my new shoes. Is there a Coach place here? I have to find a red handbag."

"We should go to Sawgrass Mills. The outlets are less expensive. Maybe on Thursday." With the photo shoot at her salon on Wednesday, that left little time to spare. They'd be going to the Keys on Friday.

Heather wouldn't be coming, she reminded herself with a surge of sadness. How could she look at jewelry when the girl was dead? Just thinking about the scene back at the Turkish Bath made her sick. Undoubtedly the police wanted to question her further. They'd probably left messages on her machine at home. She shouldn't be wasting time here.

Intending to gather her charges, she approached the counter while Georgia stopped to look at a doughnut-chain bracelet in a display case. Justine was examining necklaces with cross pendants when Marla reached her. How could she convince the woman to consider Brianna's preferences in selecting a gift?

"These heart necklaces are popular," she remarked in an idle tone, pointing to several different designs with matching earrings. "Brianna would love to receive one of these from you."

Justine bristled. "She should have a cross. Pam's got lost, so I'd like to replace it."

Marla hadn't thought about Brianna inheriting her mother's jewelry. "Why don't you ask Brie what she'd want?"

Justine's eyes narrowed. "You know, Marla, I think the idea of Brianna wearing this item makes you uncomfortable. We haven't discussed religious differences before, but I hope you'll respect my granddaughter's upbringing. She'll expect to celebrate the holidays according to our cultural traditions. Dalton told me you don't have a Christmas tree at your house."

"I celebrate Hanukkah, not Christmas."

"Well, it won't be that way when you're living together."

Marla glared at the smaller woman dressed in a prim outfit like she was going to church. She couldn't expect Justine to understand. "We'll work things out between us."

"So I fear. The woman always rules the nest."

Marla bit her lip. She had enough problems without this aggravation clouding her mind. "Can we leave now? I'd like to stop by my salon to make sure everything is all right before we go home."

Resentment kicked in that Dalton had dropped her into such an awkward situation. He should have accepted responsibility for his former in-laws instead of sticking her with them, regardless of Justine's request. Did he care more about offending his relatives than her? What would happen when she met his parents? Would their relationship stand the strain, or were her worries enhanced by her own feelings of inadequacy?

Hastening Justine out the door before she could make a purchase, Marla felt a wave of guilt. Perhaps she should have let the woman buy her granddaughter a necklace, even if it wouldn't have been Brianna's choice. The gesture would be appreciated.

Bad Marla, she chastised herself. *Always interfering. If I could only just do my own thing, I'd stay out of trouble.*

Not necessarily, Marla discovered later when they finally returned home. The message light flashed on her answering machine. The Miami Beach police wanted her to contact them. Before she even had a chance to wash her hands, the doorbell rang. She couldn't ask her guests to get it; they'd vanished into their rooms.

"Oh, hi, Goat," she said, spotting her neighbor on her front stoop. "Is everything all right?"

"Yeah, man." The scrawny fellow shuffled his feet. "The clock ticks, and the fur licks, and before you can say shazam, the deed is done. You dig?"

She thought a moment. "Are you asking if Spooks is okay? He's doing fine, thanks. I got some Frontline from the vets, for another seventy-five dollars after I spent nearly two hundred for them to find nothing wrong."

Giving a crooked grin, Goat scratched his beard. "If I can help, let me know. You've got your hands full with all these people running around the house." He craned his neck, peering over her shoulder. "Your friend still here? Ugamaka, ugamaka, chugga, chugga, ush," he chanted, swaying his hips like an islander with his Hawaiian shirt and shorts, "a roll in the hay, a tumble in the bush."

These words she interpreted without any problem. Feeling mischievous, she cupped her hand to her mouth. "Georgia, you have a visitor."

The sales rep sauntered into view, having changed into a T-shirt and sweat pants. "Oh," she said, her face registering surprise.

Goat's skin flushed. "You'd said you might want to see my cats," he greeted her. "I have an iguana, too."

"Way cool. Marla, do you mind? I'd love to see his animals."

She smiled. "We have plenty of time before dinner. Just be careful of the snake."

Rubbing her hands together, Georgia squealed with delight. "A snake! That's wild." She grabbed Goat's skinny arm and tugged him outside.

Marla shut the door, leaving it unlocked for Georgia to reenter. After changing into jeans, she entered her study to return phone calls while the older couple took a nap. Chores had piled up on her, and she felt neglectful of her duty to call her mom, best friend, and others. Foremost in her mind was another objective: decipher Heather's desperate message before the killer added her to his target sights.

Signing on to the Net, she entered the words Heather had scribbled. The search listed a turf farm in Belle Glade. Bell Farms . . . now it made sense. But what did Heather's murder have to do with sod growers?

Chapter
Twelve

Marla wondered who would bring up the subject of Heather's death while working the next day at her salon. Unable to reach any of the Luxor crew on Tuesday, she'd left a message on Jan's answering machine at the hotel. Hopefully, their acting director had shared the news. Marla was too busy this morning with clients to spare time for phone calls. She had to clear her schedule for the photo shoot at noon.

Georgia helped her move the chairs away from the front reception area in preparation for the photographer's arrival. Marla stayed out of the man's way while he set up his backdrop screen, lights, and tripod. Hoping none of their customers would trip over the wires snaking across the floor, she greeted the Luxor gang when they arrived.

Marla relied on Luis to direct traffic, but the handsome Cubano receptionist wasn't much help when the models arrived. Turning on his charm, he chatted them up and let the phone ring too long.

Jan, who seemed born to command, was calm

and collected in a svelte black pantsuit, although she was more subdued than usual as she issued orders. No one mentioned Heather. Each team member had a task to perform, and they all got to work without much conversation.

Marla got sidetracked fixing a coloring error on a walk-in customer. By the time she finished, Jan was urging Sampson to finish his fancy updo on one of the models. Using Marla's station, he chatted with the girl while wielding his curling iron with aplomb. From the awed look on the girl's face, Marla guessed he must have been bragging about himself.

Ron had just completed a geisha look on one model. Putting down his implements, he called for the next one. None responded, the girls just stood there, exchanging solemn glances among themselves. Ron approached Marla.

"Wasn't I supposed to work on Heather now?" he demanded, planting himself in front of the reception desk from where Luis avidly watched the proceedings. "Jan said she was killed yesterday. I can't believe that's true. Do you know what happened? You're the one who left the message."

Marla swallowed. She'd known someone would broach the topic before long. Stumbling over her words, she explained how Heather had summoned her and what she'd found, omitting any mention of the piece of paper in Heather's hand.

"Who would do that to her? She was so beautiful." His brows folded. "What did she say on the phone?"

"Just that she had important information to share."

"Why you? You're not one of us." He must have seen the stricken look on her face, because he hastily corrected himself. "I mean, you haven't been with Luxor as long as the rest of us. I'm just curious why she'd wanna talk to you."

Marla tilted her head. "Probably because I hang around with a cop boyfriend, and she saw Detective Masterson at the show. She must have figured I'd pass on whatever she told me, assuming it related to Chris's murder."

"You think?"

"Definitely."

He cursed. "Now we'll have to get someone else for the shoot in the Keys."

Hey, show a little grief, pal. We're talking about a woman you tumbled in your room. "I've been thinking about who we could get to substitute, at least for today. I need to talk to Jan about it." She thrust a hank of hair behind her ear. "In the meantime, ask the photographer who he wants to do next."

Leaving Ron, Marla walked toward Janice. Not all of the crew were present. Amy and Miguel were visiting their accounts in the area, so she wouldn't see them again until Friday. Tyler lounged in the back room, drinking coffee while calling in Luxor's orders from the weekend. Liesl assisted the artistic team, not very happily it appeared from the sullen look on her face.

Marla's own staff, accustomed to her shenanigans, took the commotion in stride. If she knew her friends, this event would be fodder for gossip for the next week. She just hoped they didn't resent her distraction from the salon and understood the boon it would be for business in the future. This photo session had to go well.

"I have in mind someone we could use as a model, since Heather, you know, isn't here," she told Janice, who wore a disapproving frown as she studied her clipboard.

"I was wondering when you'd get around to discussing the poor girl." Jan's face sagged. "I haven't wanted to disrupt our flow. This whole thing makes me sick. Heather was so young and vibrant."

Marla launched into her story, wishing she didn't have to convey sad tidings. Her voice clogged, and she faded to a finish. Georgia, filing her nails, glanced at her with concern.

"The show is jinxed," Sampson cried. "I want to go home."

"You can't," Ron replied with a cynical edge. "That detective said we have to stick around town."

"Does he know we're going to the Keys on Friday?" one of the models squeaked. "Oh gosh, I'll miss Heather."

"Two down," said Tyler, sauntering into view. "Don't things happen in threes?"

"God forbid." Marla exchanged glances with Nicole, her colleague at the next station, and Jennifer across the room. The short blond stylist was doing her best to stay out of their conversation, but Marla noticed that her hand holding a comb had halted in midair.

Just as their tableau seemed frozen, into the salon barged Arnie Hartman, owner of Bagel Busters a few doors down. She'd ordered salad platters for lunch, and he had called to say he was running a bit late. Grateful for the interruption, Marla hastened toward him. As usual, he wore an apron over his T-shirt and jeans. His dark eyes twinkled over a prominent nose, mustache, and firm mouth.

"What's up?" he said, with a wide grin.

His cheerful manner lightened the mood, and

work resumed. Marla helped lay out the food in the storeroom for the staff and signed the credit slip. Jan had promised to reimburse her.

"We've been talking about the girl's murder in the *shvitz*." She'd described her weekend when she placed her order that morning, but they hadn't had much chance for discussion. Marla would have liked to take the time now, knowing she could always rely on Arnie for support. A longtime friend, he'd been a wannabe suitor until she fixed him up with her friend Jillian Barlow, an actress and public relations specialist.

Reflecting on the busy lunch hour, she decided not to inflict her problems on him. Nonetheless, his solid presence soothed her nerves.

"We've been getting set up for the photo shoot, but now we're one model short," she added.

"Sounds to me like something isn't kosher with this group," Arnie remarked, his brows raised.

"I agree, although Goat suggested that Christine may have had other business in town. She arrived a couple of days before the show started." Arnie had met her animal-loving neighbor Goat on a prior occasion.

"Don't you think the detective already traced Chris's movements?"

"Sergeant Masterson isn't sharing his findings."

"Tell me again, my *shayna maidel*, why you should care?" He eyed her while sticking plastic forks into the salads for use as serving utensils.

Marla folded her arms. "I want to work with Luxor. It's a great opportunity for publicity, as well as potential travel benefits. When we move the salon, we can use all the help we can get to bring in new customers, and to raise our recognition factor."

"That means you'll raise your prices. Did Jill talk to you about doing our wedding party? She may want to lock in the cost now, before you go too upscale."

Marla swatted his arm. "You'll always get a discount. And, yes, I've already agreed to do your wedding. Jill asked my advice on locations, so we've spoken about it."

Finished with his task, he straightened. "How about a double ceremony? You and Dalton . . ."

"We haven't decided on a date yet, and anyway, I have to get rid of his former in-laws first."

"*Oy vey*, you've gotten yourself into another pickle, haven't you?"

Marla snatched a dill spear from one of the platters. "This is the only kind of pickle I want today, thanks." She wasn't in the mood to discuss her personal situation.

"*Hof oif nissim un farloz zich nit oif a nes.* Hope for miracles but don't rely on one," Arnie said with a twinkle.

"Yeah, I need one if I'm to survive their visit. Now if you'll excuse me, I'd better see what's going on in the salon."

After Arnie left, Marla suggested Babs Winrow as their substitute model. "She's a regular client who's due in for a trim," Marla told Jan. "Babs has a photogenic face. I'm sure you'll agree when you see her."

"Okay, but make sure she signs the waiver," Jan said. "We won't be offering any compensation."

"Babs is senior vice-president of Tylex Industries. She'll do it just for kicks."

Sure enough, Babs appeared delighted. "I'd love to be your model," the blonde gushed after Marla broached the subject. She preened for the photographer after Ron restyled her short, layered hair and gave her golden highlights.

"You could have a new career as a model," Marla told her with a smile.

"Like I have time," Babs responded, tugging on her ruby sweater. "Neat idea, though, if I ever run out of things to do. Wait until I tell my friends about this."

Walking away, Marla approached Jan, who stood watching the frenetic activity with an observant air. "I wanted to make a contribution to the flowers for Christine's family," she said to the sleek redhead. "How much would my share be?"

"Oh, thanks, but it's not necessary," Jan said with a genuine smile. "Luxor will cover the cost. It's the least we can do for Chris. I thought we'd also make a donation to her favorite charity."

"That's a good idea. Tell me, where is her family located?"

"Her mother lives in an old-age home in Pembroke Pines, and she has a sister in Atlanta. The police detective has already spoken to her. She'll take charge of the body when it's released."

"Is that why Chris arrived a few days early, to visit her mother? Pembroke Pines is only twenty minutes from here."

"Who knows?" Jan shrugged. "I don't keep track of people on their off time."

"Maybe you should. Two people connected to Luxor are dead. Aren't you wondering if someone in our group is involved?"

"That's for the cops to determine."

"It's interesting how Chris died." Picking up a pile of foils, Marla stacked them one on top of the other in perfect alignment. "Someone who knew she took antidepressants slipped her a similar drug with deadly side effects. I imagine this happened during the cocktail party."

Jan gave her a startled glance. "How do you figure that?"

"A waiter brought us a couple of filled wineglasses and said the tab had been paid. Who ordered the drinks? And if the medicine wasn't in the wine, how could it have been administered? In one of her appetizers? Chris's plate seemed to be full, yet I don't remember seeing her standing in the buffet line."

"So you're saying one of us poisoned her?" Jan snapped.

"I'm suggesting you should be a little more interested in what's going on beneath the surface," Marla said, risking her future job opportunities with Luxor to make her point. Hopefully, she wasn't making it to Chris's killer. Jan could have knocked off her superior to move up the corporate ladder, but that struck Marla as too obvious.

"During the show," she continued, "Heather spotted the detective in the audience just before Sampson's performance. She was about to tell me something relevant, but we got interrupted. Afterward, she called and set up a meeting between us, but she got killed before she could reveal what she knew. What had she seen that might be construed as a threat by Chris's murderer?"

"You seem to be on top of things. If you want to deal with it, be my guest. I have enough on my plate." The look on Jan's face told Marla she wasn't completely insensitive, just that she felt overwhelmed.

"Maybe Chris's mother knows something."

"So go talk to her. Her name is Violet."

"Same last name? I gather Chris never married."

"You got that right. Chris liked men to fall at her feet, but she never let anyone get too close. She was more into controlling them than marrying them. I'd even wondered at one time if she could be a closet lesbian, until she had that affair with Alonzo. When he dumped her, Chris wore a sour face for nearly a year. But then she got over it and turned back to her usual pattern of conquer-and-control."

Marla placed the foils on a nearby cart. "Where does this Alonzo reside now?"

"I think he moved back to Spain." Jan's gaze shifted. "The photographer is signaling me. We'll catch up later, Marla."

Having a spare moment, Marla noticed Tyler getting his nails buffed at the station next to Georgia. Her friend was rambling on about Goat and his animals. Smiling inwardly, she was just about to ask Ron if he needed help when the door chime jingled.

Oh, no. Why had Ma chosen this afternoon to stop by with her boisterous boyfriend, Roger?

"Hiya, doll," Roger Gold called, waddling forward to plant a wet kiss on her cheek. He wore a green golf shirt and tangerine pants, the colors making Marla think of a leprechaun except for his size. His bulging belly bespoke of too many trips to the dessert table to feed his sweet tooth.

Hiding her distaste, Marla embraced her mother with a firm hug. "What brings you to the salon today? Your appointment isn't until next week."

"I wanted to meet your cohorts from Luxor since you told me so much about them," Anita said, smiling. "How is the photography session going?"

Marla swept an arm toward the makeshift studio. "Babs agreed to substitute for Heather, the model who, er, couldn't make it."

Roger punched her arm. "You mean, the one who bit the dust?" Marla had phoned her mother last evening and filled her in on recent events. "We'd better warn this group that you're a magnet for trouble."

Marla gritted her teeth. "Ma, can I talk to you in private? Maybe Roger would like to try one of our new shampoo products. It's on the house," she told him with a sugary smile. Not that he had much hair to wash, but like many condo commandos, he grasped at anything he could get for free. After waving him off to the shampoo chair and a waiting assistant, she ushered her mother toward the back storeroom.

"Do you know of any assisted-living facilities in Pembroke Pines?" she began without preamble once they were alone. "Christine Parks, Luxor's former director, may have visited her mother at an old-age residence there before the show started."

Anita gave her a keen gaze. "I have my list at home from when I researched those places for Aunt Polly. If you tell me the woman's name, I'll find out where she's located."

"Okay, thanks." Crossing her feet, Marla leaned against the counter. "I told you I'd been to a *shvitz*. It wasn't what I expected. Instead of wizened old men, there were muscled hunks and girls in bikinis using the place like a day spa."

Anita walked over to the coffeepot and helped herself to a cup. "It's supposed to be healthy for you, but I've never been," she said, adding cream and sugar to her drink. "My mother went to the *mikvah* in her day."

"What's that?" Marla said, vaguely remembering the term from her heritage.

Anita's eyebrows shot up. They were dark, unlike her soft white hair. "Women go to the *mikvah* as part of the marriage ritual. I'll see if there's one in the area in case you'd like to go before your wedding. Which is when, *bubula*? I have to shop for my dress."

Marla grimaced. Why was everyone asking about her wedding date today? Did she have an announcement pasted across her forehead? "Never mind about that. I don't understand how a *mikvah* is different from a *shvitz*. If it's for women only, then why wouldn't Heather have chosen to meet me there?"

"Probably because you wouldn't qualify to get in on short notice. The *mikvah* is used most often by Orthodox married women after their periods. It purifies them so they can resume sexual relations with their husbands. Even if you wore a fake wedding band, you'd still have to follow procedures."

Marla straightened her shoulders. "I've play-acted before."

"You pretended to be a nurse's aide to get a job with Miriam Pearl's family in order to snoop out their secrets. Going to the *mikvah* is much more personal." Anita gave her a knowing smirk.

"How so?"

"You must have seven clean days prior to coming to the *mikvah*. There is a certain way to tell." Anita blushed, making Marla more curious.

"Go on."

"You start counting the days once your period ends. Religious women use little white cloths and, er, insert it to make sure there aren't any stains. They do this each morning and each afternoon before it gets dark."

"Eww," Marla said, cringing at the thought. "Then what?"

"You prepare for your appointment at the *mikvah*. This is what I've heard, mind you, from a friend who used to go on a regular basis. She said that on the last evening, you take a bath at home for thirty minutes and wash your hair with shampoo, no conditioner. You have to remove all nail polish and clean the dirt under your nails. You brush and floss your teeth, and can eat no further snacks. You can't wear any jewelry or makeup and are even supposed to clean the holes in your ears, nose, and naval area."

"That wouldn't be popular with people who have belly button rings." Marla couldn't conceive of who'd want to undergo this ritual. "So once you're all clean, what happens?"

Anita sipped her coffee. "You go to the *mikvah*, where you're led to a bathroom. Inside, you take a brief shower, comb out your hair, and put on the robe provided. An attendant brings you to a private room where she examines your nails to make sure you've complied. Then you go into the chlorinated pool, submerge yourself, come up and say a prayer, go underwater twice more, then get dressed."

"Sort of like a baptism, huh?" Religious customs had more in common than people realized.

"The whole thing takes about fifteen minutes and is supposed to remove spiritual impurities."

Marla's lips twisted. "I should've done it after my divorce from Stan. I could have used a spiritual cleansing to scrape him off my skin, but I think I can live without this experience."

"Suit yourself." Anita shrugged. "It's been a tradition for three thousand years. My mother described it as an emotional journey that brought her closer to God."

"Heather is closer to God, but not through the *mikvah*."

Anita pointed a finger. "She may have been going to the *shvitz* every week, like people go to a gym. The *shvitz*, unlike the *mikvah*, is a public place to relax, sweat, nosh on snacks, and shmooze with people. Probably she figured no one would follow her there."

"Well, she figured wrong."

Hearing raised voices, Marla emerged into the salon to see Sampson in a snit with Ron.

"What's the problem?" She hastened to intercede. The two hair-design artists faced each other on either side of a chair in which sat a model, finger-combing her long golden hair.

Ron maintained eye contact with the master trainer. "Chris scheduled me to do the instructional video for our new color–diffusion process."

"Christine isn't making the decisions any longer," Sampson retorted. "Jan said I could do the demo." He jabbed a hairbrush in the air. Marla noticed it was one of his signature boar-bristle brushes that he imported from China. Liesl had told her how particular he was about his supplies.

"You've already had your share of presentations at the show." Ron's face reddened. "I'm just as qualified to do this film, and I'll present the material without an ego trip. If you brag any more about your accomplishments, I'm gonna puke. Stylists need their directions to be straight and clear."

"Is that so?" Sampson sneered. "I imagine that's why you acted so cool when Christine refused to be your next bimbo."

"She told me flat-out that I wasn't her type, but I bounced right back. Unlike you, I didn't let her intimidate me." He bared his teeth. "Isn't it convenient how everything works out in your favor now that she's gone?"

Chapter Thirteen

Marla consulted the piece of paper in her hand while facing the double front doors to the Hibiscus Blossom assisted-living facility. Her mother had called the night before with information that Violet Parks was registered there as a resident, and Marla had cleared time from her busy Thursday schedule for a visit.

Inhaling a breath of cool winter air, she reflected on the commotion in her salon yesterday. Ron had had the chutzpah to confront Sampson and point out how conveniently Chris's death factored into the maestro's plans. It reminded her of the check she'd returned to Sampson, made out to the company director. Maybe Chris's mother knew what that was all about.

Pushing open the doors, she stepped inside, wondering what to expect. A whiff of food rode along a current of heated air. She identified the mouth-watering aroma of roasted chicken and potatoes, presumably coming from an empty dining room on her left. Lunch hour must have just passed.

Approaching the reception desk straight ahead,

she unbuttoned her leather jacket. This turned into a juggling act, considering the strap of her handbag chose that moment to slip off her shoulder, and she held a potted silk plant in her other hand. Adjusting her load, she grinned at the receptionist, a fiftyish blonde with teased hair who chewed gum and doodled on a notepad. The woman's bored gaze took in Marla's arrival with the barest acknowledgment.

"Hi, I'm Iris. Can I help youse?" She had a strong New York accent.

"I'm here to see Violet Parks on behalf of her daughter. We worked together," Marla added, feeling the need to explain. She eyed a sign-up sheet, hoping she wouldn't have to leave her name, then realized the list was for relatives signing residents out for temporary day trips.

The receptionist shook her head, clinking her tiered earrings. "Such a shocker. A good girl, that one, and to come to such a tragic end. She called often to check on her mom's welfare."

Marla recognized a good source of gossip. Glancing at the lounge on her right, she stepped forward. Most likely, those elderly folks occupying the armchairs and sofas couldn't even hear them, let alone take an interest in their conversation. She couldn't be certain about the bookkeeper in the back office, however. Lowering her voice, she leaned forward from the waist.

"I'd like to assist the police with their investigation. Do you have any ideas about who might have wished Christine Parks any harm?"

"The world is full of bad people, honey. You worked with the lady. Someone wanting her job? A jilted boyfriend? If you're here to ask her mother, you won't get far." Iris's expression questioned Marla's motives.

Marla lifted the plant into the woman's view. "Actually, I'm here to deliver this. I thought it might cheer her."

"She'll love those pretty pink blossoms. Go on upstairs, honey. Violet will be glad to have a visitor. The last person who saw her was Dr. Greenberg. He stopped by on Sunday."

"Is that her personal physician? Maybe he knew Chris."

"Dr. Greenberg is a dermatologist. I think the daughter requested his visit, because she was here the first time he came. The nurse upstairs would know. Seems to me he was more anxious to talk to Christine, but that could be because her mom ain't in her right mind. Violet is in the Orchard, our special-needs section. You'll be wantin' the code to get out: seven–five–eight– three–zero."

Marla followed her instructions to the elevator down the hall, passing an old man wearing a cardigan, pushing himself along with a walker. Wheelchair-bound residents sat about, their sagging postures matching their mood, if their bleak expressions were any indication. Unpleasant odors permeated the corridor, but at least the place was clean and brightly lit. While waiting for the lift to descend to the first floor, Marla noted a wall chart listing daily social activities and another one with menu choices.

"Hello, dearie. Come for a visit?" A woman sidled over, her face showing an excess of makeup and years. Marla's observant gaze took in her topaz jewelry that matched a blouse she wore with a black skirt as though dressed for the theater.

"Yes, I'm here to see a friend's mother."

"That's so sweet. I never see my children. They live up North, you know, and it's hard for them to get away. But I stay active. It's really important, if you don't want to lose it like those folks in the Unit." She spoke the last word on a descending note, as though it were a place to dread.

"It seems as though you have a lot of activities to attend," Marla said in a friendly tone.

"Oh yes, I've even started a reading circle for those of us who can still see well enough to read." The lady chuckled.

"That's wonderful." Marla felt a pang of sympathy for this woman whose children lived so distant from her. She could see in the lady's eyes that even though she hadn't complained, she missed her kids. How many old people were deposited in institutions like this and left to waste away in loneliness and despair? Their plight tore at her heart, yet she knew also that caring for elderly parents forced a heavy burden on the adult children who had their own families to tend. She shuddered, picturing the day when Anita's faculties would falter. At least Marla had a brother with whom to share decisions.

The elevator door slid open, and she cantered inside, eager to complete her business and leave. Already her mood had swung from hopeful to depressed. This place with its forlorn residents got to you, she thought, pressing the button for the second floor.

The upper level repeated the first-floor pattern, with room after room opening off the corridor as in a hospital. The linoleum floor, dull gray walls, and harsh lighting were common to both types of facilities, but that was where the similarities ended.

Personal belongings such as framed photos, knick-knacks, and crocheted blankets adorned people's rooms here, Marla noticed as she strode by, peering curiously at the occupants.

She'd never really thought about it before, but assisted living was not the same as nursing-home care. Residents who lived here took care of their own personal hygiene and wore street clothes, unlike the people who needed a higher level of care. Marla recalled her mother had mentioned one upscale place that had apartments with kitchenettes. You could even keep your own car, or move into a place that had its own van to take residents shopping, to the bank, or to doctor's appointments. Probably the cost escalated along with the services offered, but it wasn't a bad deal for older folks who were afraid to live alone.

Those in the special-needs unit in Hibiscus Blossom, however, required extra supervision. Marla approached the rear of the second-floor hallway, where she faced a closed door with THE ORCHARD emblazoned on it in bold red paint. Swallowing, she wondered what she'd find beyond. Maybe she should have asked what "special needs" implied. Evidently, the door stayed locked, because she had to push a buzzer to gain entry. Repeating the exit code in her mind, she let herself in and faced another corridor with doors opening off each side. God forbid there should be a fire. These unfortunate souls would be trapped.

Her stomach sinking, she searched for a nurses' station. She bypassed a gentleman dragging along and muttering to himself. He held on to a rail fixed on the wall.

"Is this my room?" a woman asked in a wheezy voice. Marla hadn't seen her come up from behind. "I don't know where I belong. Can you help me?" She gripped Marla's arm. "Maybe you should call a taxi to take me home."

"You don't need no taxi, Hazel. Come on now, leave the lady alone." A buxom nurse's aide pried the woman's fingers loose and grinned at Marla. "You lookin' for someone, sugar?"

"Yes, thanks, can you tell me what room Violet Parks is in?"

"Two twenty-one. Violet is a doll. She always talks so sweet and ladylike. Are you a relative?"

"I'm a friend of her daughter's."

"Oh lordie, we were so sorry to hear what happened to the poor gal. You go on and cheer her up now. Not that she'll remember too much. You could say her condition is a blessing."

"What condition is that?"

"Why, this here is an Alzheimer's unit, sugar. Violet don't remember things, but she always recognized her daughter. Such a shame." Shaking her head, the aide guided her charge down the hallway.

Marla discovered the room a few paces down and knocked on the open door. She might as well have been knocking on her own skull for all the response it generated. Stepping hesitantly inside, she peered at the two occupants.

One woman was slumped in a chair, several feet from a television blaring a soap opera. Her roommate lay napping on top of the other bed. Both were fully clothed in colorful pants sets with their gray heads neatly combed. On the surface, it appeared their physical well-being was being looked after with diligence. But the strong smell of urine told another story. A package of disposable underwear rested atop the first woman's nightstand along with a bottle of lotion, a box of tissues, and an eyeglass case. Each item was labeled with her name, Fiona Marsh. That meant her roommate must be Violet.

Great, the old lady was asleep. *Should I wake her? Might as well. She'll be glad to have company.*

Advancing to Violet's bedside, she tapped the old lady on the shoulder. Her wrinkled face seemed peaceful in repose, but her shortened stature and curled posture reminded Marla of a shriveled flower. Is this what happened when you got old? You reverted to a helpless state, and your life's work got lost in the flux of time? Marla had a sudden clear picture of her life force developing as a bud, blossoming into full glory, then wilting into oblivion. Did it have to happen that way?

No, thank goodness. Marla's great-uncle Milton had been alert until the day he died at the ripe age of ninety-two. Some people retained their faculties and contributed to the world until they dropped. That possibility reassured her. But Marla's expectations of gaining information from Violet had plummeted. She'd be lucky to get a lucid response.

"Huh? Whassat?" Violet's eyes blinked open when Marla gently shook her shoulder.

"Mrs. Parks, my name is Marla Shore. I'm . . . I was a friend of your daughter's. Christine mentioned that you lived here, and I thought I'd come visit."

Violet's expression brightened. "Christine? Is she here?" She craned her neck to look beyond Marla.

Oh joy. Now what? "I came alone. Can I help you sit up? Would you like a drink of water?" The old lady's lips were dry, but she didn't even have a water glass on her nightstand. Hospitals put water pitchers at patients' bedsides. Were relatives responsible for supplying every personal item in this facility? She placed her potted plant on the table.

"Thanks," Violet said, sitting with Marla's assistance. She narrowed her eyes. "Have we met before?"

"No, we haven't, but your daughter told me about you," Marla replied, figuring a little white lie wouldn't hurt.

"You said Christine knows you?"

"That's right. I need some information, and she suggested I ask you about it. Have you ever heard of a place called Bell Farms?" If Heather's death was linked to Chris's, then the company director might have offhandedly mentioned something to her mother.

"Say again?" Violet turned her head, as though she could hear better with one ear.

"Bell Farms." Marla raised her voice so the woman could hear her over the blare of the television. She glanced at the roommate, who remained focused on the screen like a statue.

"Dunno about that. Did you tell me Christine was here? I don't see her." Violet reached for her walker.

Marla wheeled it closer and helped the woman dangle her legs over the edge of the bed. Her limbs were frail, her skin almost translucent. The smell of baby powder drifted in the air.

I guess you aren't ready to acknowledge your loss. I can play that game. "Chris couldn't make it," Marla said. "What do you remember about her last visit?"

"She had big plans, Christine and that doctor. Who did you say you were?"

"Marla Shore. I worked with your daughter."

Violet's eyes misted. "My baby . . . they told me . . ."

"I'm so sorry."

"For what? You have nothing to be sorry about. You look fine, although you're a bit too thin." Violet cackled, showing gaps in her yellowed teeth.

Marla took a deep breath, letting it out slowly. "Can you tell me if Chris had any other friends in the area? She came to town a couple of days before the beauty show. Besides visiting you, did she see anyone else?" Likely Chris wanted a day off to soak up the sun, but it was worth a try.

"Christine met that friend of hers," Violet said with a wink. "She was so excited about something they were doing together. Help me up. They might still be in the hallway. She wanted me to meet him. My daughter gets so fixed on these causes that it's all she talks about. She'll be glad to let you in on the deal." Gripping the handlebars on her walker, Violet shoved her feet into a pair of worn slippers at her bedside.

"What deal is that?" Impatient to learn more, Marla helped the woman to her feet.

"The one with Dr. Greenberg. You know, the skin doctor." Violet hobbled forward a few steps. "He was involved in Christine's latest project. If you ask me, I think she hoped I'd make a donation, and that's why she brought him to meet me. They must've spent an hour discussing their business and forgetting I existed. That wasn't right, not when I hardly ever get enough time to spend with my girl."

"You must miss her terribly." Keeping pace with the old lady as she shuffled toward the doorway, Marla brushed past the other inhabitant, who didn't

move a muscle except to breathe. Violet didn't have
to worry about communicating with her roommate.

Violet halted suddenly. "Are you the nurse? I
want to go back to bed."

"Exercise is good for you. Come on, let's go for
a walk." The people who worked here must have
endless patience. Hoping she'd see the nurse's
aide in the corridor, Marla urged the old lady onward. "Tell me, did Chris like her job?" she said,
trying another tack.

"Christine loved her work." Violet's expression
cleared as though a veil had lifted. "She brought
me product samples to use, in the early days when
I got out more. Wouldn't do me much good now,
with the little hair I have left. Tell her not to bring
me anything next time."

They reached the corridor, where Marla read a
sign on the wall that said the recreation room was
located down the hallway. Violet headed in that direction. Glancing at her watch, Marla compressed
her lips. She should get back to the salon. Hurry-
ing after Violet, she introduced another topic.

"Did your daughter say how she liked working
with Sampson York, our artistic director?"

"She may have told me, but I don't remember."
Violet bobbed her gray head at a passerby, a neatly
dressed lady who actually spoke a greeting. Unfor-
tunately, her garbled words made no sense. Violet
paid no heed, continuing along at a snail's pace.

"Sampson owed Chris some money," Marla prodded, realizing Violet's short-term memory surged
and receded like a tide.

"Is that so? Well, I hope he paid her back."

"Did she ever talk about her colleagues?"

"Christine was in charge. She knew how to do
the right thing. You know, too, don't you?"

Despairing of getting a relevant answer, Marla made a last attempt. "What about friends, other relatives? Can you guess who might have wanted to harm your daughter?"

"Harm my baby? Why would anyone do that?" Violet blinked. "She did say someone was taking the money . . ."

Marla's pulse catapulted. "Go on."

The elderly woman's face blanked. "It's nice of you to come visit me. Have we met before?"

Marla gritted her teeth. Farther along, she spotted a medicine cart propped outside an open doorway. Restraining her steps took strength of will, but she waited until Violet resumed her ambulation before searching for the nurse. A heavyset attendant wearing blue scrubs emerged from a room two doors down.

"Excuse me," Marla said with a lilt. "I'm a friend of Christine Parks. She told me about her, uh, project with Dr. Greenberg, and I'd like to make a donation. I can't seem to find his phone number, although I'm sure he's listed."

The nurse straightened. She wore her wavy black hair in a high ponytail, her florid complexion accented with rose-toned makeup, not the best choice in Marla's opinion.

"Dr. Greenberg, now he's got a reputation among the old folks. They all go to him for their sun spots, but I heard him talking to Miz Parks's gal about bringing in younger patients. Don't know what all she'd have to do with it, but that doesn't matter now. A shame what happened, ain't it?"

"Very sad." Marla nodded at Violet, who hunched over to grip her walker. "Her mother keeps referring to Chris as though she's alive. Is that normal for her condition?"

"You betcha. Memory loss is common for residents on this floor, but I don't think all of them have Alzheimer's. Some folks got what used to be termed senile dementia. It's nature's way of blocking out the pain of growing old and feeble. Miz Parks, she be a sweet little ole lady. Always has a kind word for everyone." The nurse wheeled the cart ahead several feet.

"Does Violet have any other relatives in the area?"

"Nope. There's another daughter, but she don't live in Florida, nor does she ever come to see her mama."

"So the last time Christine visited was right before she, uh, passed away?" The nurse gave a sad nod. "You didn't happen to overhear if she had any particular concerns, did you?"

"I'd have been too busy to take notice, sister. Now if you don't mind, I've got to deliver these pills." Flashing a quick grin, the woman whirled inside the next room.

"Mrs. Parks, will you be all right by yourself?" Marla said, retreating a few paces. She felt as though the walls were closing in on her and couldn't wait to leave the oppressive atmosphere. Another resident ambled by, humming the national anthem.

"I'll go back to bed now," Violet's voice quivered.

"Wouldn't you rather sit in the recreation hall? It's bright and airy," Marla suggested, peeking into the large space where several inhabitants sat in their wheelchairs while a loudspeaker played old show tunes. No one spoke to anyone else. It could have been a roomful of zombies with all those inanimate faces.

"I don't want to go in there," Violet said in a belligerent tone. "Christine said she was coming to see me. Take me to my room."

"All right." Her temples throbbing, Marla turned and tramped along at an interminable pace until they returned to Violet's door. After ushering the old lady inside, she dashed to the exit. Muttering the numeric code aloud, she punched the keypad and grunted with relief when the latch clicked.

Emerging outside from the first floor, Marla realized she no longer needed her jacket. The temperature had risen, and the warm afternoon air brought the perfumed scent of citrus. She shrugged free from her outer apparel, feeling like a prisoner released from jail. How awful to be confined in that place, and yet the old-age home provided good care for people who needed it.

She stretched her arms and rolled her shoulders before unlocking her car. One hour may have passed, but it seemed like twenty. She craved a long walk with Spooks, with the sun kissing her neck and a fresh breeze caressing her skin, but that would have to wait.

Crunched for time, she pushed aside her musings about Christine Parks, Dr. Greenberg, and the possibilities of their association until later that evening. She'd invited Anita over to shmooze with her houseguests, and she knew Ma's friends visited just about every doctor in town. Anita might be able to get the scoop on the good physician.

When Dalton called to say he'd stop by with Brianna, Marla decided to pull together a quick lasagna dinner. Tired from work and running errands, she didn't have a minute to relax before setting the dining room table for seven and sticking her assembled dish in the oven. Before anyone else arrived, she recruited Georgia to help in the kitchen, while Justine and Larry munched on cashews in the family room.

Georgia's eyes sparkled as she spread minced garlic on the Italian loaf slathered with butter prior to baking. "Marla, you know, I was thinking. We could squeeze in one more person if I asked Goat to join us. I'll bet the poor guy doesn't get many invitations, and I really want to ask him about his volunteer work at the animal shelter. What do you say? Besides, Spooks would love to see his dog Rita."

Marla laughed. "You present a tough case, don't you? I can see past your excuse of getting our poodles together, though. Why don't you just admit you like my loony neighbor? Go ahead and ask him to dinner, but let him know it's a crowd. Spooks and Rita can play in the backyard together."

Her plans went awry when Anita showed up with her boyfriend, Roger, and his son, Barry, in tow. Suddenly Marla had ten people for dinner, awkward introductions to make, and no chance to ask her mother about the dermatologist.

Chapter
Fourteen

"Here's a hummus dip," Marla said, when everyone had settled into the family room, where a sports game ran on television at low volume. Anita had helped her add an extension board to the dining room table, but expanding the table had been easier than expanding their meal. Mentally calculating portions, Marla figured she could stretch the lasagna dish only by cutting it into fairly smaller slices.

She'd already told Georgia to grab another garlic loaf from the freezer, but salads would be skimpy unless she added mandarin oranges and water chestnuts—fortunately, items regularly stocked in her pantry. Also fortunately, she'd renewed her supply of appetizers during her latest foray to the grocery store.

"What's hew-miss?" Justine said with a sniff when Marla placed the plate next to the eggplant dip. Justine and Larry sat stiffly on the loveseat, while Anita and Roger occupied the longer sofa. Dalton and Barry stood at opposite corners of the room, their arms folded and their postures tense.

"Hum-us," Marla corrected. "It's a Middle Eastern dish made from chickpeas, garlic, lemon juice, olive oil, and tahini, a sesame seed paste."

"How interesting." Justine's nose wrinkled when Marla offered her a piece of pita bread. "No thanks, dear, I'll stick with the port-wine cheese and crackers."

"Try this chopped liver," Roger said, munching. "Anita made it, and it's de-lish. Her daughter is just as good a *balebosteh.* You're getting a prize for a daughter-in-law."

Anita nudged him. "They're Brianna's grandparents on the *other* side."

"Oh, sorry." Unfazed, Roger stuffed another cracker into his mouth.

"What's a *balebosteh?*" Vail asked, genuine curiosity in his tone. Marla could have hugged him. He'd been making a sincere effort to learn the Yiddish words her family tossed into everyday conversation.

"It means a good hostess or homemaker," Anita explained.

Brianna, who'd been on the telephone in Marla's bedroom, sauntered in to join them. "When are we eating? I'm starved." She wore flip-flops with her khakis and red cotton top.

"The bread isn't ready yet," Marla told the teenager, wondering where Georgia had gone. She'd run out to invite their neighbor but hadn't returned. No one was keeping an eye on the oven, and the aroma of toasted garlic grew stronger with each minute. She'd better take a look at the timer. "Anyone care for a drink refill?"

Larry cleared his throat. "I could use another gin and tonic, and I think we need more potato chips. Did you get the pork rinds on my list, by any chance? They're my favorite."

Marla pursed her lips. He should know that she wouldn't keep pork products in her house. Had he said that to provoke her, or was he simply ignorant?

Vail strode forward. "Come on, Marla, I'll give you a hand with the food. I need another beer anyway."

Barry detached himself from his holding spot. "Would you like me to open the Chianti that I brought? Red wine is more appropriate with our meal."

"I could use a glass, thanks," Marla said with a grateful grin.

She glanced at Vail, ruggedly handsome in black jeans and a slate gray sweater that matched his smoky eyes. His intense expression went along with his clenched jaw. Clearly he didn't like having competition present, and Barry had done everything he could to enhance their differences. The optometrist looked like a surfer with his sandy hair and tanned skin, an image he'd embellished by wearing Tommy Bahama apparel.

She bustled into the kitchen, annoyed at both men for hovering at her heels. "Here," she said, thrusting a set of pot holders at Vail, "you can take the bread out of the oven. Barry, you'll find a corkscrew in the drawer to your left."

"By the way, Marla, I know you're tied up these days, but I was wondering if you'd like to see *Shear Madness* with me. I've got an extra ticket. That is, if your boyfriend wouldn't mind." Barry's twinkling blue eyes aimed a challenge at Dalton, whose smoldering expression would have made a rookie cop quake.

"Oh gosh, I've never seen the play, and I'd love to go." Turning off the oven, Marla grasped a spatula as she prepared to cut the lasagna. "That would be okay with you, wouldn't it?" she asked the homicide detective.

He emitted a growl that Marla took to be an affirmative response. Smiling sweetly, she kissed him on the lips. "You're a real *mensch*."

They were just emerging from the kitchen when the front door crashed open. Goat staggered inside, followed by his dog, Rita, and a harried Georgia. The black poodle dashed into the family room, grabbed a cracker from the cocktail table, and scampered into the hallway before anyone could catch her. Spooks, roused from his torpor, played a game of rush-around-the-dining-room with his gal Rita, before Goat corralled the wayward animals and ushered them outdoors to the patio.

"Ugamaka, ugamaka, chugga, chugga, ush," Goat chanted, performing his jig for the assembled company. He sported a flowered shirt over a pair of faded jean shorts. With his hair askew and his scraggly beard, he reminded Marla of Shaggy on *Scooby Doo*. Goat smelled strongly of bleach, as though he'd tried to scrub away the scents from his numerous pets.

"I helped feed his animals," Georgia explained in a breathy voice. "Did you know his snake has hair?"

"Junior got a dose of an experimental hair-growth molecule," Marla said without going into the whole *megillah*. "Goat rescued the formula from some bad people who'd tested it on animals with nasty results. He's a real hero."

Goat shuffled his feet. "Marla got screwed by the sneaky bald dude. He played a number sending stylists to their slumber, but she got wise and slashed him between the eyes."

Marla winced. "Actually, I stabbed Wyeth in the

chest, but let's not go there. The dinner is just about ready. Shall we move into the dining room?"

They were digging into their main course when Roger's voice boomed. "So, Marla, when are you joining us at Shabbat services again? Anita would really like her daughter to attend."

Marla swallowed a gulp of tangy tomato sauce. "I've been too busy lately, between the hair show and my salon." *Not to mention all these people in my house, disrupting my schedule.*

"I hope you wrote down the Passover seder on your calendar for March," Anita mentioned, wagging a finger. "You can't get too busy for your own family."

"I'll say." Justine took a sip of water, regarding Marla over the rim of her glass. "Speaking of family, Brianna has a concert coming up at school. Parents usually go to these things, you know."

Marla stabbed her fork into a slice of lasagna. "Is that so? Brie, let me know the date and I'll try to get there."

"You'll try? How can you expect to give her the nurturing she expects from you as her stepmother if you don't put her needs before your own?" Justine snapped.

Marla bit back her retort when Anita interrupted. "Marla is a very giving person. She'll do her best, but you have to cut her some slack. She's put in a lot of hard work to establish her salon and build a reputation for herself in the business community. I'm proud of her, and I know she'll be a wonderful mother as well."

"What are your plans for the weekend?" Vail asked her quietly. His solid presence beside her offered reassurance, especially when he squeezed her hand under the table. He must be feeling just as put upon by their elders as she did.

Chomping on a piece of garlic bread, she spoke between bites. "Tomorrow the Luxor crew is going to the Keys for a photo shoot." Thank goodness Larry and Justine had decided to stay behind. "They've booked rooms for an overnighter, but I'll leave early on Saturday so I can get back to the salon. Darn, that doesn't give me any time to make an appointment with that dermatologist."

"What dermatologist?" Anita chimed in, giving her only daughter an aggrieved look.

"I went to the assisted-living facility today to visit Christine Parks' mother. Violet mentioned that Chris had some project going with Dr. Greenberg. I thought I'd make an appointment to see him, ostensibly for a mole check."

"Not a bad idea. Insurance companies allow us five office visits a year in Florida without a referral," Anita told their out-of-state visitors. "You have to be careful of the sun."

"What else did the old lady say?" Georgia asked. "Jan told me that the police detective, Sergeant Masterson, might come down to the Keys with us. I still can't believe he thinks one of our crowd might have poisoned Christine at the cocktail party."

"Oh, great. That'll help everyone's mood. It's bad enough that they're all stuck here until he finishes his investigation."

"I can move into the hotel if it's more convenient."

Marla waved a hand. "I didn't mean that. I just wish . . . No one seems upset about Chris or Heather."

Brianna broke in. "Wasn't that the model?"

She nodded. "I assume Heather died because she found out something regarding Chris's death. Did it have to do with Luxor, or with that doctor? Dalton, would you be able to check him out for me, even though you don't have jurisdiction on this case?"

Roger's son, seated at the other end of the table, raised his arm. "Would that be Jake Greenberg? If so, I know how you could meet him without making an appointment." He grinned broadly as though privy to a secret no one else could guess.

"Well, don't keep us in the dark," Marla said wryly.

"If he's the right Dr. Greenberg, then he's a bigwig in the American Melanoma Society. They're having their annual ball this Sunday night. I have tickets, but I wasn't going to go because I . . . Anyway, if you'd like to come, I can probably still RSVP."

Marla glanced at Vail for his reaction. Her fiancé's expression remained impassive, but she noticed he began shredding his napkin. "Would you mind?" she asked him, intending to abide by his response.

"Go ahead," he grated. "It's the perfect opportunity."

"Will you still look into his background? I need your input."

"Gee, thanks." She didn't miss his sardonic tone. Vail pointed to his daughter. "Brie, maybe we'll let Marla off the hook this week. She has too much to do."

"No way," Marla said, shifting in her seat. "Honey, which day is your concert? Nothing will stop me from being there."

"It's Wednesday," the teenager said in a small voice, "but if you can't make it, I'll understand. It's more important to find out who knocked off those two ladies."

"Brianna, mind your conversation," Justine chastised her.

"But you're all picking on Marla, and that's unfair. She's trying her best."

"Thanks, Brie. I'm glad someone's on my side. If you'll excuse me, I'll let the dogs in the house." Scraping her chair, she rose hastily before anyone could see the moisture tipping her lashes. This dinner party had been a bad idea from the start, and it had just gotten worse. Tempted to stay out on the patio, Marla slid open the glass door and stood aside while the poodles charged past.

Georgia found her in the family room, fluffing the pillows on the couch. "Don't let them get to you," Georgia said in a hushed tone. "This could happen any time two families get together with a cultural gap."

"Oh yeah?" She swatted at a pillow until the dust billowed. "We have more like a deep chasm between us. It'll never work."

"That's not true. Dalton is totally willing to compromise, and so are you. Like, Justine and Larry aren't even his parents, for heaven's sake. For all you know, his folks might love you."

"Justine and Larry are still Brianna's grandparents. They have every right to visit her."

"And you've been very gracious in allowing them to stay at your house." Georgia grabbed the pillow from Marla's hands before she beat it to death.

"You'd think they would be grateful, but Justine is doing everything she can to sabotage me. Look at the snide remarks she makes in front of everyone, and the photos of Pam that just happen to stick out of her purse. Doesn't she realize that these things hurt? Why would she be so mean? I thought she wanted to stay here so we could get to know each other, but her actions only serve to alienate me."

Georgia put a hand on her shoulder. "Try to understand how difficult it must be for Justine to see another woman take her daughter's place. She may only want to assert Pam's personality so Brie's mother isn't forgotten. No offense, but I don't see you going out of your way to remember her."

Marla lifted her gaze to Georgia's bright eyes. "I asked about her interests."

"Yeah, but you've been encouraging Dalton to pack away her favorite objects, as though you don't want any trace of her in your new home."

Marla glanced away. Was that true? If so, it made her sound heartless. "Brianna is keeping some of her mom's collections. Dalton and I have agreed to start fresh."

"That doesn't mean you can erase Pam's existence from his life. She's always going to be a part of him, and you have to accept it. Why don't you embrace her influence instead of denying it? Making peace with the past isn't only Dalton's task." Georgia smiled gently as though to mitigate her harsh words. "Now, what's for dessert? Goat said he would show me his parrot after dinner."

"Did I hear mention of dessert?" Dalton strode into the room. "Are you okay?" he asked, kissing Marla.

She fixed a lock of his peppery hair that had fallen onto his forehead and stroked it back into place. The gesture provided pleasure, but she was self-conscious with Georgia watching. "I'll be fine. It's just difficult with two sets of parents pouncing on us." She included Roger in that assessment, linking him with her mother and their obvious attempt to land her a Jewish husband, namely eligible optometrist Barry—who seemed amenable to their goal.

"I'll entertain the in-laws over the weekend so

you can get things done," Dalton said when Georgia left them alone. "Besides, you're escaping to the Keys."

"Will it bother you if I go to that affair with Barry after we get back? Because if so, I'll change my plans."

"Go ahead. If you find a link between Chris's death and the dermatologist, it would take the heat off the Luxor group, and they could all go home. I can't wait until we're alone." Drawing her close, he gave her a mind-searing kiss. "Look, if you really hate everyone being here, Justine and Larry can come to my house."

She pulled back. "No, they'd make things uncomfortable for you. I can handle it. Anyway, they'll have the place to themselves when Georgia and I leave tomorrow."

Marla had hoped to prod Georgia about her interest in Goat during the trip south, but she didn't get the chance. As soon as they turned onto the turnpike extension toward Homestead, Georgia brought up a more compelling topic.

"Do you think it's safe for us to be staying with the Luxor gang?"

"What do you mean?" Marla gripped the steering wheel as they whizzed down the highway.

Georgia flicked a glance her way. "Someone among us might be a killer."

"Tell me about it. We'll be in a group, though, so I wouldn't worry." Thinking of the group reminded Marla that she probably should have offered to pick up some of the others at the hotel, but she didn't think she could have endured their company during the two-hour drive.

She put on her turn signal to pass a car that crawled along at forty-five miles per hour. The driver was so short, Marla couldn't even see a head until she got parallel to the vehicle. The gray-haired lady could barely see over the dashboard.

Stepping on the accelerator, she sped ahead. She'd like to arrive at their destination early so they could scout around before the rest of the crew arrived.

By the roadside, an egret took flight, its long white neck arching gracefully. Various species of palms lined the highway as did the invasive Australian pines. In a circle-wide view, the blue sky stretched under the rising morning sun. It promised to be a glorious day with low humidity and temperatures in the seventies. Under other circumstances, she'd enjoy a trip to the Florida Keys, but this was a working weekend. She doubted they'd have time to enjoy the beach or to lounge by the pool.

Sadness snatched her joy away. Christine and Heather wouldn't be splashing in the ocean anymore.

"If we eliminate you as a suspect," she said to Georgia, "who does that leave?" Her arm itched, and she scratched idly at a mosquito bite.

Georgia pursed her crimson lips. She'd gathered her curly hair up with a large clip, making her eyes look enormous with her expertly applied makeup. "For one thing, there's Liesl. It's been no secret that she likes Tyler, but Chris had dibs on him when she was alive."

"I presume he put the move on you in the lounge so as to chase Chris off."

"Didn't work too well, did it? It only made her madder and more intent than ever to get him into her bed. That sure backfired. She was nuts to accuse us of having an affair."

"Chris was sick, not nuts. She'd already begun to experience a bad drug interaction." Marla's gaze sharpened. "Get a move on it," she called to another slow driver, who hogged the passing lane. *Some of these people should go to driving school.*

"Hey, look," Georgia said, pointing out the window. "What's that tree with the red blossoms?"

"It's a weeping bottlebrush." Marla glanced at the willowy branches with brilliant red flowers resembling an elongated brush. Something tickled the back of her mind, prompting a question she wanted to ask, but she couldn't quite grasp the thought. Maybe it would surface later. "I'm trying to learn my trees so I can compete with Dalton and Brianna. Did you know he grows tomato plants? I never thought a tough cop like him would be a gardener."

"You're lucky he puts up with your snooping. But then again, he'd probably never have fallen for you if you were a timid housewife."

"I did the domestic thing with Stan, thank you, and it led to strife. I like being a free spirit."

"You won't be one any longer once you tie the knot, hon. On the other hand, you might surprise yourself and enjoy being a mother hen."

"We'll see." She swerved as a car cut in front of them. "Back to the cocktail party. Did you see anyone bring Chris a fresh glass of wine other than the waiter?"

Georgia frowned in concentration. "Amy Jeanne approached her at one point, and I can picture them both sipping their drinks. Chris may not have had anything in her hand before, now that I think about it."

"I've noticed Amy keeps to herself. She looks alert, as though she knows what's going on but doesn't want to get involved. Yet she makes a statement with her nail art which seems incongruous, like someone who seeks attention."

"No one can tell what's on her mind. I've heard her mention Chris with a trace of bitterness, but if she holds a grudge, she isn't talking."

"Not to us, at any rate." Marla squinted at the windshield. Even with her sunglasses on, she felt the sun's glare. "I wonder what she's said to Sergeant Masterson."

"He makes me uncomfortable. I can't understand why he wants to hang with us this weekend. His presence will make everyone nervous."

Marla came to the junction where the road segued into the Overseas Highway. Soon they were barreling down the bridge with the Atlantic Ocean on their left and the Gulf on their right. Pinpoints of sunlight glistened off the water.

"I'm looking forward to this experience, even if the detective is there," she replied. "It'll be my first on-site photo shoot. This could open up a whole other avenue for publicity, don't you think?"

"As if you have time."

She rolled her shoulders to ease the stiffness from driving. "You know, Luxor's models worked with Heather. I wonder if she said anything to them that might be significant. This weekend will give me the chance to ask."

Georgia gave her a reproving glance. "If I were you, I'd worry about being too nosy. Like, Heather's killer might have hung around the Turkish Bath long enough to mark you. In which case, you could be next on the hit list."

Chapter
Fifteen

Regarding the tropical scene unfolding before her eyes, Marla felt as though she'd entered paradise. Luxor had gone all out in booking accommodations for its crew. She'd taken a turn as directed down a palm-lined road and on to Great Heron Key, where a privately operated resort straddled fifty acres of luxurious landscaping bordered by aqua seas.

A bevy of signs met their approach, making Marla jam on the brakes in confusion. Arrows pointed to various restaurants, gift shops, pools, and conference centers along with villa lodgings, tennis courts, a sailing school, and marina. Where was the hotel registration?

"Way cool," Georgia burst out, her eyes wide. "I could spend a week here. Too bad it's only one night."

"Tell me about it. I have a feeling, though, that this place is out of my budget range. Maybe they gave Luxor a break because they'll be in the advertisements."

Spotting a sign for the hotel lobby, Marla headed

down the narrow lane indicated. An open-air jitney rattled past on the opposite side, holding a group of laughing guests in swimsuits and straw hats.

"Tourists," she muttered. The ocean temperature was usually too cold in January for her to go swimming, but she wouldn't mind sipping a drink while viewing the sunset on the Gulf side, or strolling the grounds where hibiscus, Hong Kong orchids, and winter impatiens bloomed. Hopefully, the soothing balm of the sea would lull her colleagues into revealing their secrets, or at the very least, seduce them into lowering their guard a bit. Was this why Sergeant Masterson planned to hang around? She didn't see how he could keep track of everyone when accommodations were spread over the entire island.

Hoping for a villa, Marla merely shrugged when she and Georgia were assigned a regular hotel room, albeit with an ocean view. "Has anyone else from our group checked in yet?" she asked the clerk, one of many behind a Disneyesque reception desk.

"Oh yes," the young man stated with a smile. "In fact, I have a couple of packets for you." He handed over a folder with her name on the front and gave Georgia a similar one. "If you check the schedule inside, you'll see you have plenty of time to get settled in and have lunch before the photo shoot at two o'clock. You're to meet with the photographer by Pirate's Cove, where your group leader will give you further instructions."

Marla glanced at Georgia. "It's a good thing I brought my portable curling iron and other tools. It's breezy today, and that could wreak havoc on the models' hair. I wonder where they're staying."

Four of the girls had agreed to do the gig, and Marla hoped to locate them to ask about Heather. Meanwhile, she accepted her room key-card and wheeled her bag to the elevator. Smells of bacon and French toast wafted into her nostrils. There must be a restaurant off the lobby, but she'd rather eat later and explore the environs in her free time. Lunch was still an hour away, and she could accomplish a lot in that interval. Thankful that Justine and Larry had remained in Palm Haven, she determined to press her advantage to learn all she could about her Luxor colleagues.

"Where should we go first?" Georgia said, claiming the bed nearest the bathroom.

Their room held enough space for a dinette table and two chairs, plus a desk with a high-speed Internet connection, a television console that doubled as their wardrobe, and two queen-sized beds. Tropical-patterned bedspreads in peacock blue, ivory, and coral matched the wall prints and carpet. Marla appreciated the separate dressing area, where she spread her toiletries before freshening her makeup.

"Let's find Pirate's Cove, and maybe we'll run into someone we know along the way," she replied.

Looking into the mirror while scrunching her hair, Georgia made a face. "I hope we don't meet that police detective. He seems too interested in me for my liking. Too bad your hunk isn't along for this ride. He'd take the heat off us."

"Not off me—he'd raise my temperature," Marla said with a grin. "I'm glad Dalton isn't assigned to this case. He can get too single-minded, so it wouldn't be much of a break. Besides, we already had our getaway. Our Thanksgiving family reunion took place at Sugar Crest Plantation Resort, and

that trip raised more ghosts than resided there."
She shivered at the memory. "Remind me to tell
you about Grandfather Andrew's playful spirit pinch-
ing me in the elevator."

They headed outdoors fifteen minutes later, not
wanting to waste time inside. The air smelled like
chlorine and coconut oil as they neared a free-
form pool in a grotto with a rocky waterfall. Georgia pointed at the sunbathers stretched out on
lounge chairs. "Oh, man, I wish we could just lie
here. I could *so* use a day off."

"Me too," Marla replied, although she could
think of other places that would be warmer in the
winter. Shifting her purse, she considered the
travel brochures she'd collected, with their photos
of exotic beaches and lush tropical greenery. With
all the events in her life, it seemed as though she'd
never get to Bora Bora except in her imagination.

Maybe she should reset her standards, she mused,
adjusting the sunglasses on her nose. Great Heron
Key offered a close second to Bora Bora. A waiter
circulated among the chaise lounges, offering colorful drinks garnished with tiny tropical umbrellas
and pineapple slices. Tempted to dally, she forced
herself to focus on her mission. The sooner Christine's murder was solved, the sooner the Luxor
crew could leave. While she enjoyed Georgia's company, having one less person in her house would
simplify things.

"Whoa, Marla, is that who I think it is?" Georgia
stopped short, bumping into her.

Marla glanced at the paunchy figure ranging toward them. No way that guy in the hip-hugging
trunks could be Sampson York! Divested of his fan-
ciful show garb, he appeared almost, well, ordinary.

"Hello, my little nightingales. Isn't this place

stupendous?" Sampson waved his arm. "I couldn't have chosen a better setting myself. Kudos to Chris for finding such a charming location for our shoot." His speech sounded slurred, as though he'd already sampled the tropical rum drinks on tap.

"It's a shame she can't be here to enjoy the Keys with us," Marla replied in a sympathetic tone, "but we'll do a bang-up job in her honor."

"Damn right," Georgia said, punching a fist in the air.

Surreptitiously studying their artistic director, Marla adjusted her blazer. She'd worn a pants set with black slacks, an ivory shell, and a cranberry jacket. It made her feel more confident to wear business attire. Going a bit more casual, Georgia had settled for fudge pants and a raspberry tank top, but she always looked put together, with her bouncy hair and confident smile. In contrast, Sampson seemed to have taken a serious dive downhill. What had happened to make him foreswear his professionalism?

"It's rather windy," Marla commented. "We'll need to use extra holding spray on the models' hair. Should I get my supplies? I left my bag in our hotel room until after lunch."

Sampson's imperious expression told her what he thought of her concern. "A windswept look is perfect for the girls. Picture the advertisements: gorgeous women in bikinis strutting on the beach, a stiff breeze blowing from the ocean, the sun gleaming off the water. Seeing those images will make consumers want to rush to the seashore. And they'll need to use our conditioners to avoid damage to their hair."

At least he sounded enthusiastic about their work. "How are we dividing our duties?" Marla persisted. "Do we each get to do one of the models?" By "each," she meant herself, Sampson, Ron, and Liesl. They were the stylists; the others were ancillary personnel. She assumed Jan would be running the show.

"Indeed. I hope you brought your makeup kit as well. The photographer will tell you if he needs anything special regarding cosmetic enhancement. He's there now checking his light meter." Sampson glanced furtively over his shoulder, then leaned forward. "I wouldn't go to Pirate's Cove yet if I were you. That annoying detective is hanging around."

"Oh no," Georgia moaned. "I really don't feel like talking to him today."

"You and everyone else." Sampson's eyes narrowed. "Don't listen to anything he tells you. Half of it is untrue. He's just trying to get a rise from you so you'll talk. I suppose you realize he's aiming to pin Christine's murder on one of us."

Marla observed him closely. What had Sergeant Masterson said to Sampson that the trainer believed to be false? Or had the detective hit too close to the mark where he was concerned?

"Marla, tell him about the dermatologist," Georgia said, squinting from the sun. Taking a sun visor from her bag, she plopped it on her head.

Restless to move on, Marla shifted her weight to her other foot. "Apparently Chris was involved in a project with a local dermatologist supporting the American Melanoma Society. Would you know anything about it?"

"Of course," Sampson began but then stopped, his gaze hardening.

"Yo, dudes, what's going on?" drawled a familiar voice from behind. Marla whirled to see Tyler, Amy Jeanne, and Ron bearing down on them.

"Did you say something about Chris?" Ron asked, frowning. "I'd hoped we could avoid rehashing unpleasant events while we're here. With all due respect to our former leader, we could use a break, especially if we're to do our best work."

With his spiked hair, metallic gray eyes, and trim frame, he could have stood in for a male model. His open-collared black shirt stretched across broad shoulders, its snug fit revealing his musculature beneath. Heather had slept with him, Marla reminded herself, before the long-legged model had ended up dead.

"Unpleasant events?" she repeated. "That's not what I would call the loss of two people we knew."

"Stew about it all you want," Ron snapped at her, "but I'm not going to let some bad group karma stop me from doing my job."

"Chill out, dude," Tyler told him. "We'll be fine." He wore a safari outfit, complete with shorts, utility belt, and button-down shirt with bulging pockets. "Come on, I'm hungry. Who wants to chow down with me?"

His words dispelled the tension that had sprung up among them. Sampson, Marla realized, had been distraught, perhaps by something the detective had said to him, and Ron's temper was on a short leash.

Georgia bustled forward to join Tyler while the master stylists marched off in opposite directions after curt parting remarks. Marla watched Ron, wondering again why he didn't strike out on his own if he hated working with Sampson. Was it merely his loyalty to Luxor that kept him in their employ, or did he have another compelling reason to stay?

"Marla, let me give you a word of advice," Amy

Jeanne said by her side. The salon coordinator was so quiet that Marla had almost forgotten she was there. Her warm brown skin glistened in the sun, reflecting the warmth in her eyes.

"What about?" Marla fell into a slow pace beside the other woman. They headed down one of the paths away from the pool. The sound of splashing water receded into the distance, replaced by the gentle swish of ocean waves as they climbed a terrace.

Amy Jeanne, her jaw moving with a wad of gum, waved her hand. Marla noted tiny angel appliqués on her violet-painted nails. "I know you'd like to do more of this work. Tell the photographer that you would appreciate referrals. We're not the only company doing ads here. Miami is very hot right now for global marketing."

"No kidding. I read a news article recently that said New York designers are bringing runway fashion shows featuring swimsuits to Miami Beach. That makes sense to me. South Florida is the perfect locale, with our palm trees and sunny weather, plus we're the gateway for Latin America and the Caribbean."

"You should schedule more photo sessions at your salon," Amy Jeanne advised her. "Have your people do the hair, then submit the photos to different hairstyle magazines. If you go for special themes like weddings, makeovers, and holidays, you'll broaden your market and increase your chance of acceptance. Add these pieces to your portfolio. Meanwhile, meet as many people as you can in the fashion industry, and spread the word that you're looking for more opportunities."

Shading her eyes, Marla gazed out to sea. A freighter chugged the waters far out by the horizon. "I may have to put my plans on hold until I move the salon. That's when I could really use the publicity. I want to get into more day spa services and raise awareness in the community. Plus, I'm supposed to get married, and that means taking on responsibility for a thirteen-year-old stepdaughter."

"Shut my mouth, girlfriend! How do you manage to keep on top of things? I'd be bowled over by all that baggage. I can't even handle my sister's whining." Amy Jeanne's lips twisted in a self-derogatory smile.

Marla grinned. "I guess I thrive on challenges. Dalton is a widower, and his former in-laws are staying with me this week. Don't ask—it's just how things worked out," she said upon noting Amy's incredulous expression. "Anyway, I have my hands full right now. Escaping to the Keys was a welcome break."

"I'm impressed." Amy Jeanne regarded her with new respect.

Signaling for her companion to follow, Marla strode ahead. They reached a plateau that jutted over the sea wall. Halting, she viewed a school of fish swimming among strands of seaweed, the water pulsating as though alive. A light breeze stirred the hairs on her arms. Sniffing the briny air, she leaned against a painted wood rail. If only she were here for fun, not business.

Not this time. Get to work. Mentally debating how to probe Amy Jeanne's knowledge of Chris's affairs, she searched for an opening remark.

"At least I have a chance to direct my future," she said mildly. "Chris's ambitions are dust. It's still hard to believe she's gone and isn't sharing this weekend with us."

Amy Jeanne avoided her gaze. "Sucks for her."

"You don't sound too broken up about it."

"I sent her sister a card, but that's the extent of my sympathy. I don't miss the bitch."

"What did she do to you?" Marla asked in a neutral tone.

"Chris didn't do anything to me personally. It's what she did to Ellen." The salon coordinator paused, her face revealing conflicting emotions. "My sister is a stylist, too. She and Chris used to work in the same salon; that's how I got connected with Luxor. You know how Chris tried to control everyone? Well, that extended to our personal lives. She set Ellen up with a bad date."

Marla repressed the urge to shout in triumph. At last, she was getting someone to open up. "Go on," she said.

Amy Jeanne's solemn brown eyes turned reflective. "Ellen didn't listen to my warnings about men. She was a victim of date rape. After it happened, she started drinking, and that led down the road to drugs. She's been in and out of rehab centers ever since. I can't tell you how it broke my heart to see my baby sister destroyed, and it was all Chris's fault."

"Chris couldn't have known what the guy intended."

"No, but she should have minded her own business."

"Someone else must be thinking that same way. Chris's death wasn't an accident."

Amy Jeanne stepped back. "Don't look at me. I wouldn't hurt anyone."

"Then do you have any idea who might have poisoned her?"

"Your guess is as good as mine, although . . . I wonder . . ."

"Yes?"

"I know there was some bad blood between Miguel and Chris over a problem she developed after consulting his brother, a surgeon. I didn't want to get involved, so I never asked him about it." Amy Jeanne rolled the piece of gum in her mouth.

"Okay, thanks. Anyone else?" Marla closed her ears to the skywriting airplane droning overhead, advertising a beer joint on the mainland.

Glancing at her watch, her colleague gestured that they should move on. "I don't like to gossip. What goes around comes around, you know?"

"Let me remind you that two people have died already. Don't you want to help catch the killer? It could be one of us. Take Jan, for instance," Marla said, hoping to provoke a response. "She's been aiming for Christine's position. Now she has a shot at being appointed director permanently."

Amy Jeanne stood stock-still. "Janice wouldn't harm a hair on Christine's head, not even after she lost all that money. She scrapes to pay her mother's medical bills and doesn't even complain that Chris gained from her loss. I hope you're not going to start any rumors about her, Marla, because I'll be the first to knock you down."

And having said that, Amy Jeanne stalked away, while Marla gazed after her with her jaw hanging open. Wow, she hadn't expected that strong of a reaction! Interesting how Amy Jeanne seemed more defensive about Jan than about her own sister. How strongly had she wanted to see Janice Davidson move up the corporate ladder?

Glancing about as she headed back toward the pool, Marla searched for Georgia to discuss these new leads with her friend. Georgia must have gone off with Tyler, because there was no sight of either one of them. Her stomach growled, making her realize lunch hour had arrived. If she wanted to eat before their photo shoot, she'd better grab something now.

She caught Liesl stuffing down a hot dog at the poolside restaurant. The blonde wore a bikini top and sarong skirt. Mustard dotted the side of her mouth.

"May I join you?" Marla asked, plopping herself into a chair at the outdoor table. Brushing a dead insect off the Formica tabletop, she reached for the single-page laminated menu.

Liesl slurped her lemonade. "Sure, it's a free country."

Marla didn't like the coldness in her tone. "If you'd rather I go elsewhere—"

"No, that's okay," Liesl reassured her quickly. "I'm sorry, I know I sound curt to you sometimes, and I'd like to explain." She lowered her gaze. "I don't often tell people about my background, because they can react badly. My grandfather, well, he was in the Gestapo."

"So?" Marla gave the girl an appraising glance. "I don't hold that against you."

"Really?" Liesl's face eased into a smile. "I've wanted to regard you as a friend, but I wasn't sure if you'd . . . if you . . ."

Marla raised an eyebrow. "I'd be happy to consider you my friend, Liesl. What happened in the past is not between us. We can learn a lot from each other."

"Bang on, luv. Like, how do you keep your figure so slim?" Liesl asked after Marla placed an order for a cheeseburger and fries. "You're not a health food and exercise nut like Jan."

"I chase criminals with my fiancé."

"In between cutting and styling at the salon? When do you find time to do everything?" Liesl dabbed at her cheek with a napkin. Her mood seemed to have brightened considerably since their discussion. She had a lilt in her voice.

"Funny, I was just discussing that very same topic with Amy Jeanne. Did you know her sister worked in the same salon as Chris? That's how Amy hooked up with Luxor."

"I didn't realize that, but, then, Amy Jeanne doesn't talk much about herself."

Do any of you? Marla wasn't about to betray a confidence if Amy Jeanne hadn't told anyone else about her sister's problems. "She's very loyal to Janice."

"Clever of you to notice." Liesl's eyes flickered with amusement.

"You don't think Amy would do anything to, uh, get Jan bumped up a level? Or could Jan have a ruthless streak that makes her dangerous?"

Liesl laughed, a pleasant sound like clinking glasses. "You're way off base. Jan may be ambitious, but she isn't stupid. She knew exactly why Chris promoted her to regional manager in the first place, but she's willing to bide her time until she climbs the next rung on her own."

"I don't understand." Marla leaned back when the waitress delivered her Coke. Her throat parched, she took a long sip.

Liesl polished off her last bite of hot dog. "At one of the hair shows, Chris bragged about an investment program that her financial analyst had recommended. It had been giving Chris a high rate of interest for several years. Jan, whose mother was ill, needed extra income. She opted into the scheme just before the market crashed."

"That must have upset her." The aroma of bar-becued beef made Marla's mouth water. Where was her meal already? She craned her neck, search-ing for the waitress who had vanished. *Figures, just when I'm on a tight schedule.*

Liesl blinked. "From what I gathered, Jan ended up losing a bundle, but she blamed herself for not reading the fine print instead of Chris for leading her on. Chris got some kind of referral fee out of the deal, and she felt bad enough about what hap-pened to Jan's money that when the regional man-ager position became vacant, she recommended Jan for the job."

"Wasn't Tyler in line for a promotion, too?"

"Sure, luv, but he didn't dare make a stink. Chris knew something about him that he didn't want to get out, and that's how she kept him on a leash."

Chapter
Sixteen

"I got the impression that you had a thing for Tyler," Marla said to Liesl. "Did you feel Tyler was too tied to Christine to notice you?"

Liesl's expression shuttered. "He noticed me all right, but maybe you've sensed it—Tyler will flirt with you and then he'll back off. It's, like, he's a big fraud."

"Do you think he's gay?" Tyler didn't come across that way to her, not with his swaggering confidence and scruffy style. But she'd been wrong before on this subject, much to her detriment.

Liesl sipped her drink. "Nope. It's something else."

Marla's meal arrived, and she fell silent while she ate. The juicy burger filled her stomach with satisfying weight. Feeling the need to boost her blood sugar, she rationalized away the calories as necessary for brain function. She had to keep her wits about her if she wanted to stay one step ahead of the criminal amongst them.

While she contemplated what topic to address next, Liesl signaled for her check. Reluctant to end their dialogue, Marla blurted out the first thing that came to mind.

"Tell me, was Luxor involved in Christine's deal with Dr. Greenberg, the dermatologist?"

Rummaging in her purse, Liesl paused to stare at Marla as though she were daft. "Luxor is donating a percentage of our profits from the sunscreen line to the melanoma society. Dr. Greenberg is on their board of directors. Why do you ask?"

"He met with Chris at the assisted-living facility where her mother lives. That struck me as odd, unless he's a personal friend of the family."

"Maybe Chris wanted him to examine her mum, luv. Lots of blokes in Florida have skin problems."

"Chris's mother mentioned that she thought he was after a donation."

Removing a few bills from her wallet, Liesl tossed them on the table. "How do you know? Did you go see her?"

"I went to pay my respects."

"Rubbish, Marla. You're just damn nosy. If I were you, I'd stick to the job at hand. Now, if you'll excuse me, I have to pick up my headcase bag from my room. Do you need a Wave Runner? I brought one along."

Marla pictured the triple-barrel curling iron. "That won't be necessary, thanks. I've got my own kit."

Left alone, she leaned her elbows on the table, not caring about her manners. She took a long sip of Coke while reflecting on their conversation. Liesl had indicated that she didn't buy Tyler's come-hither approach. Neither did she. Tyler had initially tried to hit on her when she'd met him, and when she flashed her engagement ring, he'd sidled up to Georgia. He ignored the only woman,

Liesl, who appeared genuinely interested in him. Obviously, he'd used Georgia as a buffer after the cocktail party when they were all seated in the lounge. Had it been her imagination, or had Chris threatened him? What was he holding back from the rest of the gang?

Marla looked around at the crowded pool deck, sand dunes, and paths crisscrossing the hotel grounds, but there was no sign of Georgia. Maybe she'd gone back to the hotel room after leaving Tyler. And, maybe she'd learned something relevant from him. Eager to find out, Marla concluded her meal and hastened to their room. Georgia might already be inside.

No such luck. Their belongings lay scattered where they had left them. Oh well, she'd catch up with her friend soon enough. It was almost time for everyone to congregate, and Georgia was sure to report in for duty. Grabbing a pink sweater to wear under her jacket if she got cold later, plus her bag of tools, Marla left to seek Pirate's Cove.

Following the signposts planted at appropriate intervals along the way, she arrived at a delightful lagoon fringed by coconut palms, sea grapes, and mangroves. Yearning to kick off her shoes and grind the white powdery sand under her toes, she instead focused on the group gathering under the shade of a spreading banyan tree. Jan, holding her clipboard, conducted an animated conversation with the photographer while Sampson and Ron were already at work on two of the models, seated on folding chairs. Turning her back to the ocean to reduce glare, Marla approached Jan for instructions. Georgia was nowhere in sight.

"I'm ready to get started," she declared, noting that Liesl hadn't shown up yet. Sampson didn't spare her a glance. Ron nodded in acknowledgment. At least their artistic director had donned a pair of slacks and a polo shirt along with his usual composure, unlike in their earlier encounter, when he'd let his professional image slip quite a few notches.

"You can do Vivian," Ron told her. "She'll look great with a wet style, as though she's just been swimming. Her golden rust hair goes great with that turquoise bikini. The colors should really jump out on the photos." He buffed his nails against his chest. "Give her a liberal dose of gel before you scrunch. I've got a portable iron if you need one."

"Thanks, I brought my own." Marla inspected for ants before setting her bag on a fallen tree trunk. Straightening, she got a glimpse of Georgia strolling arm-in-arm with Tyler from the opposite direction.

Catching Marla's gaze, Georgia winked.

Before they could even exchange a personal greeting, Jan bustled over, perspiration coating the skin above her upper lip.

"Tyler, it's about time you showed up." Looking harried, the regional manager thrust a hand through her chili-colored locks. Marla admired her outfit, ebony crop pants and a camisole top, thinking she appeared more approachable without her formal business suits.

"Don't worry, we'll get things done on time," Tyler drawled, perusing her with his lazy gaze.

"Here's the sequence of shots." Jan thrust him a sheaf of papers. "Make sure you match each model to the products we're advertising. Georgia can work with Miguel on which accounts to target for the promotional premium." She waved at Liesl, who'd just joined their ranks, evidently satisfied that the artistic team could handle their end.

Marla's efforts to draw Georgia aside met with futility as the hours raced by as fast as the clouds in the electric blue sky. When the crew finally wrapped up its work for the day, the early evening sun had already begun its descent. Maybe now she'd be able to find some private time with Georgia.

"What's everyone doing for dinner?" Liesl asked, her pouty expression aimed in Tyler's direction. Despite her words to the contrary, Liesl was still trying to gain his attention, Marla thought. Interesting.

"Wanna meet at the Goombay Smash restaurant?" Miguel suggested. "I could go for the black beans and rice." The Cuban sales rep had gone about his business while dancing salsa steps and humming along with music from his iPod. He'd dressed casually in denim shorts, a T-shirt advertising a radio station, and sandals.

"That sounds cool," Tyler replied. "Count me in, dude."

"I'm going for a swim, so don't wait for me." Jan raised a hand in dismissal. "I'll probably just grab a health bar and fruit Smoothie later, anyway."

"You're deserting us? How are we supposed to charge our meals to the company tab without your illustrious presence?" Tyler teased, dimples creasing his cheeks.

She glared at him. "I have to account for every penny we spend. Chris knew her numbers, and I plan to follow her example."

"You'll be great," Amy Jeanne said quietly from the sideline. She blew on a fingernail as though she'd just touched up her polish.

"Thanks, but I wasn't aiming to get ahead in this fashion. You all know that, right?"

"You have my vote," Sampson's deep voice rumbled. His piercing dark eyes swept the group. "Our work seems to flow better with you in charge."

"I'll do my best to earn your confidence." Turning her back on them, Janice tossed her clipboard into a briefcase.

Marla gazed at her companions in confusion. Did no one care that Chris had died an unnatural death? Had she so offended everyone that the only thing they cared about was that their lives moved more smoothly in her absence? Even if this were true, what about Heather? No one had even mentioned her name, and when Marla had broached the subject to the model whose hair she had done earlier, the girl claimed only the barest acquaintance with the victim.

"Is it my imagination," she said to Miguel, who stood fiddling with his music device, "or is everyone happier with Chris dead?"

He gave her a startled glance. "I know I sleep better at night, *querida*. She can't threaten my brother anymore."

"Isn't he a doctor of some kind?"

"*Sí*, he is a surgeon. Chris was suing him and making his life miserable. I wanted to wring her neck for causing him such anguish." Facing the ocean, he squinted at the horizon. "Felipe raised me after our parents passed away. I would do anything for him."

Including murder? "What was Chris's claim against your brother?"

"Some female thing. I don't like to talk about it. It gets me too upset in here." Pounding his chest, he nodded once at her before stalking away.

"I didn't realize Miguel felt so strongly about his brother," she said to Jan, tapping the manager's elbow to get her attention before she could leave.

Regarding her with annoyance, Jan said, "His family ties are very close. That's a good thing, Marla. Maybe you should focus more on yours instead of prying into everyone else's affairs."

Marla realized she could be putting her future with Luxor at jeopardy by continuing with her probes, but she couldn't let two souls haunt the earth while their murders went unsolved. No one else seemed to care, except for Sergeant Masterson. And where had the investigator gone? Peering around, she realized he hadn't remained for the photo op. Had something else called him away, like an important new clue?

Considering her options, she couldn't help but press on. *Justice, Justice, shall you pursue* had been the theme of her bat mitzvah speech, and it defined her current motto. Seeking the truth took precedence over personal ambition. If that meant Luxor would no longer request her services, so be it. Certain things were more important in life . . . and beyond.

"Just answer me one thing," she called out to Jan as the other woman turned to walk away. "Why was Chris suing Miguel's brother, Felipe?"

Jan turned back to face Marla, her eyes glimmering. "She claimed the surgeon botched her breast implants. But she could have been exaggerating."

"Do you say that because you learned the hard way that Chris wasn't trustworthy? Didn't you put money into an investment she recommended, right before it went sour?"

"My, you've been a busy little worker bee, haven't you?" The redhead's lips tightened. "I rue the day I ever listened to her. Chris lied to me, but, then, I never should have mistaken her for a friend. It wasn't until the market dived that I found out she hadn't contributed one cent to that fund, while I'd lost thousands. I'm supporting my mother and felt the loss deeply."

"You must have been really angry."

"I'll say! Chris thought the promotion would make up for her bad advice, but she was wrong."

"Now you're wearing her shoes as our acting director."

Jan's eyes hardened. "Let me make something clear to you. I would never harm someone to push myself up the corporate ladder. Hard work and being a team player are the things that get you ahead. I wouldn't have it any other way. Nor should you, if you want my recommendation."

Marla swallowed. "I appreciate your honesty. I hope you realize that I care about those people who died, and that I also want what's best for Luxor. Covering up the truth benefits no one and just leads to problems down the road."

"It already has." Jan's gaze softened. "You're right, this has all been very painful. We should welcome your intervention, especially because you've helped the police solve crimes before. I just don't want Chris's death to impede our progress. She felt very strongly about donating our profits to the melanoma society, and I intend to fulfill her purpose."

Before Marla could pose a question about the dermatologist or launch a probe about Heather's role, the director slipped away. Marla turned back to the group, but people had dispersed after planning to meet at the restaurant at eight o'clock. Darkness rapidly approached. Swatting at a mosquito buzzing near her ear, she decided it was time to go inside and lather her skin with insect repellent.

"Georgia, we have to talk," she said, signaling to her friend, who lingered by a fallen coconut. Georgia's face held a wistful expression as she gazed out to sea. Starting down the path back to the hotel, Marla skirted a fallen palm frond and a lizard on the prowl. "What did you learn from Tyler earlier? I got the impression that he told you something important. Did you find out what Chris had on him?"

"You won't believe it," Georgia said, giggling. She glanced around to make sure no one in the vicinity could hear them. "Tyler is divorced. He has custody of his daughter, and he feels very strongly about parenthood. That's kinda why he comes across as a big jerk. He acts like this real cool guy and then he backs off, because he thinks most single women won't understand his responsibilities. Plus, he doesn't want to do anything to rock the boat in terms of his relationship with his daughter."

"So where did Chris fit in?"

"She knew about the child and used the situation to her advantage. Christine threatened to spread rumors about his promiscuity if he didn't sleep with her. He was afraid it might jeopardize his custody agreement, but he wouldn't give in to her, despite her manipulation. When Chris passed him over for promotion, he felt it was her way of exerting control. She gloated over his disappointment, but he still wouldn't bend."

"What a witch."

"It certainly made me see Tyler in a new light. I respect him a lot more after he shared this. I know it took guts." Georgia faltered, clutching Marla's arm. "You're not going to say anything to him, are you? I really don't want him to know I've betrayed his confidence."

"All right," Marla said reluctantly. "Sounds like

you two have reached a new understanding. Where does that leave you and Goat?" she asked to lighten the mood.

Georgia laughed, resuming her pace. "Like, Tyler and I are just pals. He's cute but totally not my type, especially with a kid. We can have fun with each other, but that's as far as it goes. Omigosh, look at that sunset. Awesome!"

Marla twisted her head to view the crimson trails ribboning from the persimmon and ruby artist's palette in the sky. Truth be told, she'd viewed sunsets enough times in Florida to take them for granted, but on a clear night like this the vivid colors still had the power to captivate. Her mood changed, however, as the red rivulets reminded her of blood, bringing home the fact that Luxor was two people short on this trip. She'd heard a lot of reasons why her teammates wanted Chris dead, but what about Heather? Had the model inadvertently uncovered a clue leading to the killer? Was that why she had to die? And what of the paper in her hand mentioning Bell Farms? What did that mean?

"I want to take a look at the boats in the marina," Georgia said, nudging her. "Do you mind if we go there first?"

"I have to put my kit away," Marla replied, lifting her bag. "Why do you want to go there? Are you hoping to catch a ride on one of the yachts?"

"Not this late." Her grinning friend's teeth reflected the light from the lampposts, which had flicked on just a moment ago, illuminating the grounds. "I can daydream about how the other half lives, though. You probably see this stuff all the time, but for me it's way cool. Flowers blooming in January, palm trees, green lawns, and ocean breezes. I could dig living in the tropics—except now it's actually gotten cold! You didn't tell me the temperature could drop this much at night."

"The weather is variable this time of year. Do you want to wear my jacket? I'm okay with just the sweater."

"All right, thanks." Georgia shrugged into Marla's cranberry jacket, while Marla donned the sweater she'd brought for extra warmth. "I wish we had time to do some of the other fun things in the area. Do we have to leave so early in the morning?"

"Afraid so," Marla replied, mindful of her other duties. Passing the poolside tiki bar, she glanced at the patrons sipping their drinks and chatting. Too bad this weekend couldn't stretch into a week. She agreed with Georgia on that score. Someday—she comforted herself—she'd make it to the tropical paradise of her dreams. Someday.

"Where shall we meet?" Georgia asked, twirling a curl around her index finger. "I may not get upstairs before dinner. I'd like to take a walk on the beach after I see the boats."

"In the dark? You can't see anything on the sand, where you're walking." Marla supposed that wouldn't matter to a northerner, so she explained: "You'd better keep your shoes on so you don't step on any jellyfish. If you start getting itchy, head inside. The no-see-ums come out at dusk."

After delivering those words of warning, she headed toward the main hotel building while Georgia split off to tour the marina and sandy beach. The perfumed fragrance of blooming jasmine filled the air, but Marla thought about the biting insects, the hidden predators that also surrounded them, targeting sweet, innocent flesh—much like the killer who had zapped the life from Christine and Heather. A shiver rolled through her. She would've felt a modicum of protection if Sergeant Masterson had been present. The Luxor group could be harboring a menace.

Her nape prickling with unease, she hurried into the brightly lit lobby and paced toward the bank of elevators. She didn't feel safe until she'd entered her room and checked for intruders before locking the door. Then she pulled out her cell phone, connected the charger, and punched in Vail's number. She needed the reassurance of his voice.

While the ringing tone sounded in her ears, she remembered all the things she'd wanted to discuss with Georgia, but they had blown from her mind when her friend mentioned Tyler's situation. Oh well. They'd talk about it later. Dismayed when she realized she wouldn't have the chance to tell Vail either, since his voice mailbox clicked on, she left a brief message for him to call her.

After a quick shower and a change into comfortable slacks with a coral cashmere sweater, she checked in with her mother via cell phone. She'd taken so long with her hair that only fifteen minutes remained before it was time to meet her colleagues.

"Don't forget you have a date with Barry on Sunday," Anita said. "He'll pick you up at seven. Remember, it's a black-tie affair."

"Maybe I shouldn't go, Ma. Dalton will be upset."

"Do you want to meet Dr. Greenberg or not? Dalton will understand that you're on a mission."

"I think he agreed because he didn't want to make a fuss. All he cares about is riding a steady road where Justine and Larry are concerned. I can just imagine Justine accusing me of dating another man while I'm engaged."

"She's not the one you're marrying, *bubula*. Call me when you're home."

Marla hung up, grabbed her purse and a warm fleece jacket, and dashed out the door. Following a hotel directory, she made her way to the Goombay Smash and arrived promptly at eight. A crowd milled about the open front doors. Searching for familiar faces, she tapped her foot to the steel drum beat from a band playing inside.

"Yo, babe, we're over here," called Tyler, who stood by a mahogany tree.

Marla strode over, doing a head count. Everyone was there except for Janice, Ron, Georgia, and their artistic director. The models had joined them, evidently intent on soaking up the company revenue.

"Did you reserve a table?" she asked. Reservations were taken for parties greater than six, and there would be twelve of them. The photographer had already left for Miami, so Marla was glad she'd had the foresight to get his card and mention that she'd like to do more work for him.

"I put in our name," Amy Jeanne said in her quiet manner. "A table should be cleared in another ten minutes or so." Her expression suddenly chilled. "Shut my mouth. That can't be our eminent trainer, can it?"

Marla followed her glance and swallowed. Sampson staggered in their direction, his hair unkempt and his shirttails loose. If she had to guess, she'd say he'd hit the tiki bar for a few more rum punches. Talk about uncharacteristic behavior. He seemed unable to hold himself together today for some reason.

"It's a good thing Jan didn't come downstairs," Miguel muttered at her side.

"Tell me about it. What's the matter with him?

Do you think he's upset about Chris's death?" A delayed reaction to her murder could cause him to lose his inhibitions.

"Are you kidding? York couldn't be more glad she's out of his way." Miguel twisted the wire attached to his omnipresent earbuds. "Everyone else scampers to obey his orders, but our boss lady was the only one who could make him dance."

"And why was that?" Marla asked, noting Ron rushing around the corner. Spotting her, the master stylist halted, looking shocked but then he just as quickly recovered himself. He must have gotten a look at Sampson's disheveled appearance. Marla missed Miguel's response, because just then the hostess called their group. "Wait, Georgia isn't here yet."

"She'll find us inside," Liesl said, looking very hip in an off-the-shoulder ribbed lavender top. "Let's go, luv."

Twenty minutes later, Marla got worried when Georgia hadn't shown up. Her friend knew they were meeting everyone at eight o'clock. Had she gone to their room to change? Taking her cell phone from her purse, she punched in Georgia's personal number. No answer.

Excusing herself, she found a hotel phone and dialed their room number. The ringing tone persisted until Marla gave up. Now what? Could Georgia have met some guy at the marina and decided to chuck her plans? *Possibly, but she would've told me, knowing that I'd worry.* She'd wait a while longer just in case her fears were groundless.

Returning to the table, she sipped her water but finally signaled the waitress to cancel her order.

"It's unlike Georgia to be this late," she said, glancing at her watch. "I'm going to look for her. You guys go ahead and eat. I'll get something later."

Ron raised his martini glass. "Where was she headed?"

"The marina and then the beach. I can't imagine what's kept her so long."

"Maybe she found the shipwreck," Sampson drawled from where he slouched in a corner nursing his drink.

"Say again?" Amy Jeanne piped in, after spitting her chewing gum into a napkin.

"It's a roped off area at the north boundary," Sampson replied. "Some old ship ran aground there, and instead of dragging it out to sea and sinking it like they do to make artificial reefs, the hotel owners made it into a resort attraction." He hiccuped. "I suppose the wood rotted, because no one can step on it now. Maybe Georgia leaned over to take a closer look and fell through the gash in the deck. That's the first place I'd search."

Chapter
Seventeen

Once outside the restaurant, Marla hesitated while she listened to the crickets. It had grown cooler, so she zipped her ivory fleece jacket up before venturing farther. Remembering that Georgia had put on her cranberry blazer, she looked around for a flash of the familiar color. None of the people strolling past gave her a second regard.

Should she trace Georgia's steps, starting at the marina? Or would it be a better idea to try the shipwreck? The mental image of Georgia toppling through a hole on deck and being trapped in a rotten hull propelled her toward the north. Voices receded into the background, and soon she heard nothing but the surf and the occasional cry of a seagull. A roped-off area loomed in the near distance, and as she approached, she saw shadowy shapes rising from the gloom.

Sampson had directed her here. Could this be a setup to get her alone? He knew she'd seen that check he'd made out to Chris.

She became conscious of a peculiar scrabbling noise. Spinning, she examined the beach to her right and the mangroves to her left. Nothing. It must be coming from that wreck, now a tangled mass of fallen beams draped with seaweed and sifted with sand. Calling Georgia's name, she stepped gingerly beyond the barrier. Surely her friend wouldn't have been so foolish as to venture this far by herself.

Illuminated by a half moon, the crisscrossing planks presented an obstacle course of dangerous proportions. Yawning gaps led to places she didn't care to contemplate, although likely whatever fell below got washed out to sea in the rip current. Waves lapped against the wood with an angry rush as though protesting its invasion.

Mesmerized by images of how the vessel must have looked in full sail, she almost didn't hear the crackle from behind. As she turned, a blunt object impacted the side of her head with enough force to knock her over. Her ears rang as she crumpled to the ground, too stunned to move. She lay on her side, carpeted by the lumpy sand, aware that her hair had cushioned the blow.

A heavy foot prodded her rib cage. When she didn't respond, her assailant rolled her onto her back. The movement made her head spin. Her vision narrowed, becoming a faint tunnel that rapidly grew dim. She caught a blurred image of someone bending over her before the buzzing in her mind overwhelmed her senses and she blacked out.

Coughing entered her awareness. Gasps for breath, followed by more choking coughs. *It's me,* she thought vaguely, feeling her body lift, then sink. Flinging her eyes open with full consciousness, she panicked when salt water flowed into her mouth. Sputtering, she flailed her arms, but a wave smashed into her face, thrusting her under the depths. She kicked violently, breaking the surface. Her lungs sucked in air, but the wheezing breath ended in a rattle that made her cough and spit. Somehow she'd landed in the ocean, and if she didn't regain control, she would be swept out to sea.

Her soaked jacket weighed her down. Holding her breath, she wriggled it off, no easy feat when waves kept smashing her. The waves were a good sign; they meant she hadn't been carried beyond the crests.

When she regained her equilibrium, she treaded water and looked around. Lights were strung out like jewels on the shoreline. It didn't seem so far, but with the feel of the current battering at her, she struggled against rising panic. *Swim parallel. Get away from the riptide.* Her temple throbbed as she positioned herself for a sidestroke. If only she could clear her lungs, she'd gather more strength.

Something bumped her leg, and her pulse rocketed. Shark! Or maybe just a school of fish. Adrenaline boosted her energy. With her back to the swells, she scissored a slow crawl at a diagonal that would bring her closer to shore. Her breaths became shallower with exertion. After each inhalation, she felt the rattle that made her want to give a violent cough. Unable to fight against the surging waves, she focused her efforts on reaching a standing depth. Her lungs burned with fire as the need to clear them became imperative.

Cold seeped into her bones and invaded her joints. She couldn't think about that now. *Think about Dalton and Brianna. They need me. I have to survive for their sake.*

With each stroke, her muscles grew weaker, and her gasping breaths more shallow. Salt water flowed into her nostrils, tickling down her throat, stinging her sinuses. Cough, sputter. *Breathe, Marla. You can do it.*

Just when she thought her lungs would burst, her foot brushed the sea botton. Folding her knees, she planted her feet on the wet sand and stood, shaking. Water dripped from her as she bent forward to retch. After a series of choking gasps, she was finally able to take a clear breath. Pulling in a lungful of air had never seemed so sweet, but it wasn't easy between her chattering teeth. She needed warmth fast.

An hour later, she lay on her bed freshly showered and wrapped in a robe, counting her blessings. *I should call Dalton* was the first thought that popped into her mind, but what could he do from Palm Haven? Georgia still hadn't returned, and Marla shuddered to think what might have happened to her. Whoever had clunked Marla on the head might have waylaid Georgia first, intending to put them both out of action. Or else the attacker had mistaken Georgia's identity because she'd worn Marla's blazer. Did it matter? Either way, she had to find her friend.

If she'd been tailed from the restaurant, it logically followed that her assailant must have been one of her dinner companions. Unless it was Jan, who claimed to be resting in her room, or even the photographer, who could still be lurking about.

Sitting made her momentarily dizzy, so she took her time getting up. Determined to locate Georgia, she roused enough energy to brew a pot of coffee while getting dressed. She'd been caught unaware once; it wouldn't happen again.

Preparing to go out, she had just put on her spare jacket when she realized her handbag was missing. Thankfully, she'd kept her room key in her pants pocket.

Outside, she hastened toward the shipwreck, glad to find her purse half buried in the sand near where she'd fallen. After brushing off the grime, she retrieved her cell phone and hurried toward the marina, where she dialed Georgia's number, hoping she might hear an answering ring.

No luck. Water lapped against the pier as she proceeded across the wooden planks toward the slips. The smell of diesel fumes mingled with salty night air as she descended a set of metal steps, avoided a coiled rope in her path, and scanned the clear expanse in front of her. Not so much as a flag moved. The breeze had died, adding to the delicious warmth from her black leather jacket.

Disappointed when her search didn't yield any results, Marla debated which route to take next. Georgia had wanted to explore the beach. Considering her limited choices, she about-faced and dutifully picked a walkway winding in that direction. A young couple strolled past, starry-eyed, with their arms linked. It made her yearn for Vail's comforting presence. Should she tell him about the attack?

She reached a hand to her hair, blow-dried but frizzy without the proper care. A long strand covered the sensitive bruise on her head. If she didn't suffer any ill effects, she might keep quiet so as not to alarm him. He had enough problems without looking after her safety.

Halfway to the beach, Marla strained to listen. Crickets chirped a noisy chorus from a nearby bank of woods, and in the distance, waves splashed ashore. She caught the faint rhythm of Caribbean music from the poolside bar. A tern flew past, soaring overhead. This area wasn't as brightly lit as the paths near the pool, where pink and orange ground lights provided illumination. Common sense dictated that she shouldn't linger.

What did that sign up ahead say? Would it direct people to go left to the boathouse for jet ski rentals, or to the right for the gazebo? Idly scratching her forearm, Marla glanced dubiously in both directions. The trail to the boathouse led toward the beach, while the other snaked into the woods. Neither one would be a wise choice for a woman alone. But who could she trust to ask for help?

No time to figure that one out. Just do it yourself. After rotating in a full circle to make certain she was unobserved, Marla proceeded down the path to the gazebo. Georgia's sense of curiosity might have directed her toward the garden, and in any event, Marla couldn't bear to think of the ocean swallowing her friend. She'd check the boathouse next if this trail didn't lead anywhere.

Halfway along the path, she paused by a Gumbo Limbo tree. Through its branches, she could barely make out the form of a toolshed. On a hunch, she tried calling Georgia's number again. Her ears picked up a bare hint of sound on her left. Breaking off the trail, she rushed across the sandy ground to the shed, where she heard a distinct ringing tone coming from inside.

Banging on the door, Marla called out, "Georgia, are you in there? Answer me!" She stuffed her cell phone back in her bag.

A couple of muffled thumps sounded in reply.

Unable to see clearly enough, she rummaged in her handbag for a penlight. It had been handy for exploring the hidden tunnels at Sugar Crest over Thanksgiving, and she was glad she'd had the foresight to bring it along.

Shining the beam at the door, she spotted a bolt that slid sideways with ease. Slamming the door open, she aimed her beam inside—and cried out when she saw her friend wriggling on the floor. Bound and gagged, but very much alive.

"Bless my bones, who did this to you? Are you all right?" she babbled while fumbling with the bonds securing Georgia's wrists and ankles. She let Georgia remove the duct tape over her mouth, wincing at the tearing sound. *Ouch.*

"Thank God, Marla." Clapping a hand to her forehead, Georgia sat up. "How did you find me?"

She pointed to Georgia's purse lying on the concrete floor. "I dialed your cell phone and listened for the ringing tone. It's just pure luck that I came in this direction. Can I help you stand? We should get out of here. Someone knocked me on the head earlier and tossed me in the ocean."

"From your mouth to my legs, hon. We're outta here." Grasping Marla's arm, she rose unsteadily to her feet. "Just give me a minute to get my balance. I think I got cracked on the noggin, too. Something hurts me fierce right here." She indicated a spot on the back of her head.

"Come on, you'll rest later." Marla scooped up Georgia's handbag. "Let's go." Stepping outside the door, she peered back and forth, heaving a sigh of relief when they appeared to be unaccompanied.

They made haste back to their hotel room, ordered room service for sustenance, and then fell on their beds as exhaustion claimed them. Neither one seemed to have suffered any long-term consequences except for a headache and painful goose egg under the hair. They'd live, which was the main thing. But deciding who had perpetrated violence against them posed a compelling question.

Sunday evening, she told Barry Gold about both incidents when he picked her up for the charity ball where she was going to have a chance to meet the dermatologist. Folding her hands on the black beaded purse in her lap, she gave Barry an admiring glance. Sitting erect in the driver's seat of his silver Lexus, he presented a charming package with his sandy hair, bright blue eyes, and broad shoulders that seemed comfortably bound in a traditional black tuxedo.

"You take too many risks, Marla," he said, his gaze focused out the windshield.

"I didn't expect anything to happen in the Keys. That just about points the finger at one of the Luxor crew, wouldn't you say?" She smoothed her skirt. "I tried to call Dalton to tell him about it, but he isn't answering his cell phone. He and Brie had somewhere to go tonight. My mother is entertaining Justine and Larry."

"Lucky woman."

Yeah, right. Traffic east was fairly light, so Marla figured they should arrive early enough to enjoy cocktails at the event, which was being held at the Fort Lauderdale Renaissance Hotel. Her mouth watered for a glass of wine. It would help ease her guilt at leaving her houseguests behind.

"Georgia and I decided she got attacked because she wore my cranberry jacket. When the bad guy realized his mistake, he went after me next." Still able to taste the salt water from her ordeal, Marla licked her lips.

"What makes you think it's a man?"

"Logic. Sampson had been drinking before meeting the gang for dinner. His clothes were a mess, which they might have been if he'd dragged Georgia from wherever he waylaid her. If he felt I was a threat because I'd seen that check he wrote to Chris, then he'd want to get rid of me."

"You think Chris was blackmailing him, and that's what the check was all about?"

Marla nodded. "Possibly. I spoke to Amy Jeanne the next morning. She said Sampson had left the dinner table because he felt ill, and Ron had gotten up to go to the bathroom. Either one of them would have had time to crack me on the head."

"Did you tell Sergeant Masterson what happened?"

"Yes, I phoned him as soon as we got back. He seemed very interested and said he had something relevant to tell me, but it would have to wait until he had backup documentation."

"What do you think that means?"

"Masterson must have learned what it is that Sampson is hiding." Marla gave her companion an appreciative glance. It was easy to talk to him. While he chided her for rushing headlong into dangerous situations, he respected her intelligence. She was well aware that her family would consider it a *mitzvah* if she married a single Jewish optometrist who valued the same traditions. She really could hang out with him, if she didn't have Dalton. But she did have Dalton. And although she felt a special fondness for Barry, he didn't fire her jets the way the detective did. Maybe with time, she'd feel differently, but time had also taught her to follow her heart. Her heart led straight to Dalton.

"So you've eliminated everyone else as suspects?" Barry asked, lifting an eyebrow.

"Never close your mind to all the options, that's what Dalton says. Each one of my colleagues has a potential motive. For example, Janice took over Chris's position after she died. Is Jan ambitious?

Yes, although she claims to take no pleasure in getting a promotion that way. Nonetheless, we have to remember that Chris led her into an investment scheme that went bust. Now she's struggling to support her mother, who has a lot of medical bills, so she can't help resenting Chris's misguided advice that put her in a hole financially."

She took a deep breath and let it out slowly to help her clarify her thoughts. "Tyler also resented Chris, because she'd passed him over for promotion. Chris had the hots for him, which was obvious to everyone. He rejected her, so she retaliated by giving the position to Janice instead. When she made another move on Tyler and he still wouldn't give in, she threatened to spread rumors that could jeopardize his custody agreement."

Gripping the steering wheel, Barry shook his head. "Refresh my memory. Who's Tyler?"

"Our area supervisor. He didn't tell anyone he has a daughter, but somehow Chris found out. I can't help liking him. He acts like such a big flirt, but deep down, he mainly wants to be a good dad. At least that's what Georgia said."

"You think your friend is clean?"

"After someone tied her up and left her to rot in that shed? I should think so. At any rate, Georgia claims she got over her anger at Chris for screwing up her relationship with Nick."

Barry didn't respond until he'd navigated the ramp to Federal Highway north. In the distance, orange city lights reflected off the tall bank buildings in downtown Fort Lauderdale. He skewed into the middle lane, avoiding a driver whose slow crawl presented a hazard. "So who's left?"

Marla shrugged. "Amy Jeanne blamed Chris for setting up her sister with a bad date. Liesl felt Chris got in the way of a potential relationship she might have developed with Tyler. Ron made a pass at Chris and got turned down. And Miguel is defensive of his brother, a plastic surgeon Chris was suing for medical malpractice."

"Didn't you say only someone with medical knowledge could have switched the antidepressants?"

"And someone with access to prescription drugs," she added. "Those older MAO inhibitors have fallen out of favor. I doubt they're easy to get hold of by your average crook."

"What if they're prescribed for a patient who still needs them, like an older person who may have been treated with the same medication for years? Did you ever check to see what medicines Chris's mother was taking?"

"I didn't think about it. Holy highlights, you're a fountain of ideas tonight, Barry."

"Maybe you can ask Dr. Greenberg some of these questions."

"I should make a list," she said in all earnestness, annoyed to realize she didn't even have a pen in her tiny clutch bag. In any event, she'd be lucky to get five minutes alone with the good doctor to ask him about the items already in her mind.

When they arrived on-site, she surveyed the crush of people and wondered how they'd find him. The cocktail hour was in full swing in one of the ground-floor meeting rooms, with dinner to follow in the ballroom next door. Clutching Barry's arm, Marla surveyed the glitterati with a hard swallow.

Groups of people milled about balancing drink glasses and plates of hors d'oeuvres. A long, curtained table situated down the center of the room held platters of fruit and cheese and warming trays of meatballs, stuffed mushrooms, egg rolls, spinach wrapped in phyllo, chicken drumettes, and more. Off in one corner, one chef tossed a stir-fry concoction while another offered fettuccine Alfredo. Who needed dinner? She could eat her fill right here.

Nudging Barry, she spoke in a low tone. "Do you see him?"

"Not yet. Why don't you get our place number while I have a look around?" He indicated a white-clothed table where name cards were laid out. "I'll stop by the bar. What would you like to drink?"

"I'll have a glass of chardonnay, please. I don't see anyone that I recognize," she added with dismay.

"Don't feel alone. Neither do I." Barry winked, before slipping into the crowd.

Marla obtained their place card before getting in line for the buffet table. She got her kicks from admiring the women's sequined gowns, accessories, and makeup. When she was married to Stan, they used to attend lots of functions like this. She only realized how hollow they were when she outgrew him.

"Jake, I'd like you to meet my wife, Sherry," Marla heard as someone bumped her elbow. "Sherry, this is Jake Greenberg, one of our board members. He's been very generous in donating his time to the American Melanoma Society."

Marla spun so fast she nearly spilled the drink of the person behind her. "Sorry," she muttered, laser-beaming the guy with the reddish gold hair, impish twinkle in his eyes, and lightly freckled face. He looked to be mid-fortyish and had a stocky figure. Too many charity dinners, she guessed.

"Hello, my name is Marla Shore," she said to him, sticking out her hand. "I've been wanting to meet you. My friend Chris raved about your contribution to the cause. Christine Parks," she added at his puzzled look.

His shoulders slumped. "Oh yes, poor Chris. She was my friend as well. We shared the same goal regarding the society."

Marla was grateful when the other couple drifted away. She only hoped Barry wouldn't choose this moment to come looking for her and interrupt the conversation. "I'm a local stylist, but I've been working with Luxor for the beauty show. Chris mentioned that a percentage of our profits from the new sunscreen line would go to the organization."

He grinned, showing an even row of teeth that were dazzling white, as though artificially brightened. Looking more closely at his hair, she noticed gray roots. So the good doctor had a touch of vanity. That might be useful to know.

"Chris was one of our best proponents. She was well aware of the damage the sun can do to your hair as well as your skin," Greenberg said. His expression sobered. "Too many people who live in warm climates ignore the danger in favor of what they perceive as a healthy tanned look. That's why melanoma is on the rise."

"So Chris worked directly with you regarding the donation from Luxor?" Marla asked, attempting to focus their conversation before she got a lecture on the disease.

He waved to someone across the room. "Actually, she pounded out the details with Heather."

"Who?"

"Heather Morrison, my physician's assistant. You may have met her. She worked as one of the models at the hair show."

Chapter Eighteen

"**Y**ou're connected to Heather?" Marla said, thunderstruck.

Dr. Greenberg nodded. "Terrible thing, what happened to her, isn't it? Who can believe someone would attack her in the sauna? I still look for her in the office when she's not there."

"I think her death is related to Christine's murder, but I'd really like to talk to you about it in private. Actually, I tried to make an appointment for a mole check, but you're booked up for the next month. I was hoping to give a donation to the society in Chris's memory at the same time."

Greenberg laid a heavy hand on her shoulder. "Call my office in the morning and tell them I said to fit you in. They may give you a hard time because you're a new patient, but we can squeeze you into the schedule if you're having a problem."

Did he purposefully misconstrue her statement? She wanted to talk to him about the victims, not her skin condition. "Thank you, I'll be sure to do that."

He smiled, the sides of his mouth creasing like double parentheses. "The number of melanoma

cases keeps increasing. We can't do enough to ed-
ucate people, and your donation will help. Now if
you'll pardon me, I see someone I must greet."

Barry sidled up to her, drinks in hand. "That
was a short conversation."

She took her glass and sipped the fruity wine.
"Short, but significant. Heather the model worked
in his office as a physician's assistant. I guess the
modeling thing was a moonlighting job. Chris must
have set her up with Luxor."

"Interesting. So Christine Parks arranged to do-
nate a portion of the proceeds from Luxor's sunscreen line to the melanoma society through Dr.
Greenberg. His assistant, with ties to both groups,
ends up dead."

"You got it. That has to mean something. I just
have to find out more."

She had her chance the next day when she made
an appointment to see Dr. Greenberg. Fortunately,
he'd had a cancellation, because otherwise a Monday morning would have been too busy for him to
have fit her in. Guilt assailed her for fleeing her
houseguests again, but it couldn't be helped. Jan
had left a message that Masterson would be releasing
the Luxor crew by the end of the week, so she had
to move fast to tag the killer. She hadn't heard back
from the detective and assumed he didn't have
enough evidence if he was letting the suspects go.
Justice wouldn't be served until someone was behind bars.

The Weston location assured Dr. Greenberg of
affluent clients, and his plush waiting room reflected
the region's upscale reputation. Framed prints of
Mediterranean vistas, potted palms, a play area for
kids, and a tropical aquarium vied for attention
with a selection of glossy magazines.

Posters by the reception desk made her nervous with their reminders: READ YOUR PATIENT'S BILL OF RIGHTS, NOTIFY THE FRONT DESK IF YOUR INSURANCE HAS CHANGED, and PLEASE TELL US IF YOU HAVE A RASH. Half the people in this crowded room probably had a rash, she thought, averting her gaze from the other occupants.

Folding her purse under her arm, she took a seat and for a few seconds watched the Skin Care Network's offering on the television mounted in a corner.

"Has your skin grown over your belly button?" Marla heard a white-coated lab assistant say before she closed her ears. At the far end of the room was a display case with medicated skin creams, a poster for an eye compound to cover dark circles, and a wallboard announcing IT'S NEVER TOO SOON TO TAKE BLOOD PRESSURE SERIOUSLY. Oh joy. If you didn't feel sick before going into a doctor's office, you surely would by the time you left. The woman next to her coughed. Feeling her skin crawl, Marla jumped up and strode to the brochure rack.

Tired of your thick, discolored, or flaky nails? she read on one pamphlet that discussed fungal infections and the prescription medicine available to cure the problem. Another flyer offered a tablet to increase nail strength. Then there was one on Rogaine to prevent hair loss. She knew dermatologists treated hair and nail problems but hadn't realized the pervasiveness of drug companies pushing their wares.

Her opinion was confirmed when she finally entered a treatment room. While she shrugged out of her cashmere sweater to put on a short, disposable gown with a Velcro closing, she noted the gorgeous redhead in an ad for Restylan, which the poster proclaimed could be used alone or with

Botox for a smoother, more youthful appearance. "Oh yeah, as though any treatment would make me look like her," she said aloud.

Dangling her legs on the examination table, she squared her shoulders when Dr. Greenberg burst in. He examined her while a nurse stood nearby. Marla scanned the room's contents while he prodded at her moles and blemishes. Her gaze passed over the disposable gloves, syringes, gauze pads, and solution bottles, then rested on a certificate saying the doctor was a participant in the Botox Cosmetic Physicians Network. You could certainly tell where they made their money these days.

"Everything looks okay," the doctor told her. "This is an even-colored lesion," he said, focusing a dermoscopy instrument on her ankle. "If it gets bigger than a pencil eraser, then I'll be concerned. The scope lets me look into the skin and see the architecture of a mole. See this spot on your arm? It's a freckle-like area, no problem there. The one on your neck is almost papular. We call that type an intradermal nevus. When a mole has hair like this, that means it supports normal tissue and is healthy."

Glad he hadn't discovered anything adverse, Marla nodded. "Thanks, but I really came here to talk about—"

"Do you know the danger signs in a mole?" Greenberg continued, oblivious to her remark. "Look for asymmetry, color change, or growth."

Following his lead, Marla commented, "Living in Florida, we have to be especially careful." If only the nurse would leave, she'd ask him about Heather.

"Just a moment while I dictate my report." As the nurse stood by holding Marla's chart, he spoke with rapid-fire dictation into a handheld device. She didn't understand a word of his medical jargon.

Afraid he'd walk out of the room before she got any answers, Marla decided she needed to keep him talking. "My father had a lesion removed from his forehead once, but I don't think it was dangerous," she said after he'd turned off his recorder.

Greenberg's eyes narrowed. "Basal cell and squamous cell are the more common types of skin cancers. Those don't usually spread like melanoma. People should realize how prevalent this disease is becoming. This year, there will be up to sixty thousand new melanoma cases in the U.S. alone. Maybe thirteen percent of those patients will die."

"That's scary. Education about the warning signs is so important. Tell me, did Christine's involvement stem from a personal history?"

His mouth turned down. "Her uncle died from it. She learned the hard way that you have to be careful." Taking her chart from the nurse, he scribbled something on a front sheet that was probably her billing code.

"How can it be prevented?" she asked, staring at the nurse as though willing her to leave the room. The middle-aged woman in the green scrubs just smiled at her blandly.

Greenberg gave Marla an indulgent grin. He must think she was unduly concerned about the disease. Didn't he understand why she'd really come? "To know how to prevent it, you have to understand the pathology. Melanoma begins in the melanocytes, cells that are normally present in the epidermis, or the top layer of skin. They produce a pigment called melanin, which gives the tan or brown color to skin and helps protect the deeper layers from the sun."

"I'm familiar with melanin," Marla replied, warming to the topic. "Melanocytes are the cells responsible for hair color. They're generated within the follicles in the scalp. One of the theories about why hair goes gray is that these cells die off with aging or else they malfunction. Either way, they fail to produce enough melanin."

Nodding, the doctor touched his head. "People with red or blond hair and light skin are at higher risk for skin cancer. Having blue eyes also increases the potential. The disease most often appears on the trunk of men and on the lower legs of women, but it can show up other places as well. People with lots of moles or atypical lesions should be especially observant."

"Is there any heredity factor involved?" Marla asked out of genuine curiosity.

"Only to a minor degree. Approximately ten percent of people with melanoma have a family history. Frequent sun exposure is the biggest contributor. It damages the DNA of certain genes, causing cellular changes that may lead to melanoma down the road. The best prevention is to stay out of the sun."

"Can't I avoid it if I use sunscreen?" Marla considered all the rays she got while walking her dog. It couldn't be helped in Florida—every time you went outside, you got zapped.

"Ultraviolet radiation is the culprit, and, again, this can result from excessive sunlight or from tanning booths. Children and young adults often receive intense UV exposure that may not result in an actual cancer for years. This early exposure starts the change in melanocytes that may eventually turn into melanoma. As such, the rate of melanoma increases with age, but it's one of the few cancers that is also found in younger people. In fact, it's one of the most common cancers in people under thirty."

"I didn't realize that," Marla said, appalled.

"You want my advice? Avoid the midday sun between ten and four, when UV light is strongest. Remember that sunlight reflects off water, clouds, sand, concrete, and snow. You can also protect yourself by wearing a long-sleeved shirt and a wide-brimmed hat when you're outside. Keep in mind that baseball caps shade your head but not your ears or neck. As for sunscreen, you need a minimum SPF factor of fifteen. Look for products that protect against both UVA and UVB, the two most damaging forms of UV radiation. Use it even on cloudy days."

"Apply it about twenty minutes before you go outside so your skin can absorb the protective agents," the nurse piped in. "Sir, I believe Mr. Andrews is waiting in the next treatment room."

"I always try to use sunscreen," Marla said quickly. Sliding off the treatment table, she stood and faced the doctor.

Dr. Greenberg, clearly in his element, wagged a finger at her as he said, "Apply it on all exposed areas, but be aware this will not allow you to sit in the sun longer. If you do, you'll end up getting the same amount of UV exposure as if you hadn't used sunscreen at all."

A buzzer sounded, and the nurse slipped outside the door into the corridor.

"Speaking of life-threatening matters," Marla said, recognizing her opportunity, "I believe Heather's association with Luxor may have gotten her killed."

Dr. Greenberg stepped toward her. "What do you mean? I've spoken to the detective on the case, but he didn't say much except that she'd been stabbed at a health club."

"It seems more than a coincidence that first Chris was murdered, and then Heather."

"And you're concerned because . . . ?"

"I want to continue my association with Luxor but not if there's danger involved. What do you know about Bell Farms?"

He shook his head. "Doesn't ring a bell. Ha-ha."

Marla wasn't amused. "Did Detective Masterson tell you how he thought Chris had died? Whoever poisoned her must have had access to an older anti-depressant medicine."

"So I understand. I hadn't been aware Christine had experienced such a degree of depression that she needed medication." He clucked his tongue. "She always seemed so upbeat. Her loss is felt deeply by our society members."

"Was Chris's mother on this type of medicine? I know you visited her in the assisted-living facility."

"I only got a brief look at Violet's chart. I don't believe she was taking any medications."

"Were you really there to examine her, or to meet Chris?"

Dr. Greenberg's gaze chilled. "Both. She wanted me to check out a lesion on her mother's arm."

"One of the aides told me you had a lengthy discussion with Chris while you were there."

"We discussed the arrangement between Luxor and the society, not that it's any business of yours. She'd found some irregularities." A puzzled frown creased his forehead as though the memory disturbed him.

The nurse peeked in the room, spurring Marla to ask her remaining questions before she lost the doctor's attention. "Irregularities?" she repeated.

"In the bookkeeping department. I said I'd ask Heather to look into it. You don't possibly think this is how their deaths could be connected?"

"It's possible."

He placed a hand on her arm, making her self-conscious about the drape she wore. She itched to put her shirt on.

"I realize you're eager to help," the doctor said, his hazel eyes intense, "but let me handle this. You don't have to get any more involved than you are already. If you want to continue with Luxor, heed my advice." He grinned. "In the meantime, come back in a year for another checkup, and stay out of the sun. You know the drill."

Yeah, I know the drill, Marla thought during the drive home. *Shut up and let the professionals handle the case—except Masterson isn't getting anywhere.* She wanted to follow this new lead but had promised to spend the afternoon with her company. With Vail at work and Brianna in school, it was left to her to entertain them.

She stopped for groceries, having invited the Luxor crew to her salon on Tuesday for a farewell party, and took the opportunity to restock her town house as well. Keeping guests well-fed quickly depleted her supplies along with her patience.

"How did your doctor-visit go?" Justine asked, helping Marla put away the groceries when she finally finished her errands. Larry lounged in the family room watching sports on television, while Georgia had spent the morning doing her hair and nails.

"Tell us, hon," Georgia said from where she sat at the kitchen table, blowing on her wet plum polish.

"I learned a lot about skin cancer," Marla told them. "Dr. Greenberg is very adamant about prevention. I can see why he gives his time to the melanoma society. Heather acted as the link between his charitable organization and Luxor. I imagine that's how she ended up as a model at the show."

"Huh? I don't get it," Georgia said.

"Chris arranged for the donation to the society through Greenberg, and he let Heather manage the details. He said Chris had found some sort of irregularity in the bookkeeping."

"From Luxor's end, or the society's?"

"He didn't seem to know." She stuck a bottle of milk into the refrigerator. "Anyway, Chris may have offered the modeling job to Heather out of appreciation, and you have to admit the girl had a great figure. Or maybe Chris just wanted her close at hand, to question her about the discrepancy."

"No kidding." Georgia narrowed her eyes. "Something smells fishy about this whole arrangement, if you ask me."

"Tell me about it. I need to learn more."

Justine handed her a carton of eggs. The older woman wore a silk blouse, navy blue skirt, hosiery and matching heels. Her navy and gold button earrings complemented her attire. She'd made up her face and looked as though she merely needed to grab her purse to go out on the town.

"Thanks," Marla said, feeling an ounce of warmth toward her guest for not sitting on her butt and letting Marla do all the work. Maybe Justine was just beginning to appreciate how many different hats Marla juggled while caring for others.

"What do you guys want to do this afternoon?" she asked, deliberately changing the subject. "How about the water taxi, Flamingo Gardens, Bonnet House, or Las Olas?"

Spooks barked for attention. She tossed the poodle a treat and watched him scurry from the room to enjoy it in private. Thankfully, he seemed to suffer no bad effects from the tick and had returned to his normal, playful self. Now if only her life would follow suit. While the others debated what they wanted to do for the day, she whipped up turkey sandwiches for lunch.

She had just swallowed her last bite when the phone rang. Taking the call in her study, she was surprised to hear Sergeant Masterson at the other end.

"I thought I'd share some information with you," his gruff voice said, "since I am dismissing the suspects on Thursday. That doesn't mean I'm giving up on the case. I need more hard evidence, and you might be able to help."

Marla broke in, excitedly telling him about her interview with Dr. Greenberg. "Isn't it important that Chris found something wrong with the book-keeping? Do you think the donations from Luxor aren't being recorded properly?"

"I've already checked into the organization's finances," the detective replied. "The amount reported in the society's books is less than what Luxor says is being donated."

"Someone is diverting funds," Marla deduced, her mind racing. "But at which end? If it's Luxor, was Chris working the scheme by herself?"

"She'd need a partner, either the bookkeeper at her own company or somebody at the society."

"Maybe she was in league with the dermatologist. He could have double-crossed her, after planting Heather as a model at the show and giving her the dangerous drug to put into Chris's drink. But then, who murdered Heather?"

"Possibly Dr. Greenberg, if your line of thought rings true. To play devil's advocate, why would he confess that Christine Parks had found something wrong with the accounts if he wanted to cover his own tracks?"

"Good point. And why would he kill Chris? Had she been about to turn the tables on him?"

"Personally, I don't believe he's our man. I've been consulting with the Miami Beach police, considering how both our victims were related. Either Heather was involved in embezzling money from the American Melanoma Society, or else she may have found out who is. But that could just be a smoke screen in this whole mess." He paused. "Did you know Miguel Santiago's brother is on the society's board of directors? Parks had been suing him over a botched surgery."

"I knew about the brother but not that he was involved with the charitable organization. How is his record otherwise? Could he be the one skimming the cream?"

"Santiago has a respected reputation, and he's in a stable financial position. I was thinking more along the lines of Miguel wanting to protect his brother from a harmful lawsuit."

"The brother, a surgeon, would have access to drugs."

"I've thought of that. I feel like I have all the dots in place, but I just can't see how to connect them. This case bugs me, Miss Shore. I don't want to see these people go free when I know one of them is guilty. Be assured I'll be watching the doctors like a hawk, but I'm hoping you might learn something in the meantime from your pals at Luxor."

"I've invited them to my salon tomorrow. You're welcome to come."

"I have to check out another lead. It's a long shot, but I don't believe in letting any stone go unturned. I'll be talking to you."

Marla hung up, frustrated that she had to spend

the afternoon squiring her guests around when there were so many other things she'd rather do. Nonetheless, she was determined to play the perfect hostess despite the distraction of realizing that time was running out. If she didn't get answers by Thursday, the person who'd left two women dead would be allowed to walk.

By Monday evening, her nerves were so frayed that when she found herself alone with Justine and Larry, Georgia having accepted an invitation from Goat to walk the dogs, she balked at Justine's suggestion for a heart-to-heart talk.

"Look, I'm not really in the mood," she said, staring out the kitchen window at the fading sunlight. "I'm sorry Brianna had choir practice tonight and couldn't see you." She'd noticed how Justine's face fell during an earlier phone call to her granddaughter. They hadn't had nearly as much time together as the elderly couple had wished. *They would have had more time if they'd stayed at Vail's house.*

Larry cleared his throat. He occupied his usual slouch on the sofa with the television blaring. The noise grated on her nerves, making her clench her teeth. She craved time alone, but since the killer might still be out there, plotting another attempt on her life, it was probably best to have company right now. *Safety in numbers,* she thought, trying to reach a state of calm by taking slow, deep breaths.

"Have you stopped thinking about yourself enough to realize how difficult this is for us all?" Justine snapped at her side. "You're about to become Brianna's stepmother, and yet you still show little regard for the woman who birthed her. That hurts me in here." Justine beat on her chest, her face a mask of anguish.

Marla wheeled around. There was no avoiding

this conversation. "That's not true. I respect and admire Pam. She did a great job of raising Brianna. But I feel she comes between me and Dalton. Or at least she did, until he agreed to move to a new place. I don't feel comfortable in the bedroom where they shared their lives or in the house your daughter decorated. I'd like to honor her memory, but not in a manner that keeps reminding me of the past."

Dalton wasn't the only one having trouble moving on, she realized with sudden clarity. Justine clung to her daughter's memories because letting her go felt like a betrayal.

"You reject everything of hers that you find."

"Because you stick it in my face. You're not making it easy for me. I love Brianna as though she's my own child. I want to be a good role model for her, and I can't do that if you keep putting me down." Marla regretted hurting the older woman, but she'd kept her emotions bottled to the point of eruption, and now the eruption had come.

"Being a role model isn't as important as being a parent."

"In my mind, they go together. Why don't you stop fighting me and realize I have the same goal as you do?"

Justine covered her face with her hands. "I miss my baby. No one will ever take her place."

"I'm not trying to, Justine. Trust me. I want to do what's best for your granddaughter."

Justine sniffled. "Losing a child is something you never get over. I feel a terrible ache inside, like a piece of me has been ripped out." She clapped a hand over her heart. "I yearn to hug my little girl."

"I'm so sorry." Marla understood the hollow feeling. She'd seen the agony of Tammy's parents after the toddler drowned in their backyard pool. As her baby-sitter, Marla had been held accountable, and she'd revisited her private pain many times over. Maybe that was why she'd tried to deny Pam's existence—because remembering that Pam had died made her recall the small child who never had the chance to grow up.

Her eyes glistening, Marla embraced Justine. "You can hug me. I'm not your daughter, but I promise to remember her. And, Justine, she'd want you to live your life as fully as possible."

"Thank you, dear," Justine choked, patting her on the back.

A sense of peace stole over Marla. No longer leery of spending time with the elder couple, she sat with them in the family room. "So tell me about Pam when she was younger," she said in a gentle tone.

As she listened to their stories, she enjoyed the tentative rapport they'd established and the momentary calm of her life, but she knew the peacefulness wouldn't last. When Luxor's crew gathered at her salon the next day, she'd ask some hard-hitting questions. Sooner or later, someone would crack.

Chapter Nineteen

Tuesday afternoon Luxor's crew entered the Cut 'N Dye salon in a jovial mood, having received word from Sergeant Masterson that they were free to go in two days' time.

"Yo, Marla," Tyler called out, "you hear the news? You'll finally get rid of us." He swaggered toward her.

Just finishing her last client, she spritzed the lady's gray head with a flourish. "I'll see you next week," she told the woman, unfastening her cape. "Luis will get your tab up front." After sweeping the hairs off her chair with a blow-dryer, she turned to the area supervisor, whose grin split his face like that of a child who'd been let out to play.

"I know you're all eager to get back to work in your hometowns," Marla told him, "but I can't say I'm happy to see you go."

Swatting her shoulder, he winked. "Is that your roundabout way of saying you'll miss me?"

"Actually, I was thinking more along the lines of missing Chris and Heather. Someone got rid of them, and I think that person is right here."

She leaned forward, getting a pleasant whiff of

his musk aftershave. "We both know Chris liked you. I understand that she threatened to jeopardize your custody agreement when you turned down her overture. Why do you feel it's necessary to hide being a father? Are you afraid it'll ruin your image of the big man around town?"

"Carting a little girl along ain't gonna get me a whole lot of dates. Women don't fancy that kind of baggage."

"Sorry to tell you, pal, but a woman can sense when a guy doesn't want to commit. Having a child acts as your excuse."

Tyler scraped a hand through his caramel hair. "Whoa, babe, you're cuttin' me."

She scrutinized his face and noticed the lines tightening his mouth. "Or maybe you're just too scared to get serious about anyone else. What happened to your wife, Tyler?"

He glanced away. "She left me for some rich accountant dude. Said she wanted a guy who worked in an office, and it embarrassed her to tell people what I did for a living."

"So how did that make you feel, like you weren't good marriage material? You shouldn't let that get you down. If you show what a giving man you can be, the right person will come along who respects your career choice and devotion to your daughter."

"We have a great relationship. I don't want to spoil it."

"You won't." She sucked in a breath. "My fiancé and his daughter got along fine before I came along, and I didn't distract from their relationship. If anything, I've added to the family circle. You should be proud that you stuck to your guns and didn't give in to Chris. It would've been easier to yield to her demands in order to protect your child."

Tyler gave a furtive glance over his shoulder. "Since you're so interested, I think there's something you should know. Like, Jan has been depressed lately over her financial situation. She's got the burden of supporting her mother, who's ill, plus she's racked up a hefty credit card debt. I think, like, she's been taking happy pills lately."

Marla stiffened. "Antidepressants?"

"Yup. I didn't want to get in trouble by telling that detective anything, but I don't mind talking to you. You're a cool cat, and you'll know what to do." He jabbed two fingers at her. "You're the bomb, Marla. Thanks for the advice."

Anytime, Marla thought, eliminating Tyler as one of her prospective assailants. He wouldn't have been so open if he meant her harm. Turning her attention to Jan, she contemplated the acting director, who kept her problems private. She'd have had the perfect opportunity to switch Christine's medication if she'd gotten into her boss's room earlier. When exactly had Jan arrived at the hotel? Could she have dropped into Chris's suite after her superior went to visit her mother?

Sauntering over to where Jan had plopped into a chair at an empty manicure station, Marla leaned her hip against the counter. "I'll bet you're glad to be going home soon. Too bad your time off was taken with police interviews and photo shoots instead of relaxing on the beach. Or did you get in early too, like Chris?"

Jan shot her a shrewd glance. "I arrived Thursday so I'd have time to get organized before our prep meeting on Friday. I had to make sure the models were contacted and our equipment was delivered as ordered."

"Did you happen to stop by Chris's room at any time during the day?"

"Hell, no. I was busy."

"Chris didn't want to review her directives with you?"

"She went out that afternoon on personal business."

"So you kept track of her movements? What did you do while she was gone?"

"What is this, an inquisition?" Jan said, anger flashing in her hazel eyes. "I told you, I had work to do."

"A little birdie mentioned that you're taking pills for depression. It would be easy to hate Chris after she screwed your investments. She was responsible for putting you in the hole financially, wasn't she? Is that why you switched medicines on her? You knew she couldn't tolerate the brand you're taking?"

Jan shot to her feet so fast that her chair crashed back. "If I wanted to poison Chris, I wouldn't have had to go to her hotel room. I'd have slipped the stuff in her drink at the cocktail party."

"Exactly." Marla smirked before noting that other conversations around them had fallen silent and everyone's eyes were on them. "Hey, go back to work," she yelled to her cohorts, stepping forward to right Jan's chair.

"Yeah, well, it wasn't me who bought the bitch a drink."

"Could anyone have gotten hold of your medication, taken one of the pills to switch it for Chris's?"

"I'm on the newer kind without the bad food interaction. Come into the back room a minute, Marla." Jan waited until Marla followed her into the storage room and they stood crowded amongst the tubes of coloring agents and developer bottles. "Promise me you won't let this go farther than this room."

Marla bit her lower lip, unwilling to withhold information that might contribute to the murder case. "I'll be discreet," she hedged.

"Amy Jeanne and I . . . we were together." She must have noted the puzzlement on Marla's face because her skin reddened. "We have a relationship," she explained, nodding as though that would prompt Marla to comprehend.

Marla's eyes widened. "Oh! I mean, I would never have guessed. The two of you are . . ." Her cheeks warmed. They'd hidden their sexual proclivities well.

"Amy was just as resentful against Chris as me, but neither one of us could kill anyone. We didn't shed any tears when Chris died, but we're not murderesses. Go ask my girlfriend. She'll confirm what I say."

Marla took Amy Jeanne aside, ostensibly to review her inventory of Luxor supplies. But once in the rear, she confronted the salon coordinator with Jan's statement.

The sleek dark-skinned woman pursed her lips, expertly filled in with mahogany gloss. "Shut my mouth. Janice didn't tell you about us!"

"Tell me the truth, Amy. Did you know Jan was taking antidepressants, and if so, why didn't you tell Masterson?"

"It had nothing to do with his case. Jan made sure to count her tablets. Not one was missing, so she didn't see any sense in blabbing her personal history. At any rate, her medicine isn't the same kind as made Chris sick." Opening a gum wrapper, she popped the stick of gum into her mouth.

"The detective did a background check on all of you. What do you think he found?"

"Nothing that makes the cops suspect us," Amy Jeanne said, chewing. "Aren't you forgetting about Heather?"

"What about her?"

"I've been thinking about our conversation down in the Keys. I didn't mention this at the time, because it didn't enter my mind, but Sampson went ballistic when she accidentally took one of his hairbrushes."

"Huh?" Marla shook her head, confused by the new tangent.

Amy Jeanne's eyes glittered. "Luxor ships in special brushes for Sampson. They're made out of boar bristles in China. I always believed Chris catered to him just to appease his ego, because the cost must have increased the company's expense budget quite a bit. She'd been looking for ways to reduce cash outflow, and that expense could have been on her list to pare down. Go ask Jan. She'll know more about it."

"You may be onto something," Janice said to Marla when she queried her. "The containers are shipped from China and off-loaded onto trucks at Port Everglades. From there, the cargo is delivered to a local warehouse, where it's packed into smaller cartons before being sent to our main supply depot. Chris was considering eliminating the middleman as a way to cut costs. She hoped we could increase our donation to the melanoma society if our profit margin improved."

"That's interesting. Sergeant Masterson told me that not all the money being donated to the cause gets into the group's coffers. Someone is skimming at one end or possibly both. Were you aware that Heather worked for Dr. Greenberg, who was Chris's contact at the melanoma society?" Maybe Heather, not the dermatologist, had schemed to rip off the charity. Had Heather been in cahoots with someone from Luxor? Chris could have found out and been killed for it. Then Heather's partner might have knocked her off to avoid exposure.

Jan tilted her head. "No, I didn't know that about Heather. I think Chris mentioned something about checking out the warehouse. She may have driven up there before the show."

"Do you have the address?" Marla didn't see how Sampson's hairbrushes entered into the equation, but she remembered wanting to ask about them. Regardless, Chris's movements were important to track. It was more likely the former company director had discovered a bookkeeping deficit, in which case Marla felt at a loss. No one present from Luxor would have been responsible for writing the contribution check. That would have come from the home office, or so she assumed. Chris might have been authorized to write a check to the society and hand it to Dr. Greenberg while she was here, but that didn't account for the rest of the year.

Financial trails were too hard for her to follow. She'd have to leave that to Sergeant Masterson's skills. Otherwise, she'd waste time interviewing financial officers at Luxor and at the charitable society's headquarters. She had neither the resources nor the time to accomplish that task. However, driving to a warehouse somewhere in the area was within her grasp.

"I may have the place written down somewhere," Jan told her, riffling through one of the folders in her possession.

Marla shot a glance at Sampson, who'd been demonstrating a feathering technique to a couple of Marla's stylists. His animated face and gestures showed he was enjoying his teaching role. Remembering the check he'd written to Chris, she wondered if it had anything to do with the special orders. Maybe he gave Chris a kickback for ordering his hairbrushes.

"Why are the imported hairbrushes so important to Sampson?" she asked Jan. "I mean, I know boar bristles are softer and less damaging to the hair than other kinds. I prefer using them myself. But can't you buy them in this country? Or are they mass-produced elsewhere and just sold at retail outlets here?"

"Sampson orders at bulk rates." Jan lifted a paper from her folder. "This is peculiar, now that you mention it. Here's a bill of lading. It lists Luxor Products as the buyer and gives an address in Belle Glade."

"That's a bit north from here. May I see that paper, please? It must be the warehouse where the shipments go before they're repackaged." Her heart thudded when she saw the heading.

Bell Farms.

So Heather had been onto something significant.

"May I keep this?" she asked Jan.

"Sure, although I don't know what you hope to do with it."

"First I'd like to ask Sampson what's so important about the shipments and why he can't get them wholesale in the States."

Sampson puffed out his chest when she approached him with that question. "Boar bristles are almost identical to human hair," he said, waving a comb in the air. "They come from the first cut of boars that are raised on farms. The animals are sheared like sheep. They are well cared for, and their bristles are harvested repeatedly."

"No one breeds boars in the United States?"

"Not to my knowledge. The best come from China. I prefer a mahogany wooden oval brush with a pneumatic cushion. The bristles distribute your natural oils and gently massage the scalp. You should use one for your fine hair, Marla. For thick-hair types, I recommend brushes with stiffer black boar bristles. They'll manage the tangles better."

"But why do you need so many that they have to be shipped in containers to the port?"

Overhearing their conversation, Ron sauntered over after checking his reflection in the mirror. "Luxor sells them," he said. "Don't you have any on your shelves? I would've thought Georgia added them to your inventory." His gray eyes regarded her with an odd light. He must be wondering why she was making such a big deal out of Sampson's pet project.

"Maybe she did. I'll have to check. It just seems like such a large order coming from overseas. An *expensive* order."

"An artist must have his brushes," Sampson told her in a haughty tone.

Ron grasped her elbow and drew her aside. "Let it go. The maestro doesn't like to be crossed. What's a few hairbrushes compared to the talent he contributes to our company?"

"It's a lot of money, that's what. If Chris was looking to cut costs, she may have decided to eliminate this expense. Or at least to have the brushes shipped directly to company headquarters instead of going through a middleman."

Ron grinned, but he looked menacing rather than friendly. "Come now, I'm sure you value your role on the team. This isn't an issue that needs your attention. Leave it to the higher-ups, and focus on technique. Would you like me to shape your hair? It's getting a bit long, and I can show you how texturizing shears will add dimension."

"Perhaps some other time, thanks." She did need a haircut, but she realized his offer was meant to distract her. *Just wait until tomorrow,* she thought. She'd scheduled only one client for an early perm, and afterward it might be a perfect day to invite her guests along for a ride. They might even stop for lunch at the Clewiston Inn on their way to Belle Glade.

Marla kept up a running commentary while driving north on Route 27 the next morning. Georgia sat beside her in the passenger seat. Justine and Larry occupied the rear. She had already pointed out the grassy plains of the Everglades to their left, but now they were entering sugar country.

"This is where the big sugar corporations grow their crops. See those fields? That's sugarcane." She indicated the tall stalks that grew next to a fallow field. "There's always talk about pollution runoff, but it seems to get buried."

"Florida is so flat," Justine remarked in a tone as flat as the landscape. She'd dressed in a white and emerald skirt ensemble more suitable for a tea party then their present outing. The large beads on her neck clicked with each movement.

"I love the sky," Marla said. "We don't have any haze like up North." Nor could northeasterners enjoy the three-hundred-sixty-degree view of pene-trating blue with fluffy white clouds like South Floridians. She enjoyed gazing at the vast expanse stretching as far as her eyes could see. Earthbound, they were walled in by sugarcane. Bordering the fields to the east was Lake Okeechobee, but she couldn't see any water because of the surrounding grassy mound known as Herbert Hoover Dike.

"Is this the big city where we're eating lunch?" Justine said, her pitch rising.

Clearly the approach into Clewiston understated its importance as the unofficial capital of the Florida sugar industry. Marla could understand why. While the town claimed the highest per capita income in the area, if you blinked, you'd pass right through it.

She turned into the drive for the hotel, an at-tractive colonial-style inn with a two-story white ex-terior. After letting her company off at the pillared portico entrance, she pulled into a parking space.

"The U.S. Sugar Corporation originally built the hotel for their visiting executives. The concrete walls are reinforced with steel rods to withstand hurricanes," she informed to Georgia as they walked inside.

Her friend nodded at the comfortable wood furnishings. "It's charming, Marla, but I'm eager to get on to the turf farm." Georgia's glance met hers frankly. "That's where we'll get answers about Heather's death, and taking us to lunch here is merely a delaying tactic because you're afraid of what we might find."

"That's not true. Justine and Larry could care less about sod growers. This is a part of Florida they've never seen." She led them into the dining room for a leisurely southern lunch.

An hour and a half later, they resumed their

course north. The trip into Belle Glade lacked any of the charm of Clewiston. Dominated by trailer parks and fishing camps, it reeked of rural backwater Florida. Marla found the road to the sod farm and drove down the pitted dirt lane, jostling her passengers.

"Well, I never," Justine exclaimed. "Where on earth are you taking us? I thought we were going for a scenic drive, but this place is pretty decrepit."

Marla explained the purpose of their excursion. "When I called Detective Masterson, he said that Bell Farms is owned by Sampson York's family. He'd made a cursory visit but hadn't found anything significant. I'm hoping we'll have better luck."

Georgia's curls bounced when she looked at Marla. "Isn't this the same address as the warehouse where Sampson's hairbrushes get shipped?"

Marla gripped the steering wheel tighter. "Yep, and Chris wanted to cut out the middleman to save money, remember? If Sampson is running some kind of operation here, he'd want to stop her. Maybe that check I found was a bribe that she refused, so he had to kill her."

Larry snorted in the rear. Unlike Justine, who had a look of displeasure on her face, he seemed amused by their discussion. "What operation? Shipments of hairbrushes?" he scoffed. "So the fancy boar-bristle thingies go directly to company headquarters instead. York would still get his custom-ordered supplies."

"But he loses a lucrative contract if his family farm serves as the intermediate shipping warehouse," Marla explained. "Where do the trucks off-load? I only see a greenhouse structure, and a brick building in the distance."

Arriving at a parking lot, she squealed the brakes

to a halt in a cloud of dust and switched off the ignition. A couple of other vehicles were present: a black car coated with grime and a pickup truck riddled with dents. A burly fellow in a plaid shirt and jeans sauntered from the greenhouse in their direction. Tattoos decorated his biceps, and he wore a baseball cap on backwards.

"Yo, lady, this place ain't open to the public," he called after her group emerged from the Camry.

"I know, but I need some information." Vaguely aware of the others gathering beside her, she plowed on. "I work for Luxor, a hair-care company. We've reason to believe that our artistic director, Sampson York, is sending hairbrush shipments to this location for processing."

"Are you crazy? We grow grass here. Look at those fields."

"But the shipping manifest gave this address."

His weathered face crinkled. "You must have your facts mixed up, lady. Sampson comes from a family of turf growers. See that house, yonder? It's his old homestead."

Georgia tapped Marla on the arm. "I thought Sampson said his dad was a dentist. His teeth are so perfect, he could be in a toothpaste commercial."

"Maybe his teeth are as false as his awards," Marla muttered, getting an inkling of what Chris may have had on Sampson. But how to prove it? "May we have a tour while we're here?" she asked sweetly. "These are my, uh, cousins who are visiting from up North, and I wanted to show them our Florida agriculture."

"Dalton likes plants," Justine remarked, gesturing toward the greenhouse. "Too bad he had to work today, or he'd have been here. Maybe we can bring him a gift." She shaded her face with her hand to regard her companions. "Well, are you coming?" Lifting her chin, she strode ahead without waiting for the others.

"Ma'am, you can't go in there," the man said.

"Perhaps we should see the manager," Larry suggested, brushing past Marla as he hurried to keep pace with his wife.

"I am the manager. Parnell Gunther, that's me. And I say this place is off-limits to visitors."

"Just what is the purpose of the greenhouse on a sod farm?" Marla asked, tugging Georgia's elbow on her way along the trail. A rich earthen scent entered her nostrils as the sun warmed her back. Grateful she'd worn slacks, she ducked inside the glass enclosure and immediately felt the humidity.

A thunderous scowl on his face, Gunther charged after them. "We experiment with different types of seeds—you know, for hybrids."

"Really?" Marla scanned the flatbeds sprouting with thin green blades. "Wouldn't that best be done at a horticultural station? I don't see any laboratory equipment."

"Unnecessary," Gunther grunted. He glanced nervously over his shoulder. "Look, y'all, you gotta leave."

"What's growing in these pots?" Marla stroked a smooth ceramic planter. A spindly stalk rose from soil inside that crumbled in her fingers. "This is pretty dry."

"Keep away from that pot. It's a delicate seedling."

Oh yeah? I've never seen grass that looked like aloe.

Marla yearned for a closer look. Georgia had meandered toward a draped table holding a coiled water hose patched with a piece of duct tape. Desperate to search the environs, she glanced at Justine. The older woman caught her gaze and gave her a half smile that nearly knocked Marla's socks off.

"How many varieties of grass do you grow here?" Justine demanded of the manager, plopping her prim self in his direct path. She wore her most formidable expression, her lips pinched and her eyes narrowed. "Do you have samples you can show us?"

"If I tell you, will you go? I need to get back to work, lady."

"Indeed." Justine inclined her head in acknowledgment.

"Over here." He gestured at a display of sod laid out on plastic sheeting. "This one is our most popular variety, called *Floratam,* but you may know it as St. Augustine grass. It's a dense sod that spreads by sending out runners. As with all St. Augustines, it requires regular watering, so you'll want to have a sprinkler system. *Floratam* also needs at least five hours of sunlight per day."

"You don't say," Justine said in her best pedigreed voice. "What if I need to put sod in a shady spot?"

With her ears cocked to their conversation, Marla noted Georgia kicking her foot under the draped table. Sidling over, she raised her hands in question.

"I'm hitting something solid under there," Georgia whispered. "We should take a look."

"Hey, Marla," Larry said, his crinkly eyes alert with curiosity. In the dappled greenhouse light, he appeared thinner, his cardigan sweater loose on his slim shoulders. His face had the kindly look of a gaunt schoolteacher. "This is odd."

He'd noticed the pots, too. They seemed incongruous for growing grass, tall ceramic containers with short green blades. She glanced over her shoulder at the manager, who had his back to them while he spoke to Justine.

"Seville, Bitter Blue, Palmetto varieties are more shade-tolerant than St. Augustine," he was saying. "They can also be used in full sunshine, so if you have a yard that's part shade and part sun, you might want to cover the whole area with one of these grasses."

"When is the best time of year to lay new sod?" Justine said as though this were the most interesting topic in the world.

While Georgia stooped to push aside the drape and see what was under the counters, Marla plunged her hand into the soil in one of the pots.

"I wouldn't install shade grass in the warmer months because you might encourage fungus. We'll only sell this type from the fall to spring. Bahia grass is less expensive, with a higher drought tolerance. It spreads by sending up long, narrow stalks with black seed pods at the end." A silence, during which time Marla didn't dare turn around. "Y'all stay put, I'm going outside to make a phone call."

While Marla sank her forearm deeper into the pot, she noticed Justine following the guy from the corner of her eye.

"Wait," the older woman said. "How do you take care of the Bahia grass? Does it need as much water as St. Augustine?"

"Lady, you can have a nice, thick lawn with regular watering and use of fertilizer. Gather your friends. You're leaving."

Marla didn't know if he was making a cell phone call or continuing his discussion with Justine, because just then her fingers touched an uneven shape amongst the dirt.

"Oh, heck," she said, taking the pot and dumping its contents upside down on the ground.

A small object, less than a foot long, slid out amid clumps of soil. She tore open its waterproof wrapping, her eyes widening at what was inside.

A stone statuette of a warrior with distinctly Asian eyes.

Chapter
Twenty

Thrusting the statue into her large handbag, Marla signaled to Georgia that it was time to go.

"Not yet," Georgia said. "Look what I found. Cartons that haven't even been opened. They're stashed under these counters."

Grabbing a pair of pruning shears lying nearby, Marla hastened in her direction. Larry came along to peer over her shoulder. "That label says those are hairbrushes from China," she noted upon closer examination. She couldn't leave without seeing what was inside. But when she went to move the box, it wouldn't budge. *Must be something awfully heavy in there*, she thought.

Georgia leaned forward, adding her muscle. Together they dragged one of the boxes into the light.

"Let me help," Larry said when she had trouble opening the heavy container. Marla cried out when she chipped a fingernail. That tape was too damn tenacious. She rocked back on her heels while Larry wrestled with the packaging. Grunting in triumph when he managed to cut a slit in the seam, he threw down the gardening tool and pried open the box.

Layers of shiny new boar-bristle hairbrushes were nestled inside. Disappointment sagged her limbs. "This can't be all." Digging in up to her elbows, she scrabbled around but felt nothing except the soft bristles tickling her fingers.

"What are you expecting to find?" Georgia asked, her dark eyes dancing with excitement.

"More of these." Marla stretched her handbag so Georgia could see what was inside.

"Way cool. Let's open another one."

Marla glanced at the entrance, but Justine must have been doing a bang-up job of getting the manager's advice on growing grass. Neither one had reappeared. Good. It was imperative that she find where the statue had come from and what it meant.

Larry made a fast job of opening the second carton, but then he gave a groan and rose. "My knees," he explained. "Will you be much longer? I'm going to see what my wife is up to. That fella probably knows she's spinning a tale."

"Tell me about it," Marla muttered, thinking she'd never heard Larry speak so many lines at once. Maybe boredom caused his silence at home, not indifference. She let Georgia search the box while she listened for an exchange outside. Silence reigned, prickling the hairs on her nape.

Her attention was diverted by Georgia's sharp intake of breath.

"Omigosh, Marla, we've hit the jackpot. Look at this." Georgia buried her arm in the second carton brimming with hair-care items. She surfaced with another wrapped statuette.

"I have a hunch—But we need to get out of

here," Marla urged. "It's unlike Justine to be so quiet."

"Sampson has to be responsible, right? He's the one who ordered these things, and his family owns the farm." Rising, Georgia stuffed the weighty object into her bag.

Marla got to her feet, wincing as a muscle spasmed in her lower back. "We can talk about it later. Obviously Sampson is involved. Chris must have known, and she was blackmailing him." She brushed dirt off her pants. "That would account for the check he wrote to her that he didn't want anyone to know about. I assume it's the reason why he killed her."

"Hey, that's good, but you're only partially right," said a familiar voice from the entrance.

Ron Cassidy strolled inside, pointing a gun at them. Behind him, the manager ushered Marla's companions in his wake.

Marla's pulse skipped. "You! Why are you here? We expected Sampson York. Or are you in league with him?" Their rivalry could have been a front, playacted to serve us a diversion.

Ron sauntered closer, a smug grin on his face. "This is my operation. When York started bringing in the shipments from China, I saw the possibilities. I'd made some contacts during my time in the slammer, and I got in touch with them."

"You were in jail?" Marla motioned behind her back to Georgia, whose gaze fixated on the gun barrel pointed at them. They both had cell phones in their purses. If one of them could call for help . . .

"I'd pissed some people off in my rise to fame," Ron said, scraping a hand through his spiky hair.

"You mean the Great Rinaldo, hairdresser to the

stars, won't have a spotless reputation? What if word of your background gets out?"

"A little notoriety can't hurt. It may even attract clients when I open my Beverly Hills salon."

"I imagine the overhead is quite costly there," Marla said in a wry tone.

He gave a harsh chuckle. "No kidding. Smuggling in Asian artifacts is quite a lucrative sideline, but I won't be doing this forever. I've almost got enough cash to bid for a place."

Marla's glance fell to the pruning implement on the ground. "And here I thought you wanted to remain under Sampson's wing," she taunted.

"I needed York for this location. If anyone discovered it, they'd blame him, especially when they exposed his lie."

Waving his gun, Ron motioned her back against the counter. Marla slid her foot toward the shears, a single nudge at a time so he'd believe she was fidgeting. "You mean he's not part of your scheme?" she said, anxious to keep him talking.

Ron scowled. "He's just a dupe. The only thing York gets out of the deal is a legitimate payment from Luxor for use of the premises."

"Sampson did his own share of duping people, though, didn't he?" Marla said quickly when she saw his jaw clench. "When did Chris find out that Sampson is a fraud?"

"A couple of years ago."

"You mean he's no better than you?" she said, hoping to goad him when his gaze flickered with impatience.

"Don't think I'm stupid, Marla. I know you're stalling, but while we're chatting, I'm thinking about what to do with you."

Marla ignored his remark. "Tell me about Sampson."

"Ha! Sampson York, the great educator, is nothing more than a farm boy whose *chutzpah* exceeds his ego." Ron sneered. "York saw a way to make money when he visited Miami Beach one summer. Stylists in upscale salons who catered to wealthy customers were getting rich enough to own boats and such. Given that York had some talent, he presented a forged license to get his first salon job. The rest is history."

Marla shifted her hips while edging the shears closer. "Did Sampson kill Chris because of what she learned about him?"

His eyes hardened. "Chris was blackmailing Sampson. She donated the money to the melanoma society, figuring his deceit could be put to good use. I'm the one who eliminated her. But it's going to be more difficult to get rid of four people than two."

Justine, who'd been standing motionless under the watchful gaze of the brawny manager, gasped. Larry held her arm, as though he feared she might topple over. His mouth was set in a firm line, and Marla hoped he wouldn't try anything foolish. He wouldn't stand a chance against the muscular younger men.

"Two people?" she queried Ron. "So you were responsible for Heather's death, also."

"No shit. Chris wanted to cut costs by removing the middleman for Sampson's shipments. She would have sent the hairbrushes directly to company headquarters, but I needed Luxor to repackage the stuff here."

Marla tilted her head. "Of course, you had to retrieve your illicit cargo. Listen, there's something else that puzzles me. Do you know who was stealing from the melanoma society? I'd just like to hear it wasn't Dr. Greenberg." The shears touched her sandal. Now if only she could devise a way to snatch the tool and toss it at Ron's gun hand.

"Don't worry, the good doctor wasn't involved. It was my idea," Ron boasted, patting his chest with his free hand. "I recruited Heather to help. The Luxor bookkeeper wrote the contribution check, which Heather deposited in a dummy account. Then she transferred a lesser amount into the society's bank account. We split the difference."

You're a rotten egg all the way, aren't you? "So when did Heather become a liability?"

Ron snorted. "She wanted money to boost her modeling career, but the chick became a problem when she noticed the bottle of antidepressants in my hotel bathroom. You didn't know that my mom, like Chris's mother, lives in a home for the aged. She's been taking those pills for years, the old kind, since they always worked for her. Heather put two and two together. I tried to brush her off, but then she became annoying."

"So you followed her to the Turkish Bath?"

He shrugged. "I didn't have to. I already knew that she went there on a regular basis, so I hid and waited for her."

"How did you poison Chris?" Marla wondered if this might be one question too many, but Ron seemed to be enjoying the opportunity to boast of his cleverness.

"I understood the toxic side effects from the older drug because of my mother," he explained with satisfaction. "Chris had no need for precautions with the newer dose. It was easy to buy a couple of glasses of wine at our cocktail party, slip the drug inside one of them, and direct the waiter to deliver that glass to Chris. She wouldn't refuse a gift from an admirer. I couldn't risk her closing down my little operation here."

"Were you afraid of what Heather told me? Is that why you attacked me in the Keys?"

"You're too nosy for your own good," he said with a snarl. "Snooping around, asking questions. When Heather set up a meeting with you, I realized your turn came next."

"Did you mistake Georgia for me because she wore my jacket?"

"Yeah, but then I decided it wasn't such a bad thing to take her out, too. You might have shared everything you knew with her. When I heard you were both safe, I decided to let you come to me. Sooner or later you'd figure things out and show up here." His eyes were cold as he raised his weapon. "Outside, everyone. I've thought of the perfect method of disposal. A car accident will work if we find a deep enough canal. People crash into the water all the time around here. Gunther, what do you think?"

"Works for me," the thug growled. "There's a canal running along the main highway."

Frozen to the spot, Marla heard Georgia cough beside her. She needed a decoy, but what? Her glance met Justine's. The older woman's eyelids fluttered. Then she crumpled.

"It's my heart," Justine cried. Larry caught her, and they both hit the deck.

At the moment when Ron's attention wavered, Marla bent, scooped up the shears, and slung them with all her might in his direction. He howled in pain when the blunt end hit his forehead.

She and Georgia bolted for the door.

A wild gunshot rang out.

Georgia had the foresight to snatch a ceramic pot along the way. She crashed it onto Gunther's head as he stood aiming his weapon at the elderly couple on the ground.

"Come on," Marla shouted, knowing they only had minutes before the two vermin roused themselves.

Making a swift recovery, Justine staggered to her feet.

Larry helped her stumble along as Marla scavenged for the keys in her purse. Georgia was already dialing 911 on her cell phone when Marla unlocked the car doors, tumbled inside, and switched on the ignition. As soon as her passengers were in, she tossed the car into gear and zoomed down the dirt road.

"Well, I never," Justine said from the backseat.

"It's not the best environment in which to raise a child," Justine told Dalton on Saturday night. Marla could hear them talking in the family room while she worked on the finishing touches to dessert in Vail's kitchen. Her fiancé had invited them to dinner at his house. He didn't seem to mind anymore that his former in-laws would see the boxes stacked in the hallway.

"Marla loves Brianna as though she were her own daughter," Vail said. "She just has this propensity for attracting trouble."

"Home life won't be enough for her. She's too restless. That's why she gets involved with these criminals."

Gritting her teeth, Marla sliced the warm brownies she'd baked, crisscrossing the pan with knife marks that gouged the metal. *Just one more night,* she told herself. Justine and Larry were leaving Sunday morning, and then she'd finally have the town house to herself. Georgia had left on Thursday after a tearful farewell. She'd enjoyed her visit, despite the bad things that had happened. Marla promised to keep in touch and expressed her hope that they'd meet at another hair show if Luxor kept her on the team.

Now she felt like an outsider again, with Brie chatting on the telephone in a bedroom and Vail discussing her as though she weren't there. Even the dogs, Lucky and Spooks, played with each other and ignored her. Blinking away a sudden sheen of moisture, she set aside the knife and drew a cake dish toward her.

"Marla means well. She just has an impetuous nature," she heard Vail claim in her defense.

"You don't say." Justine's voice dripped with sarcasm. "Brianna needs someone more stable to supervise her. Don't get me wrong. I like Marla. She's a lovely girl, and I can see why you'd be taken with her. But Pam would never go gallivanting about town chasing crooks, and she certainly would be home every day after school. Any woman you marry has to uphold—"

"Justine, put a sock in it. You have to trust Dalton to make the right decision. He'll do what's best for his daughter." Larry's sardonic tone caught Marla by surprise. She crumpled the brownie in her fingers. Reaching for another to put on the plate, she swallowed hard. *Brownie points for you, Gramps.*

"He's right," Dalton said. "I'm not trying to replace Pam. I'll always love her, and nothing can take that from me. But I also love Marla. She's a great role model for Brie with her people skills and business savvy, and I think she'll make a great stepmother. Brianna already looks to her for advice. Most importantly, Marla will go the extra mile when Brianna needs her. She's a caring person, and both of us have come to rely on her more than you know."

Marla's throat clogged with unshed tears. Careful not to brush crumbs on her face, she swiped her eyes. Wow, he'd never told her all those things.

"There are other differences between you," Justine pointed out with a sniff.

"Such as religion?" Dalton retorted. "That's not an issue where we're concerned. We respect each other's traditions."

"How about moral values? Brianna is overly focused on appearance for a girl her age. Did you know that she wants to highlight her hair? She's way too young to start destroying her natural beauty."

Vail cleared his throat. "I would agree with you, except Marla made me see the light. There's nothing wrong with Brianna wanting to look more feminine. We're learning to compromise."

Justine clucked her tongue. "Well, be aware that we'll be keeping close watch on how things progress. If Brianna doesn't get the care she needs or starts hanging out with the wrong crowd, Larry and I will make our presence known."

"Brownies, anyone?" Marla breezed into the family room, pretending she hadn't heard a word. Later, when she had a private moment with her fiancé, she'd tell him exactly what she thought about their conversation.

"I heard every word," she said when the opportunity finally arose and they found a few minutes alone. "I appreciate your defense, but I think, in retrospect, you should have insisted Larry and Justine stay here for the week."

She'd just emerged from the master bathroom where she'd refreshed her makeup after clearing away the dinner dishes. Dalton had trailed after her into the bedroom while Brie and her grandparents watched a movie on TV.

"Justine was the one who insisted on staying at your place to get to know you," he replied.

"More to find things to criticize."

"She said she liked you."

Marla studied him. Despite her irritation, she had to admit he looked ruggedly handsome in his black pullover sweater and jeans. A lock of hair swept across his forehead, grazing his smoky eyes. Itching to straighten his part, she curled her fingers while her gaze meandered to the bed. It had been too long since they'd had any intimacy. Warmth coiled in her erotic regions at the thought of what they could do together.

"Yeah, right," she said, tamping down her physical reactions. "Justine especially liked being held at gunpoint by a killer. I have to admit, she showed more guts than I'd imagined, but the situation didn't raise her opinion of me."

"You solved two murders and exposed a smuggling scheme. The authorities rounded up everyone involved after Georgia called for help on her cell phone, and you told them what you knew."

"We were lucky, but it doesn't cancel the fact that two people died."

"Through no fault of yours." He kicked the door shut and paced toward her.

She recognized the gleam in his eye and shook her head. "We're not done with this conversation yet. How will you feel if Luxor asks me back to work on another event? I'd be expected to travel."

She'd said good-bye to the Luxor crew on Thursday, and Janice had expressed her gratitude for Marla's help at the hair show and for revealing Ron Cassidy's treachery. She'd promised to keep Marla on the call list if she retained her position.

Sampson York, exposed as a fraud, had been fired. Marla felt sorry for him, since he really was a talented stylist and teacher. Now Luxor had to appoint a new artistic director.

"So? You've always wanted to go places but never had the chance," Vail said. "I've seen those Tahiti brochures you carry around, although you might consider switching to the West Indies," he added with a teasing grin. "The Caribbean is a lot closer."

She ignored his remark. "I wouldn't be home when Brianna gets off from school. You heard what Justine said."

"Brie is used to letting herself into the house by now. That's not a problem. I want you to be happy, sweetcakes."

"I still think you should have let Justine and Larry stay here," she said, stubbornly refusing to quit the issue. "Did you even consider my feelings when you spoke to them about their visit?"

He drew her close and ground his hips against her body. "What about the feelings you're getting now?"

"Stop it, you're avoiding the subject." Despite her objection, her breath grew ragged. "Maybe we'd better hold off on our wedding plans until I meet your parents. They could be worse than Justine and Larry."

Lowering his head, he nibbled at her mouth. "Mom and Dad will adore you."

"Oh yeah? How do you know?"

"Because they're ready to make your dreams of going to exotic islands come true. I hope you don't mind if I've gone ahead and made plans for us again. I know I should've asked first, but then you'd have come up with some excuse as to why you couldn't get off work."

"Oh no," she moaned against his lips as he rained kisses on her face. "What have you done?"

"My parents are treating us. We're going on a cruise."

Author's Note

This story was inspired by an incident that happened when I attended the Premiere Beauty Show (*www.premiereshows.com*) in Orlando one year. Ideas for books can come from anywhere; you need merely keep your eyes and ears open for opportunities. The other outstanding bit of research I did was to visit the Russian and Turkish Baths in a hotel on Miami Beach. What fun! Like Marla, I'd expected something entirely different. The place turned out to be way more interesting than I had anticipated. I wished I'd had extra time to linger and enjoy the amenities.

Marla's next adventure takes her on a cruise. Caribbean cruises are my favorite vacation; I've been on over fifteen cruises on a variety of ships. I love the relaxed ambience, tropical ports, rum punches, and bountiful buffets. Taking notes for *Killer Knots* led me to some new experiences which I'll be sure to share in my next tale.

I love to hear from readers. Write to me at P.O. Box 17756, Plantation, FL 33318. Please enclose a self-addressed stamped #10 business-size envelope for a personal reply.

Email: **nancy.j.cohen@comcast.net**

Website: **www.nancyjcohen.com**

Blog: **http://mysterygal.bravejournal.com**

Enjoy the following preview of
Nancy J. Cohen's next
Bad Hair Day mystery
KILLER KNOTS
Coming in December 2007
from Kensington Books

"**A**re you sure I won't get seasick?" Marla Shore asked her fiancé as they approached the Port of Miami via a bridge over the Intracoastal. Squinting at the white ships lining the pier like ducks on parade, she felt a twinge of queasiness in her stomach. Hopefully, her first Caribbean cruise wouldn't be her last.

"These big ships have stabilizers," Dalton Vail replied, focused on his driving. "It'll probably be so smooth you won't even notice we're on the water."

The handsome detective spared her a glance. He wouldn't admit to being excited, but she saw the spark in his gray eyes. She looked forward to sharing this experience with him and his fourteen-year-old daughter.

From the backseat, Brianna tapped Marla on the shoulder. "Look, there's the *Tropical Sun*! Can you see it?" The teen had talked about nothing but their trip for the past few weeks.

"It has their signature lounge on top," Marla pointed out, admiring the massive vessel's sleek lines. Her attention shifted. "Do you have enough cash for parking?" she asked Dalton as he followed the signs to the garage. "It's twelve dollars a day."

"They take credit cards. Why don't you and Brie get off here with the luggage? The cruise terminal is straight ahead. I'll meet you at the entrance." After he pulled up to the curb, he helped them unload before jumping back behind the wheel and zooming away.

Marla grimaced as a stiff sea breeze blew wisps of her carefully coiffed hair about her face. Her hairstylist skills would come in handy on this voyage. Rummaging in her purse, she withdrew a few bills for the porter, who checked their bags.

"Where do we go now?" Brianna said, confusion muddling her brown eyes. She wore her toffee hair in a ponytail along with the standard teenage garb of jeans and a camisole top.

"Let's wait for your father."

Charter buses pulled up to the curb along with yellow taxicabs and a shiny metal Sysco supply truck. Cops wearing neon green vests directed the traffic that added to the noise level. Seagulls squawked. Engines idled. Porters shouted. Airplanes roaring overhead made Marla's blood pound in her ears.

Who said cruises were restful vacations? Mingling with three thousand other passengers doesn't fit my dream of a tropical getaway.

Diesel fumes warmed by the summer sun mixed with the aroma of hot dogs from a nearby vendor. A passenger next to her crunched on a potato chip, his ample belly filling his shorts and flowered shirt.

Oh joy. Eleven days to gain weight at endless buffets. It's a good thing my new salon will offer spa services in addition to the usual hair treatments. I'll be their first customer.

Marla knew Dalton was looking forward to the meals. He'd pored over the dining-room pictures in the brochure. Same for Brianna, whose growing stage made her continually hungry. Marla was more interested in checking out the shops and lounging by the pool. Forget the onboard salon. She'd take a peek, but that was one place she wanted to avoid on her vacation.

As Vail hustled across the street, she watched him with pride. His broad shoulders filled the Tommy Bahama black shirt she'd given him for Father's Day. Even with the silver peppering his ebony hair, his distinguished appearance made female heads turn in appreciation. She hoped this cruise would bring them closer together as a family.

"Let's go inside," he said, taking charge.

At the door, a uniformed official checked their passports and ushered them into the terminal. They entered the line for U.S. citizens and shuffled along like sheep in a herd until they reached the counter. Vail collected their papers and submitted their passports, cruise tickets, and credit cards for their on-board credit accounts.

"How does my hair look?" Marla asked before she grinned in front of a mini camera that snapped her photo. Just getting to the ship was an ordeal. She couldn't wait to get settled.

In the next room, another attendant handed them each a room-key card, which they signed on the back. Brianna's eyes bulged when she realized she'd be able to charge her own purchases.

"All right! I hope I meet kids my age to hang out with on the ship." Brianna stuffed the card into her Nine West purse.

"You will, honey," Marla said, giving her an indulgent smile. "They have an excellent teen program. You'll have your own activities and even your own newsletter every day."

"Over here," Vail said, directing them to the security detail. Like at the airport, they had to pass their carry-on bags through an X-ray machine while they walked through the gates. After they cleared, a guard waved them toward an up escalator. A long metal walkway open to the breeze awaited them at the top. Shaded by a blue awning, it led to the gangway onto the ship itself. But first they had to get past the pair of photographers who captured a quick picture of them in front of a *Tropical Sun* welcome-aboard poster.

"I wonder how much that photo will cost," Marla remarked. She shivered with excitement as they crossed a plank over a short expanse of water. Once on the ship, they had to present their key cards. A crew member swept each card through a machine that brought up their photo ID. Marla noticed a dispenser of liquid hand sanitizer just beyond. Great; they'd need it to prevent norovirus.

"At last," she said, once they were free to find their room. She glanced at the bank of elevators, the wide carpeted stairway, and two long corridors flanking either side of the ship. "Where is our cabin, port or starboard?" she asked Vail, relying on his sense of direction.

"We're starboard on deck eight," he replied. "That's on the right side of the ship facing forward. I usually remember because port has four letters same as left." He nodded at the crowd waiting in front of the elevators. "It'll be a few minutes before the mob clears."

"We can take the stairs." Wondering why he peered around as though expecting someone, Marla put her foot forward just as she spotted an auburn-haired woman waving at them. She'd come off the down elevator, accompanied by a tall man with receding hair, eyeglasses, and a broad grin.

"Dalton! Brianna!" The lady descended upon them, spreading her arms wide.

"Grandma," Brie responded, rushing into the older woman's embrace while Marla stared.

Grandma? Don't tell me Dalton's parents are here. Her vision wavered. She felt as though the floor had opened beneath her, and she'd dropped into Wonderland. Why did no one else act surprised? Dumbfounded, she stood there like a statue.

"You think we'd pay for your cruise and not come along for the ride?" Brianna's grandmother said. "Besides, we wanted to meet Marla. At the rate your father is dragging his feet regarding a wedding date, this may be our only chance."

She grasped Marla's stiff hand. "We're delighted to meet you. I'm Kate, and this is John. Or call us Mom and Dad."

Vail hugged his father. "Dad, I figured you'd be looking for us down here."

Marla stood back, struggling to comprehend. Dalton had known his folks would be on the cruise, and he hadn't said a word? True, Kate and John had treated them to the vacation. Presumably the elder couple meant to smooth things over after Dalton's former in-laws created a strain between them. But if Dalton's folks were anything like Pam's parents, she'd *plotz!*

Not to worry. Kate and John flew in from Maine. They'll have plenty to do on the cruise.

And she really should forgive Justine and Larry, who still mourned Pam's death. It wasn't easy for them to accept Marla as a potential stepmother for their granddaughter.

Kate linked her arm with Marla's. "You're prettier in person than in your picture," Kate said with a warm smile. "I can't wait to get to know you, but I'm sure you and Dalton would like to unpack. We'll take Brie to our cabin. Her suitcase is already there."

Vail frowned. "Huh? Why would it have been sent to your stateroom?"

"I guess you didn't notice that her room number is different from yours. She's staying with us so you and Marla can have some privacy. I hope that's okay with you, sweetheart."

Brianna's expression took on a devilish gleam. "Sure, I have my own key anyway. As long as you agree that I don't have a curfew." She cast her father a smug grin.

"Now just a minute," he began.

Vail's dad made a dismissive gesture. "Let it go, son. Brie can't get lost on the ship, and she'll have a better time if she hooks up with some young people." He exchanged a knowing look with Marla that made her like him already.

"We'll catch up to you guys later," Kate told Marla, then squeezed her elbow.

Kate was certainly a touchy-feely person, Marla thought, appreciating how she appeared totally different from Justine, Pam's mother. It might not be so bad having her future in-laws on board after all. Wanting to accommodate Brianna, she turned her attention to the teen.

"Are you certain you're all right with this, honey? You know you're welcome to stay with us. We want to spend time with you, and—"

"She'll be fine." Kate wrapped an arm around the girl's shoulder. "Take your time exploring the ship. We sail at five; then we have the lifeboat drill before dinner. We'll meet up with you in the dining room."

After trudging up the stairs, Marla and Vail sought their cabin. Feeling like a conditioned laboratory rat, she followed the coral carpet down a brightly lit corridor that seemed to stretch to infinity. Brass plates displayed room numbers, and when they reached theirs, Marla noticed an envelope tucked into a seashell decoration by the door.

"Look at this," she said, showing Dalton the scrawl that addressed the message to Martha Shore. "Someone must've spelled my name wrong." After sticking it inside her purse, she unlocked the door to their cabin. "Yikes, my closet at home is bigger than this place!" Plopping her bags on the floor, she surveyed their home for the next week. There was barely enough space for their suitcases, let alone her and Dalton.

A queen-sized bed stood against the opposite wall, where a wide picture window showed a view of the pier. Other furnishings included a small nightstand, a desk that served as a dresser with drawers, a desk chair, and a small loveseat facing a television mounted on a ledge.

She noticed Dalton eyeing the TV and said, "If I'm going to lose you to sports games, you can find me on the pool deck." Upon peering in the bathroom, she said, "Hey, look in here. If you turn around when you brush your teeth, you'll be taking a shower."

Vail excused himself to use the facilities while she examined a pile of papers on their bed: the *Tropical Tattler* newsletter, announcements about a preview art auction, gift shop flyers, and spa treatment specials. Always on the lookout for bargains, she stuffed them in her purse to read later and turned to her carry-on bag to remove her cosmetics.

From the bathroom, she heard a thump, followed by an explosive whoosh and a loud curse. The detective emerged looking shaken. "Jeez, if you sit on that thing when you flush, you risk losing some vital body parts. They aren't kidding when they say to close the lid first."

Marla laughed, then put her things down on the bed and walked over to kiss him soundly. "I can see one benefit to this cabin. We'll have to snuggle closer." They spent a few minutes doing just that until a knock sounded outside the door.

"Hello, my name is Jovanny," said their cabin steward, a short young man with a swarthy complexion. "May I assist you with luggage?" Their suitcases had arrived. Marla and Vail stood by while Jovanny dragged the luggage inside. "Your cruise guide will tell you what goes on each day," Jovanny said, with a flashy grin, while Marla strained to understand him. He spoke as though he had a wad of cotton in his mouth. "Today we have lifeboat drill at five-thirty. Life jackets are in closet. Your station is deck seven, C-4. Okay, lady and gentleman? If you need anything else, please call me on telephone."

As soon as he left, she returned to unpacking her bag. A loudspeaker blared, making her jump.

Ding dong, ding dong.

"Attention, all passengers," announced a deep male voice from a console on the desk. "According to SOLAS, International Convention for the Safety of Life at Sea, we are required to hold a lifeboat drill within twenty-four hours of sailing. When you hear seven short blasts and one long blast, this is the signal to proceed to your lifeboat assembly station. There will be no eating or drinking during this exercise. This is a mandatory drill even if you have cruised with us before."

The man's voice droned on, issuing further instructions, but Marla closed him out. She'd opened the envelope addressed to Martha Shore and pulled out a piece of paper inside. Narrowing her eyes, she stared at the typewritten words:

I know what you did and I have what you want.

Her blood chilled. Who would send this weird message?

She'd done a few bad things in her life, but mostly they'd been resolved. No one on board could possibly know about the erotic pictures she'd posed for when she was nineteen. That hadn't been the best moment in her life, but she'd needed the money to pay for an attorney after Tammy had drowned in a backyard pool. As her babysitter, Marla had been held accountable by the toddler's parents. She'd finally put the tragedy to rest, so why would it rear its ugly head now? Nah, this had to be a mistake.

"What's wrong?" Vail asked, giving her a curious glance. He'd started hanging up his suit jackets.

"Look at this note." She thrust it at him.

Scanning the words, he scowled. "Gotta be some sort of joke."

"Or it's been sent to the wrong person." Flushing with guilt, she grabbed the paper and tossed it into a drawer. Nothing would ruin her vacation. "Forget about it," she said. "Let's explore the ship. I'd like to make sure Brie is happy with her arrangements."

Vail opted for a snack, so they headed for the Outrigger Café on deck eleven. Unsure of where to go, Marla suggested they follow the trail of people holding drink cups. They found the dining room with several buffet lines, and Vail filled his plate with a juicy hamburger, French fries, pasta salad, and herb-roasted chicken, while Marla allowed herself coffee and fruit.

"How can you eat so much? It's nearly time for dinner," she said, sipping the brew.

"Don't worry, I'll be hungry again," Vail answered, his mouth full. "How's the coffee?"

"Rich and robust, with no bitter aftertaste. I saw a notice alongside the dispenser that says the brand is Hair Raiser. They must have the concession throughout the ship."

His eyebrows lifted. "I hope that isn't a portent since you do hair for a living."

You and me both, pal. This is one week when I want to lie out and catch the sun, not help you catch killers. "Maybe I should serve the stuff in my salon. I'll look it up on the Internet when I get a chance."

After bolstering their energy, they strolled outside to preview the pool, Jacuzzis, and solarium. Then they went indoors to ride the glass elevator down and ended up by Hook's Champagne Bar on deck five. Marla stared at the nine-story central atrium in confusion.

"How did we miss the salon, spa, and fitness center?" she asked. "Weren't they on the same deck as the pool?"

"I don't know. They could be at the other end. We need to look at a diagram." A couple of long blasts on the ship's horn sounded. "Forget it, we're about to cast off. Let's take the elevator back up."

Completely disoriented, Marla pointed to the carpet on their way aloft. "It's a good thing the design tells you what day it is. I could easily lose track of time here."

"I wonder if they change the carpet at midnight."

"You can stay and watch. I'll be too tired tonight."

As soon as she stepped outdoors into the afternoon July sun, she felt the vibration increase and realized the ship had begun moving. Jostling for a position by the rail, she felt a rush of excitement. She watched the pier recede before they entered the outlet leading to open sea.

Strains of "Hot Hot Hot," played from a steel band by the pool, where a costumed man on stilts led a line dance. Waiters hawked strawberry piña coladas as the drink of the day while the ship glided past Parrot Jungle Island, a fleet of anchored sailboats, cars racing by on the causeway, and mansions fronting the Intracoastal. A Jet Ski skipped along the water as the *Tropical Sun* neared the last strip of sand.

Marla tilted her head back, enjoying the fresh air and the warm sun that kissed her skin. They were embarking on a grand adventure, and her final view of the shoreline came with the realization that they'd have more than a week free from phone calls, work hassles, and chores.

Ding dong, ding dong.

"Good afternoon, ladies and gentlemen," boomed a male voice on the public address system. "This is Captain Rick Larsen speaking to you from the bridge. Our mandatory assembly drill begins shortly. When you hear the emergency signal, please proceed to your assembly stations with your life jackets. Staterooms and public areas will be checked to ensure that all guests have exited these locations. Smoking, drinking, eating, and the use of cellular phones is prohibited during the drill. Thank you for your attention and cooperation."

"Come on," Vail said, signaling. "We have to go below."

"Let's take the stairs. I need to work off all the calories I'm going to consume."

She gave a last glance at the late sun reflecting off the tall buildings of the Miami skyline. Forced activities might be the only cloud on the horizon, but she could tolerate even those if they took away the decision-making process. She'd dreamed of lying on a tropical beach with no decisions to make except which rum drink to try. That being her only goal for the cruise, she could be flexible otherwise.

Then again, she felt like a sailor at military inspection when they reported to their lifeboat assembly station. Upon their arrival on deck, a uniformed officer recorded the cabin number emblazoned on their vest fronts and directed them to join a group of passengers lined up in jagged rows. Squashed between an overweight fellow who sweated profusely and a mother of two whose youngest child wailed at loud decibels, she struggled to fasten her life vest. The bulky jacket forced her neck up at an uncomfortable angle.

Vail cursed beside her. He'd gotten himself tangled in the straps and flailed helplessly while attempting to snag the buckle. Knocking into a muscular guy in the row behind, he mumbled an apology. The fellow must have been easily over six feet tall. He wore a bandanna and tattoos like a biker dude.

"No problem, buddy," the tattooed man said with a grin.

"You have it on backward," Marla said to Vail. She bit her lip to suppress a smile. It wasn't often that she saw her fiancé at a disadvantage, and when she did, she just wanted to take care of him. She assisted him in putting the vest on correctly.

A female staff member wearing all white—blouse, skirt, shoes, and visored cap—glared at her charges. "Listen up, people." Everyone snapped to attention while she strode back and forth. "Make sure those straps are tight. Otherwise, if we have to pull you out of the water fast, we'll yank on the vest and you'll be left behind to sink like a stone. Come on, squeeze closer. This is how crowded it gets in the boat." She pointed to the vessel suspended overhead.

"Do we get to sit in the lifeboat?!" hollered one passenger.

"Sit, stand, or lie, you'll be crammed in there. Oh, and another thing, if you have to jump overboard, cross your arms in front like this. Otherwise, the jacket may hit your head upon impact."

"Oh joy. Something else to worry about," Marla murmured.

"Your automated light will flash when you enter the water," the officer continued. "It serves as a beacon. You can use the whistle to draw attention to yourself. Now, are there any questions?"

At Marla's side, Vail blew the whistle attached to his vest.

"Nice move," Marla crooned, "especially when you don't know whose mouth it touched last." She shifted her feet as she heard the familiar *ding dong, ding dong* from the loudspeaker.

"May I have your attention, please?" said a disembodied voice. "The general emergency signal that began the drill consists of seven short blasts followed by one long blast through the ship's whistle and internal alarm system. If you are in your stateroom when you hear this signal, grab some warm clothing, gather any medications you may require along with your life jacket, and proceed to your muster station. If you are not in your state-room, go directly to your station, where in a real emergency, a life jacket will be issued to you. Do not use the elevators, as they will not work in a power failure. Lighting along the floors and stair-ways will show the route to the assembly stations."

Marla tuned him out, preferring not to dwell on the unpleasant possibilities. Instead, she contemplated how many times during the day these announcements would disrupt them.

Sweat dribbled between her breasts while she listened to the speaker repeat his message in several languages. "How long is this going to last?" she groused. "I'm dying from the heat."

Vail regarded her from under his thick brows. "You'll build up a good appetite for dinner. I wonder where Brie and my folks are. You don't see them, do you?" He stood on his toes to peer over the heads of taller figures.

Marla's gaze caught on a handsome older man who murmured something into his companion's ear. The woman, a blonde who looked about half his age, shrugged away. Not that it was any of her business, but she wondered if that was his wife or his daughter. She caught another person staring at the couple, a fellow with tousled dark hair, a shifty expression, and a camera with which he shot a quick photo of their profiles.

You're imagining things, she told herself. *He's probably just snapping a picture of the lifeboat beyond. People are here to have fun, and so are you.*

As soon as the ship's horn blasted the all-clear signal, she unstrapped her vest and yanked it over her head, mussing her hair. Jostled by other sweaty bodies, she proceeded indoors and followed the mob down the staircase to deck eight.

With a sigh of relief, she opened the door to their cabin and bounded inside to air-cooled comfort. "Man, is that thing bulky," she said to Vail, as they tossed their life jackets onto the bed. "We'll let the cabin steward put them away."

"I need a shower, but it's time for dinner already," Vail replied, raking a hand through his hair. He gave her a rueful glance, as though he would have liked to linger.

Hustling to the dining room, Marla despaired of having a minute free. She could end up being busier on this trip than in her salon at home. *At least you don't have to cook or wait on customers*, she thought gleefully as they were ushered to their table by the restaurant manager. Elegant white linens, vases with fresh orchids, subdued jazz music, and scores of uniformed waiters soothed her nerves as she took a seat.

"Typical of Brie to be late," Vail said in an indulgent tone. He grabbed a bread stick from a basket on the table.

"You're just eager to stuff yourself. We're the first ones here." Marla nodded at the other empty chairs. "I'm glad we have a table for ten, so we'll meet new people. Do you suppose the waiter will wait until everyone arrives to take our orders?" She glanced around the room, decorated with crystal chandeliers and floor-to-ceiling windows. "Some passengers may choose to eat in the café upstairs."

"Who knows? Can you pass the butter, please?"

As Marla complied, some of their other table companions appeared. She was startled to recognize the older couple from the lifeboat drill. Even though the newsletter indicated this evening's dress code was casual, they'd changed into fancier outfits than they'd worn on deck.

"I'm Oliver Smernoff, and this is my wife, Irene," the man said in a baritone voice. He wore a black suit that contrasted sharply with his graying temples. Most of the hair on top of his head had receded, leaving him partly bald, but his even features and tall stature made him attractive for a man in his fifties. His wife wasn't as young as she'd seemed at a distance, judging from her hands more than her face. The veins stood out on her overly tanned skin, making Marla rub her own hands and wish for lotion.

Irene attempted to smile, but her stiff facial muscles turned it into a grimace. She wore an elegant blue sheath dress and a necklace that shimmered with diamonds.

The newest arrivals, on the other hand, boasted a distinct age difference. "Thurston Stark at your service, and this is my wife, Heidi," the man boomed to Marla and Vail. He was a big guy with a confident smile, hazel eyes, and wheat-brown hair. With his broad shoulders, he might have been a football player in his earlier days. Heidi looked about thirty years younger, a typical blond trophy wife with a vapid expression. She wore a black dress so revealing that if the ship rocked, her boobs would risk tumbling out.

While Thurston and Oliver exchanged hearty greetings, their wives acknowledged each other with tepid nods. It appeared they already knew one another. Before Marla could inquire as to the nature of their acquaintance, more of their tablemates arrived.

"We're out of seats," Marla noted to Vail in an undertone. "What happened to Brie and your parents?"

"You're right." Half rising, he scanned the dining room. "I don't see them anywhere."

Marla's stomach sank. "Great, and I figured nothing could go wrong this week."

Vail gave a snort of disbelief. "The way you're a magnet for trouble, sweetcakes, we'll be lucky to get off this ship alive."